ALL *of* THIS

ANNA SCHAEFFER

WESTBOW
PRESS®
A DIVISION OF THOMAS NELSON
& ZONDERVAN

Scripture taken from the Holy Bible, NEW INTERNATIONAL VERSION®.
Copyright © 1973, 1978, 1984 by Biblica, Inc. All rights reserved worldwide.
Used by permission. NEW INTERNATIONAL VERSION® and NIV® are
registered trademarks of Biblica, Inc. Use of either trademark for the offering
of goods or services requires the prior written consent of Biblica US, Inc.

WestBow Press books may be ordered through booksellers or by contacting:

WestBow Press
A Division of Thomas Nelson & Zondervan
1663 Liberty Drive
Bloomington, IN 47403
www.westbowpress.com
1 (866) 928-1240

ISBN: 978-1-4908-9024-1 (sc)
ISBN: 978-1-4908-9026-5 (hc)
ISBN: 978-1-4908-9025-8 (e)

Library of Congress Control Number: 2015910787

Print information available on the last page.

WestBow Press rev. date: 07/24/2015

To the Giver of purpose

Chapter 1

When I was little, I would hold my breath whenever I felt emotions I couldn't understand. I wouldn't release it until my little lungs burned for air, my cheeks screamed red, and spots danced in my vision—until my mom held me tight, whispering assurances that everything would be okay. Then I would open my mouth and gulp as much air as I could, gasping and choking and feeling. As long as I focused on holding my breath, I couldn't think about what hurt.

As I stood alone in the crowded Atlanta airport, I began to feel those familiar emotions of fear and uncertainty wrap their stiff fingers around my throat. I was sixteen, but still I'd have given anything to have my mom standing beside me, comforting me, like all those years before. Around me, crowds of people shoved their way toward their destinations while I remained still. My feet were blocks of concrete in my jogging shoes, and I had to make an effort to scrape them along the terminal.

I shifted my beat-up backpack to my right shoulder, clutching the strap like a kid on her first day of kindergarten. I finally got my stubborn feet to move as I stuck my elbows out and forged ahead. An advantage of growing up in Seattle was that I'd learned how to make my way through a crowd.

I reached the end of the terminal and stopped. *Deep breaths. Breathe in; breathe out. Repeat.* Around me, my flight mates clutched their friends and relatives, laughing and crying—finally home. Beside me, a little girl ran into the arms of her father and buried her face in his neck.

Before I could stop myself, my mind flashed back to my own dad. The disappointment in his eyes, the resignation on his face, the way he dropped me off at the SeaTac airport to face whatever waited for me over the next few months.

"I don't even know them," I'd told him as we pulled into the drop-off lane.

"I don't know what else to do, Sadie. They'll take care of you," he said as he handed my backpack to me.

"They're probably a bunch of rednecks."

Dad sighed and rubbed his neck. "Get it together, Sadie. I'll see you in August."

Shaking my head to bring my mind back to the present, I brushed my wilted, sandy bangs out of my eyes and searched the sea of unfamiliar faces.

What if they forgot? I asked myself. *What if they changed their minds? What if—*

"*Say-dee!* Over here!"

My ears perked at the sound of my name, and my gaze followed the direction of the voice.

A tall, freckled, redheaded guy waved just to the right of me. Next to Ronald McDonald stood a petite, pregnant brunette.

I shuffled through the rest of the quickly dispersing crowd, my heart pounding in my ears like the percussion in a climactic movie scene. I swallowed my nerves and offered a small wave as I approached.

"Sadie! Hey!" I was fewer than three feet away, but my uncle had to yell to be heard over the din. I immediately picked up on his southern accent. He offered me a crooked, boyish grin and proceeded to wrap an arm around me in a hug. I awkwardly patted his back once, if only to prove to myself that this was really happening and I'd really left all I'd ever known.

"Here, let me take that," my uncle said. I gratefully slid out of my backpack. "It's good to see you, kid."

"Oh, but look at her, Kurt! She's all grown up!" Aunt Melina exclaimed, slowly lifting her hand to indicate my height. "I'm so glad you're here." She stretched out her arms for a hug, and I allowed myself to fold into her embrace. It was a little uncomfortable, given that I was at least a couple of inches taller than she was and had to bend over her belly. She hugged me tightly and then pulled back. "Hold on. Let me just look at you for a minute."

Melina held me at arm's length, and I could feel her bright-green eyes scan my weary frame. Her vision clouded as she brought her eyes back up to mine.

"Just look at you, Sadie Grey," she whispered.

That's all it took. I felt my insides begin to crumble, and I quickly averted my eyes so I wouldn't cry. Looking into a face so unknown yet so familiar and hearing my middle name that was only used by one other person in the entire world—it was almost too much.

Apparently, Melina thought so too. She squeezed my shoulders and flapped her hand in front of her face to dry her eyes.

"Well!" She clapped. "Let's get your luggage."

Although it had been a pain to pack my stuff and send it across the country the week before, I was grateful because I had to wait for only one large suitcase to make its way around the baggage carousel.

Melina kept her hand splayed across my back while we waited, and I tried my hardest not to stiffen beneath her touch. I grabbed the old suitcase my mom had used nearly nineteen years before when she'd made the opposite of my trip. Kurt offered to pull my suitcase once we reached the parking lot.

I passed him the luggage, which resembled a tacky sofa cushion. A wheel popped off and rolled under a minivan. Kurt and Melina stared at me.

"Bad case of jet lag, I guess." I shrugged.

Kurt's big hand jovially patted me on the back, and it was all I could do to regain my balance so I wouldn't kiss the concrete.

Once I buckled into the middle seat of their old golden minivan, Melina shifted her weight so she could look at me from the front passenger seat. "So how was your trip?" she asked.

"Not as long as I thought," I admitted. "I slept practically the whole way since I had to leave so early."

"That's right," Kurt added as he merged into traffic. "You're on Pacific time."

"Yeah. Like, right now, it feels like it's ten instead of one o'clock. I'd usually be eating breakfast, but it's more like lunchtime." As if on cue, my stomach growled. *Loudly.* Which was totally embarrassing.

Kurt laughed and nudged Melina with his elbow. She swatted at his bicep. "Oh, come on!" he said. "You're out of excuses."

I watched their volley in confusion. "Did I miss something?"

Kurt turned briefly to look at me, although his brevity was way too long, considering the other cars zooming past us. "Nope, but you're in for a treat."

Twenty minutes later, Kurt pulled into a parking garage, and Melina mumbled, "Hallelujah."

"You forget I grew up in this city, dear," Kurt said as he climbed out of the car. Melina responded with a comment about how growing up in a big city didn't make him invincible, but I tuned her out and took in our surroundings.

The restaurant was called the Varsity, and it was huge. The building looked like an old drive-in with its vintage signs and red and white colors. Kurt held the door open for us, and we stepped into chaos. The place was packed with customers trying to maintain some semblance of a line in front of the long counter. The staff wore red T-shirts and red-and-white paper hats. Above them, the menu stretched across the wall, displaying a mind-boggling list with combos of burgers, chili dogs, and fries.

We merged into the crowd. As each customer made his or her way to the front of the line, the server called out, "What'll ya have?" and then rapidly worked to get the person's order ready. It was all so fast paced and overwhelming.

"Sadie and I are going to the restroom while you order, Kurt," Melina said. "Surprise us?"

He turned to me, and I nodded before following Melina through the crowd.

I studied my appearance while I washed my hands in the restroom. My mascara had faded into circles beneath my gray eyes, and when I blinked, I noticed my taupe eye shadow had collected in two creases. I splashed some water on my face and blotted with a brown paper towel to get rid of the sheen that had built up. With no more makeup, I felt exposed, like somehow my aunt and uncle would be able to see through me more easily.

On the plane ride over, I'd resolved not to form attachments in Georgia. Because if anyone got to know the real Sadie Grey Franklin—I couldn't afford to think like that. I wasn't exactly crazy about spending my summer vacation on the other side of the country with relatives I barely knew, but my dad told me he couldn't do it anymore. Isn't that sad? He all but told me he didn't want his only kid. Never mind the fact that he couldn't even handle himself most days, but taking me away from the only place I'd ever known? Ouch.

I jerked my hair into a messy bun, pulling myself out of my thoughts, and then followed Melina to our table.

Kurt passed out the food. "You've never had real food until you've eaten at the Varsity," he said as he slid a tray in front of me. "This place is an Atlanta landmark."

I looked down at a burger slathered in chili and cheese, a pile of greasy onion rings, and a hot dog covered in shreds of white, purple, and green stuff. "What is this?" I asked, poking at the creamy stuff with a plastic fork.

"It's coleslaw." Kurt watched me like he was watching an Olympic sport—brown eyes wide, unblinking, expectant.

I wasn't too excited about trying it, but I picked up the hot dog and took a bite. I chewed for a minute, trying to figure out what, exactly, coleslaw was. Some sort of cabbage and carrots was my best guess. I swallowed and reached for the cup Melina mercifully slid in front of me. I took a big gulp of what looked like iced tea but tasted like a bag of sugar. I attempted to discreetly spit most of the beverage back into my cup and wiped my mouth with a napkin.

"So what do you think?" my uncle asked.

"The tea is a little sweet, isn't it?" I could almost feel my blood sugar spike.

Melina nodded. "Sorry. I forgot you wouldn't be accustomed to sweet tea. It's kind of a southern thing."

"Just like fried stuff covered in chili, cheese, and slaw?" I ventured a guess.

Kurt smiled and reached for Melina's hand. "Mind if I pray?" he asked.

Was he really going to pray in the middle of this crowded restaurant, where everyone could hear him? I didn't respond—just looked down at my tray and tried to pry a piece of slaw out from between my molars with my tongue.

Kurt and Melina closed their eyes. "Father," Kurt began, "thank You for Sadie." He glanced up at me, and I ducked my head. "Thank You for new opportunities and the summer that's ahead of us and the chance for us to be a family together ..." He went into giving thanks for the food, but I tuned him out.

Family. Even though I had never met their children, Kurt and Melina seemed to have the ideal family. I could tell in the way they interacted with each other with jokes and smiles and kindness. The idea of a real family was something I'd never had a chance to experience. Kurt's prayer felt like a barb in my heart, reminding me of all I'd never had.

The topic of family dominated our lunch conversation. "You'll get to meet the kids as soon as we get home," Melina said as she dipped a fry in her chocolate milk shake. "They're with a sitter. Our oldest is Tristan. She's eight. I was expecting her when"—she paused, but I knew what she was thinking—"when we last saw each other." Although I could tell she was trying to hide it, she sighed. I'd spent the past eight years trying not to think about that day. It was enough to suffocate me. But I knew we were all thinking about my mom, so why didn't she just say the word *funeral?*

We ate in silence for a minute. Melina dipped another fry. "Then there's Jackson. He's six, and I'm pretty sure that boy could take his father out in wrestling." Kurt elbowed her. Not hard, but it startled her, and she dropped her fry. I stifled a smile.

"Cooper's our third." She held up three fingers. "He's two and barely has a chance to get a word in edgewise around his older siblings." She handed me a milk shake–covered fry. "Try this. It's heaven."

I took the fry and popped it in my mouth before it could drip. It was a strange combination—the warm saltiness of the fry mixed with the cold sweetness of the milk shake. But it was so good. "And then," Melina said as she held out another fry, "there's Butter Bean. Due to make his or her debut on Labor Day, ironically." She laughed.

"Butter Bean?" I asked as I slid the rest of my slaw dog across the table to Kurt.

"Mm-hm," Melina said. "The first time the kids saw the baby on the sonogram, he or she was the size of a little butter bean. Since we're keeping the gender a surprise, we decided to use Butter Bean as a nickname."

"I see." I was starting to suspect my relatives were crazy.

As we drove east on I-20 after lunch, I closed my eyes so I wouldn't be interrogated the entire two-hour drive. I wondered what my nickname would've been. I was probably either Oops or Oh-No-What-Have-We-Done.

I opened my eyes to air out my thoughts. I couldn't let myself go into all of that. When I looked out the window at the endless blur of green pine trees lining the interstate, it was hard to be sure that I wasn't really the one standing still while my surroundings zoomed by, completely unconcerned with Sadie Grey Franklin.

Chapter 2

The gravel driveway jostled me awake. Somehow, I'd managed to doze on the way to the Elliots' house. I slowly opened my heavy eyelids and peeled my cheek off the window. The driveway ran alongside a yellow wooden house. The one-story building had a big front porch complete with a swing and a couple of white wooden rocking chairs. It was cute in a quaint sort of way and exactly how I pictured a southern home.

Kurt drove around to the back of the house and parked beneath a large, shady tree.

"Home, sweet home!" He turned off the engine and unfastened his seat belt.

Melina groaned and pressed a hand to her lower back. "Thank goodness." She turned to me. "This house actually belongs to your grandparents, Sadie, but living in Pecan Creek would make a long commute."

"They work overseas somewhere, right?" I hadn't had much contact with my grandparents after my mom died, but they still contacted me on Christmases and birthdays.

Melina nodded. "They're in Russia. They won't be back in the States for another year or so. We miss them, but we know that's where they're supposed to be." She smiled, but she looked a little sad. I, for one, didn't understand how people could leave their lives and language and move to another country.

I drew in a deep breath through my nose, pushed it all the way down, and held it as I unbuckled my seat belt and tied the lace on my shoe. I allowed the air to slowly leak through my lips, taking the tension with it, and rolled my shoulders. *This is it. A new beginning. Start over. Move.* That last order was for my feet, which refused to cooperate when Kurt opened my door.

I finally stepped out into the sticky humidity of Pecan Creek, Georgia. I was from a place known for its rain, so I came with built-in tolerance for humidity, but this was different. Everything was extremely dry, but somehow the air still felt like a damp, fleece blanket. I grabbed my backpack and followed Kurt and Melina into the house.

A burst of cool air greeted me when I stepped into the kitchen. The walls were a cheery yellow, and tall windows let in a view of the sun as it began to sink into the line of trees in the backyard. Across the room, three kids and the babysitter sat clustered around a table. Kurt leaned my dilapidated luggage against the dark cherry cabinets and motioned for me to do the same with my bag. I trailed behind Kurt and Melina to where the kids sat like plastic garden owls, their eyes wide and unblinking as they assessed the intruder.

"Hey, babies!" Melina sang. "We brought your cousin home!"

Home. The word taunted me like the word *family.* Blinking back the unwelcome thought, I stepped toward Melina's outstretched hand.

"Here we go. Time for the intros," she said as she clapped her hands.

"There's our girl Tristan, but she goes by Trissy unless she's in trouble." My aunt winked at me and leaned to kiss her daughter's cheek. The girl's curly red hair, fair skin, and freckles looked like her father's, but the eyes she turned in my direction were a vibrant shade of green like her mom's.

"Hi, Trissy." I tried out the unusual nickname. My cousin smiled, revealing gapped teeth, and then went back to her coloring project.

Melina turned to the boy sitting next to Trissy. "This is Jackson." She tousled the boy's hair. He had his mom's black-brown hair with his father's eyes and freckles. He waved briefly before reaching for a crayon that started to roll off the table.

Kurt caught the crayon and handed it to his son. "There you go, man."

"And this," Melina said as she lifted a toddler from his booster seat, "is little Cooper. Isn't that right?" She hoisted the towheaded toddler into her arms and tickled him beneath his chin. I waved at him, and he buried his face in his mom's shoulder. Melina kissed the top of his head and handed him off to her husband, who tossed him gently in the air until he giggled.

Melina gestured to the girl who seemed to be about my age sitting at the other end of the table. The girl stood and tucked her long, wavy brown hair behind her ears.

"I'm Becca Shepherd," she said as she stretched out her hand to shake mine. I didn't exactly shake hands when I met people my age, but the gesture seemed natural for her so I clasped her hand and shook.

"I'm Sadie Franklin."

"Becca's also known as an angel disguised as a babysitter," Melina added, "and your first friend in Pecan Creek!"

Becca's smile reflected in her deep hazel eyes. "I don't know about *angel,* but I love these kids. Speaking of kids, I promised my little sister I'd watch a movie with her tonight, so I should get going. They've all been fed, and Cooper had a bath after a pudding incident."

Melina took a check out of her purse on the counter. "Bless you," she said, although I hadn't heard anyone sneeze. "Thanks for your help, Becca."

Becca took the check and hugged each of the kids. Turning to me, she smiled again. "It's great meeting the niece of the infamous Kurt Elliot."

"Infamous, huh?" Kurt set Cooper on the floor.

I stood back and watched the easy banter take place among my aunt, uncle, and Becca before she slipped out the door.

Once the door clicked behind her, I stood in the middle of the kitchen, not sure what to do with myself. Melina glanced at the clock. "You probably don't want a big dinner, Sadie, so how about I just fix you a snack? Trissy, why don't you show Sadie where she'll be staying, okay?"

Trissy reached for my hand. "I'll show you our room," she said.

10

Our room? I grabbed my backpack and suitcase instead of her hand.

I followed Trissy through the living room and down a short hallway. She pushed open a solid-wood door to reveal a room that looked like some sort of bubble gum monster coughed up a cotton candy hairball. In other words, the place was *pink*.

And I was supposed to share a room with an eight-year-old? All I knew about little girls was that, once upon a time, I was one. But I'd spent the past eight years trying to block out my eighth year of life.

"Well, here it is!" Trissy didn't know the definition of shy. She gestured in the direction of the bed.

"Where do I sleep?" I wasn't dumb, but I had to ask.

"With me, silly!" She took my backpack and tossed it on the bed. A fluffy orange cat hissed and dashed out from under the bed and out the room. I jumped. Trissy giggled. "That's Marigold. He's super mean."

I was less concerned with the cat than the thought of sharing a bed with a sparkplug of energy. Especially since we'd just met, like, ten minutes ago.

Trissy clapped her hands, reminding me of her mom. "I have two closets, and Mama helped me clean out some of my little kid toys so you can put your stuff in one."

Finally. Something didn't I have to share. I fell back on the pink patchwork quilt and sank down beside my backpack. For the first time all day, the full force of my exhaustion hit me like a freight train. I was glad bedtime would come three hours earlier tonight.

While Trissy droned on about how my other things were still in their boxes in the storage shed and how we could pretend we were opening presents when we unpacked them tomorrow, I let my eyes close. I could get used to this bed. It was so soft, so plush, so—

"Sadie! Your snack's ready!" Melina's voice rang through the house.

I groaned and rolled off the bed. Trissy put her hands on my lower back and shoved me in the direction of the kitchen. Personal space was obviously a foreign concept to this chick.

Melina apologized profusely that my first "real" meal in Georgia (Kurt seemed put off that lunch at the Varsity didn't count) was a peanut butter and jelly sandwich.

"I promise we'll eat something of substance for dinner tomorrow," she said as she set a glass of water in front of me. Kurt took the kids out to check on their garden, and Melina joined me at the table. She offered a short and sweet (sweet because it was short) prayer for the food and then lifted her eyes to mine.

"I still can't believe you're here. And so grown up and beautiful too." Her smile was soft, motherly. "You look just like Melody when she was your age, you know?"

I looked down at my slumped, weary position in the chair and swallowed hard. I never really considered myself to be all that pretty, but being compared to my beautiful mom brought tears to my eyes. "I've been through a lot," I said quietly. The confession surprised me. That was supposed to stay in my head, yet I'd just put it out there in the open for my aunt to interpret. I hadn't meant to play the vulnerability card.

Melina took a sip of her water. "I can't begin to imagine. Do you wanna catch me up on your life a little bit? We've got a few minutes before the troops come in."

"Actually, I'd like to take a shower and go to bed, if that's okay. It's been a long day." I had neither the desire nor energy to go into all of that.

"Oh, okay." Melina swiped at the condensation left by her glass on the table. "I understand. Trissy is staying in the boys' room tonight, so you can have a chance to acclimate." I sighed in relief. I had been planning to camp out on the squishy suede sofa in the living room, but a whole bed to myself would be so much better. "Go get your stuff, and I'll show you the bathroom."

Even though the sun had just gone down, I went straight to bed after my shower. I sighed as I closed the bedroom door, grateful for a few hours of solitude. I wouldn't call myself antisocial or anything, but when you're used to a lot of alone time, a whole day surrounded by people speaking in an accent that might as well be a foreign language is draining.

I felt like I was at a hotel. Melina had already turned down the quilt to reveal silky, lavender sheets. The lamp sitting on the bedside table had a paisley pink and purple shade and emitted a soft, inviting glow. It almost made the utter pinkness of the room bearable.

I clicked off the little lamp and crawled into bed.

Chapter 3

When I awoke Saturday morning, I stretched and glanced out the window. The sun was already high in the sky.

I climbed out of bed slowly and pulled on a pair of gym shorts and a T-shirt before sneaking down the hall to the bathroom to brush my teeth. My nose picked up the smell of bacon, and I followed it into the kitchen.

Melina and Trissy sat at the table, each with a mug of coffee between their hands because, obviously, Trissy wasn't hyper enough without caffeine.

"Mornin', sunshine!" Trissy called. Too perky.

Melina looked up from her mug and offered me a sweet smile. "We saved you some pancakes and bacon. It wasn't easy."

"Yeah," added Trissy. "You should be thankful. I about had to smack my brothers."

"Where are the boys?" I yawned.

"They're in the backyard with Kurt. Might as well enjoy the peacefulness." Melina motioned across the kitchen. "I know my Seattleite wants some coffee, right?"

I found a clean mug sitting by the coffeepot and poured a cup. Trissy waved me over to a seat next to her, and I sat down to eat a plate of the fluffiest, butteriest, most delicious pancakes and chewiest bacon I'd ever eaten. The mother-daughter duo watched me eat with amusement.

Six pancakes later, I sat back and rested my hands on my stomach. "That was so awesome."

Melina plopped yet another pancake on my stack. "You're rail thin. Eat another one." Actually, I was proud of my weight. Despite the insane amounts of fast-food and microwave meals I consumed while fending for myself, I'd managed to stay slim.

Since I'd eaten breakfast an hour before the next meal, I skipped lunch and finally started unpacking. All of my stuff fit into the closet except for socks and T-shirts, which I put in a drawer Trissy loaned me. All of my makeup went in a drawer in the bathroom I shared with all of the kids. I tried not to be ungrateful, since the Elliots were being so nice to me. But I'd had my own bedroom and bathroom almost forever, and it was hard to imagine sharing the space with three kids.

It didn't take long to unpack my suitcase, but then I had to unpack the boxes of stuff I had shipped over the previous week. There wasn't much in them, really, just a few more clothes and a couple of trinkets from my room.

"What? No posters?" Trissy popped her head in the doorway, and I jumped.

"Um, nope. No posters."

"Really? But they're fabulous! Look at mine!" She jabbed the air in the direction of the bed. Oh yes, those posters. How I managed to get any sleep with a herd of horses staring me down was beyond me. Especially when some of the horses were pink. With sparkles.

"Yeah, those are some great posters, Trissy. But I don't have any."

Trissy looked dejected, like her horses had just lost the possibility of ever making any friends. "Hm. Do you have some pictures?"

"Pictures of what?"

"Of you and your mom and dad, silly!" It was all I could do not to kick Trissy out of the room. She was just a kid. A tactless kid, but a kid nonetheless. "No, actually, I don't." I did have some pictures, of course, but the truth was they hurt. They were reminders of what had been and would never be again. Trissy didn't need to know that.

"Well, how about—"

"Trissy," I interjected as gently as possible, "can you please let me finish unpacking? Alone? Then I'll go outside with you, and you can show me your swing set or something."

For a minute, I was afraid I'd hurt her feelings. But then a smile broke out across her freckled face. She said, "Please! The swing set is for my little brothers. I'll show you the trampoline."

After an afternoon of swinging while watching Trissy's flipping skills and Jackson's attempts to impress me with his remote-controlled car, I went inside and splashed water on my sweat-coated face.

Trissy decided at some point during the day that she would be my shadow, so she also splashed her face with water. Damp curls still clung to her cheeks as she reached into a drawer under the sink and pulled out a tube of lip balm.

"I like to look fresh for supper," she explained.

Melina called Trissy into the kitchen to help with dinner preparations, and I followed my skipping cousin into the kitchen. My eyes started to water as soon as we reached the kitchen. I wasn't crying; it's just that I hadn't smelled real food in so long my senses were spazzing out on me.

Melina stood at the stove, a whiny Cooper wrapped around her leg. She waved a gravy-covered spoon in our direction. "Trissy, get the plates out. Sadie, Trissy will show you where the cups are so you can get those out."

I barely had time to salute and parrot Trissy's "Yes, ma'am!" before a funny look passed over my aunt's face. She blinked. "I'm sorry, Sadie. I'm so used to being in mommy mode, it's kinda hard to snap out of it. You don't mind, do you?" Mind if she was in mommy mode or mind getting the cups down? Actually, I didn't mind setting the table at all. It was the whole I'm-the-mom thing that was getting me. Melina must have picked up on this, because she quickly added, "Anytime you think I'm treating you like one of my kiddos, you let me know, you hear?"

I managed a half smile and a nod and then followed Trissy to the cup cabinet.

The Elliots eyed me curiously throughout dinner. I guess I shocked them when I mentioned the closest thing I'd had to a real meal in the past six months was hand-tossed pizza. I'd had a stomachache ever since gorging on pancakes at breakfast, but I indulged again that night on what Melina called "comfort food": country-fried steak, mashed potatoes and gravy, green beans, and biscuits.

Kurt assured me she was just trying to make a good first impression, and she shoved him. My aunt and uncle amused me. They were easy to like as long as I remembered none of the current circumstances were their fault, although they did have a herd of kids that would no doubt drive me crazy by the end of summer.

After dinner, Melina sent the boys into the living room to play while Kurt, Melina, and Trissy established the ground rules that came with living in the Elliot home. I don't know who saw the wisdom in letting Trissy in on it.

"First," Kurt said around a bite of blackberry cobbler, "we're very happy you're here. We want you to be comfortable and feel like this is your home. Or home away from home. Whichever suits you."

"I hate to do this," Melina dove in, "but I need you to do your own laundry. I'm up to my eyeballs in dirty clothes these days, but I can teach you how if you want." If only she knew I'd been washing my own clothes for the past eight years. "And once you meet some new friends, they're welcome to come over to hang out. Just ask our permission." She paused and placed a hand over her middle. She stared at her plate for a minute. "I'm sorry. Bean distracted me. I think that's it for now, though."

"Don't forget the no-boys-allowed-in-the-bedroom rule!" Trissy interjected. I coughed. *What?* She pointed her fork in the direction of the living room. "I made that one up. When my brothers come in to play, they destroy it. I think you'll like this rule, Sadie."

"That's a good rule, Tris," Kurt agreed. I barely knew these people, but by the way he tilted his head and looked at me while he said it, I knew he wasn't just talking about playtime with the kids.

I poked at my cobbler until my fork was loaded. I understood the need for ground rules, but really, who did they think I was? How much had Dad told them about me?

"Okay, I know I'm not from the, *uh*, ideal environment, but I'm not going to make a habit of sneaking guys in to sleep over."

I glanced at Trissy, who watched me over the rim of her milk glass. I was never around kids, so I completely forgot to filter what I said. I held my breath and avoided eye contact with my aunt and uncle.

"Really?" Trissy's eyes blossomed with excitement. That couldn't be good. "Oh, Sadie, I can't believe I get to have your first sleepover party with you. It'll be so fun!"

I choked on a chunk of blackberry until the fruit dislodged from my windpipe. I dared to glance at Melina and Kurt. She had her hand over her mouth, and he still had his loaded fork in his hand, but the corners of his mouth twitched. I felt my eyes water and held back a cackle.

I got to experience the "fun" a few hours later. It was still earlier than my usual bedtime, but I found myself completely exhausted again. I chalked it up to all of the unpacking and fresh air. That, and I knew Kurt and Melina still wanted me to catch them up on the life of Sadie Franklin. I curled up on about a fourth of the double bed, as far away from my cousin as possible. If there was one thing I was not, it was touchy-feely. Like, seriously, don't touch me unless you're swatting a mosquito carrying the West Nile virus. At least Trissy assured me Marigold the cat wasn't under the bed today and was sleeping on top of the dryer instead. "He likes the bumpity-bumpity," she'd said.

I was so tired I fell asleep before Trissy could finish explaining why she couldn't wear socks to bed. My last thought of my second night in Pecan Creek, Georgia: *Someone save me.*

***

In my dream that night, I sat with my mom and Melina at the Elliots' kitchen table, laughing and talking. Mom's sandy hair was pulled back into a smooth ponytail, her blue eyes sparkling. She had this radiant glow about her, and her smile made me smile too. I leaned over to hug her, but Trissy burst into the room, dressed in a bright-pink sundress. Without a word, she took my mom by the hands and pulled her to the car waiting outside the house. And then

Mom was gone. Disappeared. Melina turn to me and said, "Looks like it's just us now, Sadie Grey."

***

I woke up in a cold sweat. For a full minute, I couldn't remember where I was, but then I heard Trissy's deep, undisturbed breaths beside me, and it all came flooding back. I hadn't dreamed about Mom in a long time, but then again, her memory clung a little more tightly to my thoughts since I'd come to stay with the Elliots and Melina had tried to fill the mother-sized gap in my life. My heartbeat returned to a normal rhythm, but I was restless and needed to walk around.

Unfortunately, I hadn't memorized the layout of the house very well yet. By the time I reached the living room, I'd hit my hip on the dresser, stubbed my toe on a threshold, and walked into a closed door. I was relieved to find a lamp turned on in the living room. Not just because it saved me from breaking my foot on a block tower but because I was tired of the dark.

I sank into the plush suede sofa and pulled a quilt off the back of the couch. After tucking it around me, I drew my knees to my chest and stared at the light, trying to ward off the shivering. I was still exhausted, but I was scared of what I might see if I closed my eyes again. The memories—even the good ones—haunted me like ghosts. I liked to remember Mom, but whenever I thought of her, I saw the horrific scenes, heard the terrible sounds, felt that suffocating sense of terror that stole so much more than just my breath.

For a while, I sat there in a daze until I heard footsteps padding across the carpet. I glanced up in time to see Melina sinking onto the couch beside me, one hand on her abdomen, the other on her back.

"Hey, Sadie," she said as she yawned.

"I'm sorry I woke you up."

"Oh, you didn't." She yawned and patted her stomach. "Baby Bean is a night owl, which means it's only three o'clock and I've already been to the bathroom four times."

I'd never been around a pregnant woman before. One of the girls from school got pregnant the year before, but she'd moved to Portland to live with her dad's family.

"Can you feel it move?" I asked

Melina shifted her weight so she faced me. "Feel what move?"

"The baby."

Melina nodded excitedly. "Oh yeah. Here, give me your hand." She grabbed my wrist, and I watched her drag my hand over her stomach. "Now, just wait here for a second."

Melina poked herself in the side. I held my breath and waited. For what, though, I wasn't sure.

A moment later, something jabbed my hand, and I jumped. "Whoa!" I clamped my free hand over my mouth. "What was that?"

Melina winced. "That was a foot."

"No way. That's so cool," I whispered. This whole thing fascinated me, and I kept my hand hovering over Melina's middle. It was really awkward when I thought about it, getting in someone's space like that.

But Melina didn't seem to mind. She placed her hand on top of mine and slid it to the side. "Over here. I think the baby is boxing now." Melina crossed her eyes, and I laughed.

"Does it hurt that bad?"

She slid my hand a little more to the side. "A little, but I wouldn't trade this feeling for anything. If I can feel my baby, I know he or she is healthy. And that's completely worth it."

"You love your kids, don't you?" The question popped out of my mouth without warning.

"I'm completely in love with them." She looked straight at me. "And I know your mama felt the same way about you."

I looked down quickly before she could see the shadow pass over my face. I felt her warm hand on my back.

"I know this change isn't easy for you, Sadie, but I'm here if you need to talk." She squeezed my shoulder. "Not to try to replace your mama, of course, but to be your aunt, your friend."

Had she heard my thoughts? I slid out from under my blanket. "I should get back to bed."

Melina sighed. "Okay. I'll see you in the morning. Good night, Sadie Grey."

"Night, Melina."

Chapter 4

When I was about five years old, Mom told me the truth about the moon. We were sitting on the couch in the living room one night before my dad came home from work, looking out the window at the full moon. Mom had pointed at the sky and told me the moon didn't actually glow like a star or the sun.

"Then how does it shine?" I asked.

"It reflects the sun."

I wasn't sure what "reflect" meant, but I knew light made everything look happy and friendly. After that night, whenever I looked up at the moon on a really dark night, I felt safe because it meant the friendly sunshine was still there, somewhere. I couldn't see the sun, but the moon could.

Now, many years and many miles from that night, the Elliots' screen door complained as I slipped out of the house and into the predawn. I looked for the moon—looked for a promise that the sun was coming—but it wasn't there. Instead, the world was bathed in confusing gray hues. The cars, the trampoline, the swing set—all gray, like an old photograph. Without the light of the sun or the reflection of the moon, nothing felt certain. I identified with that.

The air was cool as I raised my arms over my head, attempting to loosen joints still sore from a night of tossing and turning. There was something about being around Melina that brought on the memories and dreams, maybe because she was so similar to my mom. Despite the good dreams, I was scared they'd turn into the terrible memories of her death, so I ran from them.

The street was still sleeping at six o'clock as I walked to the edge of the driveway. I tightened my ponytail and glanced down to make sure my laces were tied. I hadn't left the old yellow house since I'd arrived two days earlier, and I didn't know where I was headed, but facing the unknown was familiar and somehow invigorating.

I turned left and broke into a light jog. My muscles, stiff at first, slowly warmed up to the exercise. I gradually increased my speed, watching the neighborhood pass by in my peripheral. Melina told me all of these houses were old, like, early-twentieth-century old. The pecan and oak trees surrounding them had to be at least that old too. The streetlamps clicked off for the day as I passed under them, and I laughed sardonically. *Story of my life. Here comes Sadie. There goes clarity.*

As I ran, I breathed in through my nose, sharp but paced, letting the air travel through me and mingle in my lungs before leaving my mouth. The sidewalk was cracked and uneven, so I veered slightly until I was on the road. My feet pounded the pavement, the sound mixing with my breaths, creating the only soundtrack I needed. Or wanted.

I stopped pumping my arms long enough to press a hand to my lower abdomen. My side burned, probably because I hadn't run in several days, but I kept going as though I could outrun the pain. I alternated between jogging and running until the sun began to make an appearance over the tall trees, occasionally stopping to take jagged breaths, bending over, heart pounding before making myself go again. Acknowledging the growing pain in my side wouldn't help me move past it.

By the time I reached the end of a cul-de-sac, my breathing came in the form of heaves as I tried to gulp enough air to quench my burning lungs. I'd pushed myself too hard. My abdomen felt like it was being squeezed by a small clamp—one of those you use to hold a stack of papers together when a staple won't cut it. Running was addicting, though. The endorphins releasing into my system, the adrenaline propelling me forward, the focus on breathing taking my mind off everything.

Sitting on the curb, I rested my arms on my knees and focused on breathing. My legs burned, sure, but that ache in my side meant there was no way I could jog back. I glanced down at my watch and realized I'd been going for over an hour. No wonder I hurt. I slid down to the asphalt, going through some stretches. Toe touch, count to fifteen. Stand. Cross right leg over left, bend down, touch toes, count to fifteen, switch legs. I stood and started walking, one fist pressing into my middle.

I reached the end of the cul-de-sac and stopped. *Oh, come on, Sadie!* I thought. *Did you seriously just get lost in this blip of a town?* Apparently, I did. I had no clue where I was, no cell phone to call for help, no anything. When I set out earlier that morning, I'd planned a quick jog around the block. I'd stayed in a residential area, but for all I knew, I might not have been in Pecan Creek anymore. My favorite part of running was the ability to block out the world, but today that proved to be a stupid idea.

I tried to recall familiar landmarks as I walked. All of the houses had large front porches and giant trees flanking them. The streets ran together, all of them named after something floral. *Chrysanthemum, Hydrangea, Iris* ... It was nearly eight o'clock now, and more cars were on the streets. Sweat meandered from my hairline, down my cheeks, and off my chin. I flapped my shirt, trying to cool off a little. The exercise, combined with the day's growing humidity, was intense.

After using my fine-tuned deduction skills—trying out several wrong streets—I arrived at a familiar road sign. Magnolia Street. Finally! Only, I came in at the opposite end from the one I'd left.

My muscles were warm and loose, but that crazy abdominal pain somehow made my head throb. I needed water. I quietly slipped into the house, hoping everyone was taking advantage of sleeping in on the last day of the weekend.

"Oh, thank goodness! There you are!" I froze in the doorway as Melina rushed toward me, the skirt of a turquoise wrap dress swishing around her knees. She reached to hug me but took a step back when she noticed my sweat-damp T-shirt and, most likely, my stench.

Her eyes cooled from a look of relief to one of accusation. She brought a hand to her forehead, silver bangles jangling on her wrist. "Where have you possibly been?"

"I couldn't sleep. I was running. I'm a runner." *That should clear things up.*

"Sadie, I—" She ran her fingers through her bangs. "I was so worried. Kurt and I—oh! Kurt!" She stepped over to the counter and grabbed her cell phone. I waited while she placed a call, sweat still dripping down my back.

"She's home," Melina spoke into the phone. "Uh-huh. I don't know yet. Okay. Yeah, you too." She hung up and slid the phone back on the counter. "Kurt has been driving from here to kingdom come looking for you. You didn't have your phone, did you? Why, Sadie?"

I shrugged and motioned to my shorts. "I didn't have a pocket to put it in."

Trissy chose that moment to skip into the kitchen holding out a ribbon to match her yellow sundress. "Mama, I'm ready for you to fix my hair."

Melina waved her off. "Just a minute, Tris. Go check on the boys and make sure Cooper is okay."

Trissy sighed loudly and left the room. "Mornin', Sadie!" she called over her shoulder.

Melina turned her attention back to me. "I wasn't talking about your phone. We were so worried."

I stepped around her and sat at the table, hunched forward a bit because of the pain. "Can I get a glass of water?"

My aunt silently retrieved a cup and filled it with ice and water from the refrigerator. She set it in front of me and then sighed as she eased into a chair across the table. I noticed for the first time she already had her makeup on, and her silky hair was curled a little on the ends. Even though she was thirty, she usually looked like she couldn't be any older than twenty-five. But right now she looked weary.

I took measured sips of water until the cup was empty while Melina waited on me to talk. "I didn't think I needed to ask permission to exercise," I said. *Especially from someone I've lived with for two days.* "I'm not a little kid. I'm almost seventeen."

Melina sighed again. We were reaching the point where I was afraid she'd run out of oxygen. "Sadie, I—you—we—"

"Us?" I offered.

She rolled her eyes and once again looked younger than her years. "Not now. We're all leaving for church in twenty minutes, so we'll talk later."

"Church?" *Um, not.* "I haven't even had a shower." *Or a desire to go to church.* My inner thought train was starting to irritate me. I needed another distraction.

Kurt entered the kitchen, dressed in basketball shorts and a T-shirt, and dropped his keys on the counter. "Y'all okay?"

Melina huffed. "Can you take Trissy and Jackson to Sunday school, Kurt?"

"Come talk to me while I get ready, Mel." He gently helped her to her feet and led her out of the kitchen.

"Sadie," Melina said as she turned around in the doorway, "shower, change, and meet me back in the kitchen, please."

***

"What a poor, deprived creature you are, Sadie Grey." Melina emptied the contents of a little plastic cup of cream into her coffee and stirred. For most people, being called by their middle name meant they were in trouble. Melina used it as a term of endearment, which was how I knew she'd calmed down. This family was backward in so many ways.

I took a sip of my own coffee. "It's not my fault, Melina."

"I just never thought a child from Seattle could be so sheltered." She dumped another cream into her coffee. That made three. "I mean you've seriously never been to the Waffle House? Have you even had grits before?"

"What are those?" I tilted my head to the side as she gasped. "I'm kidding. Of course I've had grits," I reassured her.

Melina and I sat at a booth, facing each other. At the end of the table, Cooper sat in a high chair, quietly scribbling on a kids' menu. The little guy was ridiculously shy around me. Melina told me he was perfectly capable of carrying on a conversation; he just chose to sit back and observe life. I'd only heard him say a maximum of two words since I'd met him.

Now, though, he glanced up as a waitress set a chocolate chip waffle in front of him, his green eyes wide. "Yum," he declared without any inflection in his voice. My aunt smiled and leaned over to kiss the top of his head. I leaned back as a waitress set a plate of food in front of me that I'd watched the cook prepare on a griddle right out there in the small, dining area.

"Here's your All-Star Special," the waitress said, her penciled brows rising into her curly, brown hair. She retrieved two more plates from the counter and set them in front of me. In total, there were four—I counted *four*—plates in front of me. Waffle, bacon, sausage, ham, scrambled eggs, grits, and toast. I loved eating food from different cultures, and there was nothing extremely out of the ordinary about the meal, but I was quickly learning southern America was a whole other world from the Northwest.

"Is all of this mine?" I whistled as the waitress left to greet a table of new customers.

"All yours." Melina wrapped her slender fingers around her coffee mug. "I ate this morning. I just thought we needed a chance to talk. Plus I'd hate to waste all of the effort I put into getting ready to leave the house this morning." Melina closed her eyes. "I'll pray. Dear Lord, thank You for a beautiful summer morning. Thank You for this food, and thank You for Sadie. Amen."

By the time I realized what was happening, she had already finished her prayer.

"So," Melina said as she began cutting Cooper's waffle into bite-sized pieces and I stared at my food, unsure of where to begin, "I'll be honest." I held my breath, waiting for her reprimand. "Kurt's the one who's good with teens. I tend to hang out with the younger crowd." She slid Cooper's plate back to him. "Don't I, bud?" My little cousin nodded resolutely, but his eyes looked confused. "So I'm learning, Sadie. I'm trying not to treat you like one of my kids, but I also know I can't just turn you loose on life, you know? See my dilemma?"

I didn't really, so I didn't say anything, just focused on poking butter into all of the little squares in my waffle.

"Here's my idea." Melina stared at me until I looked up at her. "Let's forget this morning, okay? Let's start fresh." She cradled her mug in her hands and took a slow sip of the cup of sugar with a touch of coffee in it.

I picked at the crispy edge of my waffle. I still wasn't sure where she was going with this.

"I want to be your friend, Sadie." Oh, so *that*'s where she was going. How many times had adults told me that, only to turn around and yell at me later? "But I also want to be your aunt—the woman figure in your life."

A piece of bacon lodged itself in my throat, and I coughed. I'd grown up without a "woman figure" in my life, and unlike a movie, I couldn't rewind to the crucial scenes in my life when I could've used a woman to help me figure out life. As far as I was concerned, it was too late for that. I sipped my coffee and noticed Cooper staring at my second piece of bacon.

"Can he have that?" I asked. Melina nodded, so I dangled it in front of the kid. He eyed me for a minute, one eye slightly squinted, before slowly reaching out and taking it.

"Say thank-you, Coop," Melinda prodded.

"Sanks." He shoved half the slice into his little mouth.

He really was cute. I smiled and stuck a spoon in my grits. I already knew I didn't like them, but I didn't want them to go to waste.

"Your cousins are going to love having you here, Sadie Grey," Melina said.

My middle name again. Why did it bother me when she said it? For one thing, it wasn't very creative; I have gray eyes. For another, it was spelled the English way with an *e* rather than an *a*, which made even less sense. I set my spoon aside and gulped a few sips of my coffee, even though it was still way too hot. Maybe it was because Melina, who was *not* my mom, used my middle name like my mom did. Not even my dad did that. I took another sip of coffee, watching Cooper turn his waffle chunks into racecars.

"I'm not going to pretend to know your life, Sadie," Melina said, reaching for Cooper's fork and feeding him some waffle.

"That's probably best," I said, meaning she wouldn't want to know everything.

She ignored me. "But I want you to know that your mama was more than my sister. She was my best friend. We went through a really rough patch when she moved away with your father right before you were born, but that doesn't change how much I loved her. I want to remember her, Sadie, and I know you do too, so if you ever want to—"

"You don't know what I want," I said, my jaw tight and my voice quiet. "You're right about not knowing anything about my life. I've been through—"

"Little ears are listening, Sadie."

"I've been through all kinds of crazy stuff. But I've learned. I know how to take care of myself. I'm sorry if you didn't like me leaving the house this morning, but I know how to make it on my own." I tried to pick up my fork, but it clattered to the table. My hands quivered, and I shoved them into my lap.

Melina sat a little straighter. "You're right. I'm sorry. All I was saying was that if you want to talk about Melody, I'm here."

"Eight years too late," I mumbled under my breath.

"What was that?"

"I said, 'This is more food than I can eat.'"

***

"Hurry, hurry, hurry! Jack, where are you?" Trissy ran into the living room and dove onto the couch, startling me out of my Sunday afternoon stupor. "Mama! Hurry!"

I placed one arm across my middle and the other in front of my face. "Trissy, please."

Trissy pried my arm off my face. "It's two o'clock!"

"So?" I pushed myself into a sitting position as Melina carried Cooper and a laptop into the room. "What's going on?" I yawned, wondering why the boys weren't taking a nap.

"It's a tradition," Melina said. "Every Sunday afternoon, the kids get to video chat with their grandparents." She sat next to me. "Actually, they're your grandparents too." She bounced a little in her seat. "Oh, this is exciting!"

My breath quickened. *My grandparents?* I hadn't seen them in years. They always called on my birthday and major holidays, but my dad never had a great relationship with them, so there wasn't a whole lot of keeping in touch going on. How much did they know about me? My dad sure didn't keep them updated, and Melina didn't really know much about me either, so she couldn't have told them. But what would they think of me when they actually saw me? What would they think if they learned I wasn't exactly walking the straight and narrow?

I forced myself to breathe as Jackson finally entered the room, a blanket tied around his neck like a cape. The three kids piled onto the couch. Trissy stretched out behind my head like a cat, while Melina set Cooper between us and Jackson sat on her other side. "What time is it in Russia?" I asked.

"They're near Moscow, so it's already about eleven thirty at night right now."

Trissy leaned around me and stuck her face next to mine. "They live in the future!"

Melina opened the laptop and placed a video call to my grandparents. After a minute, the ringing ended and their faces filled the screen. My heartbeat quickened, and my reaction surprised me. They looked exactly like I remembered them, just with grayer hair and a few more laugh lines. But their eyes were the same. I don't know why, but I remembered their eyes the best. They were kind and gentle and full of life.

"Hey, Mom and Dad," Melina said, smiling. She balanced the laptop precariously on what was left of her lap, disappointing Marigold who was about to launch from the floor. He sauntered out of the room while Trissy and Jackson said hello, and Cooper even smiled around the thumb in his mouth. Melina shushed Trissy right as she launched into a description of the picture she'd colored at church and angled the webcam toward me.

"Mom and Dad, there's someone else who wants to say hey."

I waved at the screen, my fingers shaking slightly. "Sadie," my grandmother said, "it's so good to see you! Isn't she pretty, Jim?" My grandparents gushed over me and how much I'd grown. I actually enjoyed their praise, until I remembered they didn't even know me. They were, after all, just doing the grandparent thing.

I answered questions about how tall I was, my favorite foods, and other surface-level stuff. I told my grandparents about my trip and my first impressions of the South. I even told them my dad was doing well, just to make them happy. At some point during my mini interview, Kurt came into the room. He sat in the recliner and studied me.

After the questions, I gladly let the focus shift back to the kids as Trissy and Jackson chatted about their lives for a few minutes before everyone exchanged good-byes. Afterward, I resumed my relaxed position on the couch while Melina took the boys to their room for a short nap. When she returned to the living room and propped her feet up in the recliner, I asked, "What are Grandpa and Grandma doing in Russia?"

Melina's eyes were closed, but she smiled. "They're missionaries."

Chapter 5

Melina told me I would attend church that evening since I'd missed out that morning. She and Kurt wanted me to start making friends in Pecan Creek, even though I knew I wouldn't have much in common with church kids including, well, *church*.

Kurt and I pulled into the parking lot at five o'clock. The activities didn't begin until five thirty, but he wanted me to get there early so I could have a meet-and-greet with whomever showed up before my class started.

I stepped out of Kurt's truck and tugged my denim shorts down a little. I wasn't completely scandalous—I knew the religious people I was about to encounter didn't want an eyeful of my thighs, runner's thighs that they were.

I followed Kurt through the side doors of the building. "To get to the youth room, you go straight up the stairs, hang a left, last door on your right," he explained, but kept walking with me.

"I can fend for myself," I suggested. *I mean hello. Story of my life.*

"Oh, I'm sure you can, Sadie." He held open the door to a supply closet. "But this is kind of my job."

I snorted. "Aiming for that elusive Uncle of the Year award, huh?"

"Actually, a paycheck. But that too." Kurt laughed. "I meant that I'm the youth pastor. I lead all of the awesome stuff you're about to experience."

Someone put me out of my misery.

Kurt missed my Oscar-worthy eye roll and began handing me stacks of Styrofoam cups. "Usually," he grunted as he stood on his tiptoes to reach some more cups, "we do some Bible study on Sunday nights."

"Naturally."

"But we switched it up last week and did some pretty intense spiritual stuff on Wednesday, so tonight's game night, like we usually do on Wednesdays. You see?" He handed me another stack. At least I wouldn't have to listen to a sermon. All of the praying my relatives did at the dinner table suddenly made a lot more sense.

Once my arms held enough cups to block a good bit—like, 99.9 percent—of my vision, Kurt said, "All right. Well, I'm headed to my office. Remember, up those stairs over there, last door on your right. You good?"

If my hands hadn't been so full, I would've been tempted to salute. I settled for a *mm-hmm* instead.

"I'll be up there in ten minutes, max." His steps faded down the hall.

I inched my way to the stairwell door and attempted to shift the cups around so I could open it.

Just as I'd nearly achieved a balancing act worthy of Cirque du Soleil, the door swung open toward me, and I lost my balance. Cups went everywhere, as did my arms and legs as I flailed around, eventually landing on the floor. I uttered a short strand of choice words and then clamped my hand over my mouth when I remembered where I was. I sat like that for a moment, trying to control my anger long enough to face whoever failed to look through the handy little window on the door before shoving it open like the building was on fire.

A pair of brown loafers stood in front of me, attached to a pair of khaki pants, attached to a white dress shirt complete with—*are you serious?*—a bow tie. My eyes made it to the face, which I noticed belonged to a guy around my age. His brown hair curled just before it reached that ridiculous bow tie, and his dark brown eyes stared at me.

I flicked a cup off my knee and Bow-tie Boy sprang into action, grabbing cups like candy from a piñata. "Here, let me help you."

"Um, thanks." I ignored the hand he stretched out to me and hoisted myself off the floor.

We silently gathered the cups until the load was split evenly between us. The guy shifted his stacks to one side and stuck out his hand again. I suddenly thought of Becca and how she shook my hand when we met Friday.

I slowly slipped my hand into his cool grasp and shook once before letting go. "Thanks ... for the help. I'm Sadie Franklin." I shook my head to toss the bangs off my face.

"Nice to meet you, Sadie." Bow-tie Boy had a dripping drawl. "I'm Truitt Peyton."

And that was how I met my second peer in Pecan Creek. I ended up with a bruised tailbone and dignity all in one.

"Well, Truitt Peyton, I need to get upstairs with these cups."

"Your first time at Pecan Creek Baptist and Kurt's already pack-mulin' you, huh?" He grinned, his chin dimpling.

"Something like that." I started up the stairs, Truitt walking beside me. He had a couple of inches on me, but he wasn't tall— maybe five foot seven.

"Where are you from, Sadie?" He glanced at me as we reached the landing and began ascending the second set of steps.

"I'm from out west, staying with some relatives for the summer." I quickly made a plan. If I didn't tell him I was the youth pastor's niece, maybe he wouldn't find out. Because if he knew that, he'd probably assume I was some super-spiritual person just because my relatives were Christians. As it was, the guy was already looking at me like I was some newly discovered breed of pecan tree or something.

He opened his mouth to speak again but stopped himself when Kurt rounded the corner. For once, I was glad to see the overgrown kid.

"Sadie! There you are. Truitt, what's up, man? I see you've met my niece, Sadie."

Truitt glanced at me and arched one of the dark eyebrows on his tanned face. I groaned as my plan flew out the window. Instead of an anonymity, I was about to become an anomaly. Awesome.

"Yes, sir," he said. Of course he said *sir*. Any self-respecting, southern bow-tie wearer had to say that. "She didn't say she was your niece, though. Do you like the South, Sadie?"

"It's kind of hot and sticky, Trudy, but I'm used to humidity so I'll live."

"I'm Truitt."

"Right." I began marching down the hallway.

"Sadie?"

Seriously, the guy just couldn't take a hint. "Yeah?"

"Youth room is this way."

"Oh." I turned on my heel and followed the guys down the hall.

The Pecan Creek Baptist youth group met in a dump. I mean it wasn't dirty; it was just full of old stuff. A crooked recliner, a couch with a faded floral slipcover, and a mishmash of other dilapidated furniture.

"So, Sadie, what do you think?" Kurt grinned proudly.

"Looks like home."

The guys laughed. They didn't realize I was kinda serious. All the room needed was the smell of musty carpet and a pile of takeout boxes, and I would've done a double take.

Kurt, still looking beyond pleased, patted one of the sofas. "Some of the activities get kind of wild, so church members donate their old furniture every now and then as replacements." He gave the sofa a final pat. "Well, I'm running down to the office to speak with the pastor for a second, so Sadie, you can hang around here. The others will be here soon. Truitt can show you around, right, man?"

Once we were alone, Truitt spread out his arms and turned in a circle. "Well, this is the youth room." He flopped into the crooked recliner, and I held my breath, convinced it was about to flip him. "Okay, tour's over. Tell me about you."

"What about me?" I gingerly perched on the arm of the couch on the other side of the room. In my head, I was all like, *I'm the daughter of a single, checked-out father, I can't go back to my friends, and I'm forced to live with my uncle who happens to be a youth pastor, so you don't even wanna get me started on my life, bro.* But verbally, I refrained.

"You're Kurt and Melina's niece. That's gotta be awesome. Not the fact that you're a niece and not a nephew, though. Or maybe that's cool too. I dunno, since I've only ever been a guy. But what were we talking about?"

I blinked.

"Oh yeah, Kurt and Melina are awesome. I bet you're having the time of your life with them."

If I'd been experiencing the time of my life over the past few days, I could've rolled over and died right there. But I didn't say that. Instead, I said, "They're really nice."

I had hoped that would be enough info for him. Nope. "So, Sadie, where out west are you from?"

"Seattle."

"In Washington?"

"No, the other Seattle," I deadpanned. I didn't like answering all of his questions, and I briefly considered suggesting his ideal career might just be a greeter at the supermarket. "Yeah, I'm from Washington."

"I've never been there. Do you go to the Pike's Place Market where they throw fish and the Space Needle all of the time?"

"It's actually *Pike* Place, not Pike's Place. And I've been to those places, but I never did much of the touristy stuff."

He stuck the footrest out on the recliner, and the chair made a loud popping noise. "So you eat a ton of fish then?"

"Um, sometimes."

Truitt actually looked like he might drool over the thought of fresh fish. "Maybe one day I'll make it out there."

I didn't see a response to his comment necessary. I could only hope if he ever did go to Seattle, he wouldn't open his mouth. Locals could peg him as a tourist from a mile away. I tapped my foot against the couch and waited for Kurt to return.

Thankfully, kids started filtering into the room right about then. Kurt arrived too and stood on a small wooden platform at the front of the room. He whistled in a frequency akin to a boiling tea kettle and told the group to start introducing themselves to his—and I quote—"supertastic niece."

I stood as a petite girl dressed in a bright-pink shirt and khaki Bermuda shorts approached. "Hey! I'm Kari Taylor." The girl had cky blue eyes and long, blonde ringlets. It was the kind of hair that people forked over huge chunks of cash to get, only hers looked natural. Her accent was one of the thickest I'd encountered so far, but it was cute on her. She wasn't the kind of person I'd hang around, though. She seemed to have the princess complex that usually accompanied looks like that.

"Hi, Kari." I smiled. She grinned. She pulled me into a quick, friendly hug like we'd known each other longer than three and a half seconds. I froze, not used to such southern hospitality.

"Hey, no PDA at church!" A girl with long, dark-auburn hair approached us as Kari released me. She smiled. "Hi, supertastic niece of Kurt. I'm Lena. And I'll go ahead and put your mind at ease by telling you I'm not as touchy-feely as my best friend here." She elbowed Kari lightly in the side, her green eyes shining mischievously.

"I'm Sadie Franklin. What grade are you guys in?"

Kari giggled and stage-whispered to Lena. "She says 'you guys.'"

I leaned forward, inviting myself into their BFF bubble. "I'm sorry. What did I say?"

Lena, who stood a couple of solid inches above the other girl, rested her arm on Kari's shoulder. "You said 'you guys.'" She exaggerated her drawl. "Everyone 'round here says 'y'all.' We're gonna be seniors this fall."

"Oh, don't rub it in, girls." We turned to see Becca standing beside us. "Y'all are in the home stretch, and I'm heading into junior year. Sadie, tell me you're not a rising senior too."

I raised my hands, palms upturned. "Guilty." Although the truth was that that wasn't a guarantee. My last guidance counselor meeting of the year had left things a little iffy in the graduate-on-schedule department.

A few more girls came up and introduced themselves to me, including Willow, who had shiny, dark hair and sharp eyes that seemed to notice absolutely everything. She told me it was her second time at the church, and I was glad I wasn't the only stranger in the room. Everyone else seemed extremely close, and I knew from experience that trying to break into a group like that was pointless.

Somehow, by the way Willow watched me while I introduced myself, I knew she understood at least a little bit of where I was coming from. I made a mental note to stick close to her.

Truitt caught my eye, and I looked away—but not before I noticed him slipping his way over to the group of girls. He said hello to the others and then turned to face me, opening his mouth to speak, before another sharp whistle from Kurt cut him off.

"Okay, people, take a seat." Kurt paced back and forth on the little platform until everyone was seated. I happened to be between Becca and Truitt.

"What's up, Becca?" Truitt leaned over me and high-fived Becca.

"Hanging out with my new friend. You?"

I pressed into the back cushion, feeling like a third wheel. I wondered if those two had a thing for each other.

Kurt opened the evening with prayer, and I took the opportunity to scope out the rest of the room. There were about fourteen students total, the majority of whom were girls.

Afterward, the group played a bunch of ridiculous games, beginning with a bowling game that used balled-up pairs of tube socks to knock down the Styrofoam cups I'd carried up the stairs. For that one, I teamed up with Willow, who had terrible aim when it came to throwing socks. Her sock ball veered sharply to the right and knocked over a couple of Kari's and Lena's cups in the next lane. I couldn't help it. I started laughing, which drew attention to the scene and made everyone else laugh too. Willow made a face, which only made me laugh harder, and then tossed me a sock ball for my turn. "I'll get you for that," she whispered, which also struck me as funny. Maybe it was all of my stress trying to find an outlet, or maybe it was because so far, church was nothing like I'd anticipated. But by the time the game was over, I could honestly say I'd had fun. Although if anyone told that to Kurt, I'd deny it.

Kurt needed someone to keep track of scores for the next game, so I volunteered. It gave me a good opportunity to sit back and just observe. Becca and Truitt were a team again for a game appropriately named worm fling, but he offered to be the one catching the whipped-cream-covered gummy worms in his mouth that Becca flung blindfolded. I couldn't tell if he was being a gentleman or if he just really liked gummy worms. Every now and then, Truitt would glance my way and then pretend he hadn't as soon as I looked up. I'd caught him doing that all night when he thought I wasn't paying attention. I only watched him back because he made me uneasy.

"Okay," Kurt said as he settled on the floor this time and leaned against the wall like he was one of the teens. "Tonight didn't really have a theme to it, but it's been a crazy couple of days for my family, as I'm sure you've figured out." He glanced at me and smiled. So he was basically calling me crazy. I felt prickles rise on the back of my neck.

"It's been some kinda crazy for me too." The amount of southernness packed into that sentence surprised me. All I needed was the drawl, and I'd fit right in. Meanwhile, Kurt just grinned that goofy grin of his.

After praying again, Kurt ran through some announcements. "Don't forget your money is due in two weeks for the Chicago mission trip. The trip isn't until the end of summer, but we need to get everything together as soon as possible. Also, Lake Day is this Saturday! We'll meet here at eleven and head out to the lake, have lunch, hang out, go out on some boats, all that. I know our group is kind of slim since it's summer, so this is a good opportunity for you to invite some people. Acquaintances, friends, significant others who belong to other denominations ..." He tossed a sock ball at Kari, who made a face.

"Very funny, Kurt. I'll be sure to tell James you miss him and secretly wish you were Presbyterian." The group laughed at the inside joke, making me feel even more uncomfortable in the group. I'd totally pegged Kari as the clingy girlfriend type, although I couldn't tell the difference between a Baptist and a Presbyterian to save my life.

After Kurt dismissed the group, Willow left and Truitt and Becca volunteered to take me to the main church service. Truitt held the door to the stairwell open for us, and I got a good look at him while he was distracted by a text message. He was just so so … I don't know. *Perfect*. And not in an I'm-so-charming-look-at-my-dimple kind of way either. What I meant was he did the whole hold-the-door-open thing, he had an answer for every Bible trivia question Kurt tossed out during a Jeopardy-type game they played (did you know Moses had anger issues and broke—literally—the first set of Ten Commandments?), and he refused to slap girls in the face with gummy worms. I'd seen all types of people in my city, and I knew no one could be *that* perfect. Everyone who appeared that in control of their life had secrets. But then, I had secrets too, and I obviously didn't have a whole lot under control. These church people would throw me out the window if they knew half of it. Not to mention I'd be living on the streets if Kurt and Melina knew the kind of person I really was.

"What did you think of youth group?" Becca's question interrupted my thoughts. I wondered what secrets she held. She wasn't all girly and super cute like Kari or drop-dead gorgeous like Willow, but she was pretty in a natural beauty kind of way. She had a well-proportioned figure, and I know it's virtually unheard of for girls to wish they had *more* weight, but I couldn't help but wish I'd rounded out a tiny bit more. Despite my jealousy, something about her was different. She didn't seem like she'd already prejudged and labeled me. She genuinely seemed to want to know what I thought of youth group, so I gave her a genuine answer. "Some of the games were lame."

For a minute, she didn't say anything, and I thought I might have insulted her. But then she tilted her head to the side and said, "Yeah, some of them are. But your uncle is awesome."

We entered the main building, which Becca called the sanctuary, and I spotted my aunt and cousins. "I'll see you later," I called over my shoulder.

Chapter 6

....

"Not that I don't appreciate you trying to keep my life interesting and everything, but I'd love it if you could prepare me a bit more before sending me into these situations." I pulled apart a piece of my roast beef—left over from a big, southern Sunday lunch—and dunked it in the gravy pooled in my pile of rice.

"You never asked what my job was, Sadie," Kurt said around a mouthful of peas.

Beside me, Jackson grunted and stabbed mercilessly at his own peas. He'd attempted to spoon his peas into his napkin at the start of dinner, or "supper" as my relatives called it. I'd laughed, blowing his cover, so he'd been snubbing me ever since.

I swallowed my meat and took a sip of milk. "That too, but I meant Becca. She's the *pastor's* daughter?" No wonder Becca had been so good at appearing nonjudgmental. She was used to being nice. She had a reputation to uphold. And, apparently, my uncle thought I needed a little extra religious influence in my life. "I mean that's something I feel like I should've known at the beginning. You've dropped the information ball twice now."

"Oh, come *on*, Sadie." Trissy rolled her eyes. "It's life, not football!"

Kurt and Melina started laughing right there in the middle of my rant. "It's not funny, you guys!" I huffed.

Kurt took a sip of his sweet tea, a beverage I had yet to retry. "Sadie, please, you've got to stop."

All of the faces around the table turned serious, except for Cooper, who was consumed with his attempt to peel a pea. "Stop what?" I asked.

Kurt grimaced. "Saying *you guys*. It's incorrect grammar."

"Why?" I mixed the gravy into my rice, but my eyes didn't leave his. Had I not just had this conversation at church with Kari and Lena? "Are you some of those zealous gender-equality people who get offended when I say 'you guys' instead of 'you guys and girls?'"

Melina coughed. Kurt leveled me with his gaze. "No, Sadie, of course not. I feel a woman's place is in the kitchen and all that good stuff." This earned him a punch from Melina. He winked at her. "What I mean is we all say *y'all*."

"I know." I stared blankly.

"Then try it!" Trissy set her fork down a little too forcefully, caught up in the apparent excitement.

I sighed. "Fine. You know, *y'all*—"

"Wait!" Trissy slapped her hand on the table. "You said it wrong! Daddy, tell her she said it wrong!"

Kurt shrugged. "You said it wrong."

"How could I possibly have said it wrong?"

"You said"—Kurt raised his voice about fifteen octaves too high, even for a teenage girl—"Yo-all."

Jackson started laughing so hard his chubby gut shook, which made me laugh too. "Then how is it supposed to sound?"

"Try this." Kurt leaned across the table, his elbow nearly in his gravy. "Yuh-awl. All smooshed together."

"Okay, yuh-awl."

Kurt shook his head in defeat, but his eyes shone. "I give up. Maybe that literature class can teach you some culture."

I set my fork down carefully, but it slid off the edge of my plate and clanked against the table. Had I heard him right? "What literature class?"

Kurt glanced over at Melina, whose lips were pinched together. "You haven't ..."

Melina shook her head. "That was our after-dinner conversation, dearest."

"Oh." He ran a hand through his curly hair and glanced at me.

I looked down. "What are you talking about?" I said to my roast beef.

Rather than answer me, my aunt set about cleaning Cooper's hands and getting him down from his seat. "Trissy, please help your brothers get ready for bed, then why don't y'all watch a Veggie Tales movie or something? We'll clear the table for you, okay?"

Trissy sighed but slid out of her seat and took her youngest brother by the hand. "Let's get out of here, Coop." She looked at Jackson and tilted her head in the direction of the living room. "We don't wanna get in the middle of this, boys."

While my uncle cleared the dishes off the table and my aunt made coffee, I sat in my chair, watching them. When they came back to the table, Melina placed a steaming mug of black coffee in front of me, a sure sign things were about to get serious.

"Look, Sadie," Kurt said, his big hands wrapped around his coffee mug and his eyes glued on me. "We know about your English class, your math class, your anatomy class ..." He trailed off, but his eyes never left mine. I forced myself not to be the one to look away.

"What's your point?"

"The point is you basically failed eleventh grade."

I tried not to let my shock show on my face. I didn't know that. Honestly. I mean yeah, I knew I wasn't doing so great, but I hadn't looked at my final grades. I swore under my breath, breaking the stare.

"Sadie!" Melina gasped.

Ignoring Melina and me, Kurt plowed ahead. "What did you think you were going to do this fall, Sadie? Jump into senior year and graduate with your class, no consequences?"

I shifted in my seat, sliding my hands under my legs so I wouldn't pound the table with my fists. "I think this doesn't concern you. I'm here for the summer, then I'll be back in Washington, where I'll deal with my own issues. It's not like I'll have the opportunity to go to college, so grades are no big deal. Who told you anyway?"

"The school called Mike, and Mike called us." *Dad, you are such a traitor!* The one time he actually decided to stick his nose in my business … "And in this house, we do not swear, so I advise you to watch your language."

The most immature, most rebellious part of me wanted to do it again just to spite him, but that would definitely not end well. I swallowed my venom. "What's the point of this conversation, exactly?"

Melina rested her hands on her stomach, but her face was stern. "If nothing changes, you'll be repeating eleventh grade in the fall. College or no college, that's not good, especially when we all know you're capable of so much more." She stared at me until I squirmed under the pressure of her intense green eyes.

Like my aunt actually knew anything about me. My grades had always been average—not great, not terrible. Average. But when your social life is the most fulfilling thing you have, you let the other, less fulfilling things slip a little. I took a shaky sip of my coffee, enjoying the slight burn the hot liquid made as it slid down my throat.

"That's why," my aunt continued, "we decided to homeschool you this summer, like we usually do with our own kids during the school year. We'll pull up the grades in the classes you failed and stick you in an SAT prep class so you'll be able to retest."

Oh, so my dad had shown them my first round of SAT scores too? Perfect. It wasn't my fault a friend's birthday party had been the night before. Hangovers make it hard to focus on a nearly four-hour test.

By this point, I was angry, and I bit the inside of my cheek to keep from blurting out how I really felt about this conversation. About my education. About this family. "Do you have the right to do that?" I tasted blood.

"With Mike's permission, a stipend, and some paperwork, which we've already taken care of."

Kurt jumped in when he saw me open my mouth. "In Washington, minors are required to stay in school until they're eighteen. And you're both a minor and a resident of Washington, so this whole process doesn't need your approval."

Wow. For someone who supposedly loved helping teens, he sure seemed to enjoy taking apart my world, brick by brick.

"Okay, listen," Melina said, putting her hand on Kurt's arm. He leaned back and drained his coffee. "The classes are three days a week, beginning Wednesday. You squeaked by in algebra 2, so you'll be taking anatomy and American literature, along with an SAT prep class."

Her words were one big blob of *wobwobwobwobwob*, like how the adults in Charlie Brown's world always sound. I reached for something I could understand. "You said other students? Are they all stupid too?"

Melina fingered the ends of her hair. "You're not stupid, Sadie."

"It's basically what you're saying."

Kurt set his cup on the table, just hard enough to make me jump.

Melina looked at him, her expression still stern. "I've got this," she whispered. He didn't seem happy to agree, but he leaned back again. "Maybe one student didn't pass his classes, but the rest are already homeschooled. Everyone needs the SAT practice experience, and a couple of them are getting ahead so they can get some classes out of the way and have time to dual-enroll at community college this coming year."

"So what you're basically telling me is I'm going to be a churchgoing, homeschooling, skirt-wearing, piety princess wannabe? What's next, a purity ring?"

Kurt smirked—or maybe was a grimace. He drummed his fingers on the table and exhaled, like he was considering how to reply. "The wardrobe and—what was it?—piety princess things are optional, of course, but the churchgoing, homeschooling part is correct."

"What does my father really think of this?" He'd never taken such an interest in my well-being, and I got the feeling my relatives had done a little manipulating. Or bribing.

"Mike actually thinks it's a good idea." Melina looked tired.

"Was he sober when you talked to him?" My tone dripped sarcasm.

"Sadie," Melina said as she sighed heavily, "please don't make this harder than it is. Of course we want you to be happy, but we also want what's best for you. We've been praying about this for a long time."

I made slow, bold eye contact first with Melina, then Kurt, then Melina again. "Well, that's your mistake, not mine."

I stood, leaving my barely touched coffee, and stomped outside, letting the screen door slam behind me.

Honestly, the only thing that kept me from running away was the fact that I had nowhere to run *to*. I had options of where to run *from*—Seattle or Pecan Creek—just nowhere to go. My life had always been like that. Leave things, people, behind but step forward into darkness with no clear direction.

My legs ached to run, but my stomach hurt and I didn't want a repeat of that morning. I sat in a swing and slipped my phone out of my pocket. I tried to take a deep breath, but my breaths were still heavy and quick from storming out of the house. I couldn't let myself think about the mess I'd left in the kitchen, and despite my fierce independence, I craved a connection with someone who understood me.

It was Reese's eighteenth birthday and, at the moment, I didn't care if I hadn't left Seattle on the best terms with him. In a moment of bravado, I dialed the phone, forcing myself to calm down while it rang.

The phone rang several times, but no one answered. Eventually, the voice mail clicked on, and I listened to that annoying automated lady instructing me to leave a message at the tone. I ended the call and tossed the phone onto a bed of grass. I was so not in the mood to take orders from people.

As I pumped my legs as high as the swing would allow me to go, I realized I was glad Reese hadn't answered my call. What would I have said anyway? *Um, I'm sorry I left without telling you good-bye, but after what happened … Happy birthday!*

I stayed on the swing, pumping my legs to relieve the tension until the sun gave up and settled down for the night. Every now and then, I caught a glimpse of Melina when she passed by the kitchen window. Once I even saw her looking out at me, but I pretended I hadn't seen her and kicked my legs harder.

***

That night, I tossed in bed for at least three hours. Every time I glanced at the clock, only another minute had passed. I would give anything to just be able to sleep, to block out all of the stressors hurling themselves at me. But Trissy was restless in her sleep, like some sort of feral monkey. Right as I would settle into the covers, my eyelids growing heavy, she would flop a leg over me. So I'd slide out from under her, closer to the edge of the bed, and try to sleep again, only to have an arm whop my face.

After the second arm episode, I couldn't take it anymore. I grabbed my pillow and felt my way to the living room, hoping Melina wasn't up. When I got to the couch, I pulled the throw blanket off the back and wrapped it around myself and adjusted my pillow. Across the room, Marigold was curled up in the recliner, shooting laser beams from his eyes. Ever since I took his place in Trissy's room, he had hated me. But there just wasn't enough space in that suffocating pink room to add in a psychotic cat.

"Yeah, I'm on your turf. Deal with it," I muttered. The cat jumped off the chair and ran out of the room. I leaned back and stared at the ceiling. *It's horrible how you can be so past the point of exhaustion that you can't sleep.*

I flipped over so my face pressed into the back of the couch. It smelled like clean laundry. Not the Laundromat kind of clean laundry but real, home-style laundry. That in itself was a testament to my fatigue. *Home-style laundry? You're losing it, Sadie.*

The smell reminded me of my mom. Melina was so different from her—shorter, darker hair, brighter eyes—but at the same time, she reminded me so much of my mom. Like the way she'd sung alto in church tonight. For the briefest instant, I felt like I was little again, wearing a sundress and lacy socks and standing next to Mom on a Sunday morning. Back when Mom made sure the two of us were in church each Sunday. Then there was the way Melina's smile crinkled the skin around her eyes, and her gentleness toward her kids. The similarities both comforted me and made me want to scream, "You're not her!"

Footsteps padded on the carpet, and the lamp flipped on, causing me to pull the blanket over my head to shield my eyes. Butter Bean must've been dancing again.

"Sadie?" I heard a hoarse whisper. A hoarse *male* whisper. I slowly pulled the blanket down past my nose and tucked it under my chin.

"Hi, Kurt." His form was fuzzy as I squinted at him.

"What's up, Sadie?" *Why is he being so nice to me when I completely blew him off earlier?*

"You know, just hanging out." I thought that would make him go about whatever he was doing at two in the morning, but he slid across the floor in his socked feet, T-shirt, and plaid PJ pants. I scooted to a sitting position and rubbed my eyes as he sank onto the other end of the couch.

"Seriously, Sadie, why aren't you in bed?" What was he wanting, an apology?

"I could ask you the same thing," I snapped with a little more bite than I intended.

He gave me a pointed look, and for a moment, I thought he'd tell me off. He shook his head. "Fair enough. Mel wanted some water, and I volunteered since it's so hard for her to get comfortable. Bean wakes up whenever she moves around."

"You're a good man, Kurt." It's the closest I would come to an apology.

He shrugged. "Okay, so now it's your turn. What gives?"

"Your daughter sleeps like a feral monkey."

He chuckled softly. "I wouldn't put it past her. Mel is an animal when she's not carrying extra weight."

I gagged. "Ew. Please!"

He ran a hand over his jaw, his mouth open. "Sorry, Sadie. But it's the middle of the night. I think the fact I'm able to communicate at all is a miracle within itself."

I surprised both of us by laughing, which made me laugh harder. A moment later, Kurt was laughing too, deep and quiet. It felt good, like the rubber band of tension stretched between us wasn't pulled quite so tight.

I ended the spontaneous laughing episode with a yawn, finally feeling like I might be able to get some sleep. "Well, good night."

Kurt leaned against the arm of the sofa, crossing his arms over his chest. "Nope, this little exchange is not over until you tell me what really brings you to my living room at 2:00 a.m." All traces of jovial uncle were gone, a soft seriousness replacing the spark in his eye.

I sat up a little straighter and smoothed my hair out of my face. "I couldn't sleep. Too much running through my mind."

He nodded like he understood. "Can I ask what about?"

In my mind I told him, *No, Kurt, you cannot.* But out loud, I said, "Just ... just thinking about all that's happened over the past few days. And my life back in Seattle."

"You miss it?" He sounded surprised at my confession.

Did I? "It's complicated. I'm here now, and I couldn't go back if I wanted to. It'd be too ... too ... difficult. But I don't want to get into that."

He yawned and stretched his arms above his head, revealing muscles I didn't expect him to have. "That's your call. But I'm a youth minister and high school counselor during the school year, Sadie. You think you've got junk? I help teens work through their junk every day of my life. I can catch a curveball."

I looked down at my knees.

He stood. "I need to go get my Mel her water before she makes me sleep out here."

"Your cutesy coupleness makes me gag." I stuck out my tongue for emphasis.

"One day, Sadie, one day. You just wait 'til love gets a hold of you." He patted my shoulder and went into the kitchen.

Yet again, I was acutely aware that my uncle really didn't know me at all.

Chapter 7

The next morning, I tried to entertain the boys while Mel and Trissy cooked breakfast. I hadn't played with them before, but my aunt and uncle suggested I spend time trying to get to know my cousins. Turns out all they wanted to do was play with trucks. Violently. I'd already confiscated one of Trissy's dolls when Jackson and Cooper thought it'd make for a good time if they ran over her with their semi trucks. Trissy begged to differ.

"Vroom-vroom," I puttered awkwardly as I pushed a toy dirt bike around on the floor. My ears felt hot, and I found myself embarrassed that I was embarrassed about making *vroom* noises for a six-year-old.

"You don't do that," Jackson huffed, taking the toy from my hand. "You gotta give it lots of power, like vroom vroom!" He took off running on his hands and knees, the little bike plowing through the thick carpet.

I took that as my opportunity to bow out and stepped into the kitchen. That was enough awkward *vrooms* for one day.

"How's the bonding going, Sadie?" Melina added milk to a pot of oatmeal at the stove. She'd told me when I first woke up that we should start over and pretend the night before hadn't happened. I opened my mouth to ask if that meant the whole you're-going-to-be-homeschooled thing hadn't happened either, but Melina had interrupted with "Child, you do *not* want to mess with these hormones right now," so I'd dropped the matter and gone to play with Jackson and Cooper.

49

Trissy brought me a cup of coffee. "You do like cream in it, right?" From the look on her face, I could tell she'd figured out what had gone down in the kitchen the night before.

I took the steaming mug and inhaled deeply. *Mmmm* ... vanilla. It wasn't an espresso from my favorite local roaster in downtown Seattle, but I'd take it. "Thank you, Trissy. This smells really good."

Trissy brought a hand to her chest. "Mama! Sadie really does have a heart!"

Melina waved a wooden spoon, like she was erasing her daughter's comment. "She's kidding, Sadie. Aren't you, Tris?"

Trissy shrugged. "Sure."

I slid into a seat at the table. "What do we do today?"

"Well," my aunt said as she stirred a pot of oatmeal, "I thought us girls could use a little retail therapy!"

I felt a grin stretch across my face.

We went shopping an hour away from Pecan Creek, in what my aunt and uncle referred to as "The Big City." You'd think they'd be talking about New York City or even Atlanta, but nope. When we left the airport, I'd asked Kurt what was the nearest city, to which he'd replied, "Augusta." When I asked what was so special about Augusta, Kurt's jaw dropped.

"It's Augusta, Sadie. Not only is it the hometown of your aunt, it's also home to a famous golf tournament each spring. Tell me you've heard of it."

When I told him that the name did sound familiar and that I'd seen some of the tournament on TV before, he'd breathed a sigh of relief and returned his attention to driving.

Now, though, I got to see Augusta for myself. And when I compared it to Pecan Creek, I could totally see how it earned the name of Big City.

Kurt had a staff meeting at the church, so by the time Becca came over to watch the boys, and Melina, Trissy, and I finally pulled off I-20, I was itching to shop. The mall appeared to our right, and I stuck my face to the glass. This was what I needed. I wasn't necessarily poor, but I didn't have a ton of money. It probably wasn't the greatest idea for my dad to work at a casino. We turned just before the main entrance to the mall and Melina took us down a side road, past a sign boasting GAP, American Eagle, Aeropostale— some of my favorites. But Melina kept driving, turning off onto another road, and then another. She pulled the van to a stop in front of a—

"We're here!" she announced, unfastening her seat belt.

"A thrift store?" I asked, my face betraying my disappointment.

In the seat behind me, Trissy slid open the back door and hopped out. I saw her curls bouncing in the corner of my eye.

Melina nodded and turned her big eyes on me. They were kind but not apologetic. "This place has some really good things. I know you wanted the mall, but Kurt's job is all about saving souls, not earning heaps of money." She slid out of the car and shut her door.

The thrift store was located in a large warehouse building. It really was impressive with its department store layout and popular music selections.

Approximately two and a half minutes into the shopping spree, I realized we were going to be there a while. Melina waddled like a penguin, although a very fashionable penguin, in her white shorts and black, sequined top, and Trissy wanted to touch anything fuzzy or pink. I badly wanted to go off on my own and do my own thing, but Melina told me she'd buy me a few new outfits, and I didn't want to take her generosity for granted.

Trissy and I followed Melina to the teen section, and I began browsing the racks. "Oh, nice!" I reached for a dress. "I can't believe they have these. I love this brand."

Melina shifted beside me. "Actually, Sadie, I'd rather you not."

What now? "Why? It's a lot cheaper here than if you get it new at the mall."

"Well, it's not the price …"

Trissy's ears perked up. The kid thrived on drama.

"I don't understand." I ran my hand down the soft green hem.

Melina sighed. "It's kind of short. Even with leggings."

Trissy nodded sassily. "Yup. It's not whole."

"Whole?" I raised an eyebrow at Melina. Sure, the dress was short, but it was still a whole dress.

"She means wholesome."

I wrestled the shirt back onto the rack and ducked my head. "Fine. I'll just … I don't know. Let's move on." I didn't know what else to say.

Mel clapped her hands, her signal for moving on. "Well, I'm going to visit the restroom."

After Melina and Trissy left me to do my shopping, I spent nearly an hour stockpiling clothes that met Melina's "Modest is hottest" mantra. I'd never had anyone tell me how to dress before, and I felt smothered, even if Melina did have a pretty good fashion sense.

After shopping, we drove back past the mall and across the street to McDonald's.

"What's next?" I asked as I munched on a handful of fries. French fries could singlehandedly redeem the day. I flicked a crumb off my shirt and dunked a fry in my ketchup.

"Well," Melina said as she sipped her Dr. Pepper, "I was going to take you shoe shopping next door, but I really don't think I can walk much more."

"Why don't you stay here and we can go?" Trissy deserved a high five for that suggestion, so I gave her one.

Melina rolled her eyes and drummed her nails on the table. "I guess you two can go. I can see the store from here."

"We'll come straight back." I smiled my best I'm-so-sweet-and-mature smile.

She pulled a couple of bills out of her wallet. "I'd like change, please."

I tucked the money into the pocket of my shorts and tried to keep up with Trissy, who skipped her way to the door of the restaurant. She kept skipping until we reached the shoe store at the other end of the shopping center.

"Trissy!" I hissed. "Get over here!" I hoped the attractive sales guy didn't hear me and think she was my sister or something, although the hair alone was a pretty big indicator that we weren't siblings.

Trissy bopped her way over to me and the strappy pair of sandals I was admiring.

"What? Need some help? I'm pretty good with clothes and stuff."

I glanced down at the mismatched socks she wore with her plaid shorts. "Uh-huh. Listen, you're also a kid, and you're supposed to stick by me, okay?"

She smashed herself to my side, wrapping her arm around my waist. "How's this?"

I cringed and pushed her away. "You know what I mean. Don't touch me."

She poked out her bottom lip and flipped her hair over her shoulders. It boinged back into her face. "Ooh, touchy," she said, grinning. "Ha! Touchy. Get it? You said don't touch me, and I said you were touchy!"

I shook my head and searched for the sandal in size 6.

Twenty minutes and a hefty receipt later, Trissy and I made our way back to the restaurant and found Melina on her phone. I waved and sat down across from her. Trissy sat unnecessarily close beside me. You'd think she'd get enough of that by sharing a bed with me.

Melina continued talking to Kurt and held out her hand for the change. I masked my face in a confused expression and shrugged. Trissy giggled and fist-bumped me. Melina frowned. *Hey, she wanted us to bond. That's all I'm saying.*

A few minutes later, Melina ended her call and stood. She placed a hand on her lower back and groaned.

"Are you okay?" I gathered my two shopping bags, handing the heftiest to Trissy.

"I'll be all right. All of the walking just got Bean moving. Are you two ready to go home? I should put my feet up."

Trissy and I nodded in unison.

"Okay, let's stop by the restroom, then we'll go."

Trissy rolled her eyes. I guffawed. Melina slid her chair under the table and said, "Laugh all you want, girls, but just remember this moment when it's your turn."

Trissy and I caught up to Melina. "I don't think you have to worry about any nieces or nephews for a long time," I whispered to her, dragging out the word *long* for emphasis.

She stopped walking and looked me squarely in the face. "You see to that."

***

"Coming through!" Trissy sang as she sailed into the bedroom and flopped on the bed. "Guess what. I'm a fish!" She laughed and flopped again.

"Guess what. Go away." I went back to putting my new shirts in my drawer.

I heard breathing beside me. "What's that?" Trissy asked.

No. Not that. I quickly shoved the rest of the clothes on top of the envelope that was peeking out and closed the drawer. "What's what?"

"Wasn't that a vanilla envelope?"

"A what? You mean a manila envelope?"

"Whatever. Is that what it was?" Trissy pulled herself to her tiptoes and tried to peak through a crack in the drawer.

"Um, no. No, that was not. That was my vanilla—" I shook my head. "I mean my *manila* shirt."

If there was one thing I'd learned about Trissy in the few days I'd known her, it was that she could be a fruitcake. Case in point: she completely believed I had a manila-colored shirt.

I wadded up the last of the shopping bags and tossed them in the glittery trash can. That envelope held pictures—the only pictures I had of my mom. Pictures from the time I was a baby until just a week and a half before the terrible, terrible day of the accident. Those pictures were almost sacred to me, and I was afraid that sharing them would somehow weaken the last strands of a connection between my mom and me.

When Trissy finally left the room, I closed the door and retrieved the envelope. Clutching the envelope to my chest, I leaned against the door and slid to the carpet. I took a deep breath and pinched the little metal clasp on the envelope. I reached in and pulled out a photo, unable to help my smile. In it, I was six and sitting on the couch with my mom. She had one arm around me and the other in the air, her hand a blur as she tried to get my dad to hurry. He'd tried to set the self-timer on the camera but hadn't been quick enough to make it to his seat. Instead, the left half of the image was filled by Dad's sweater. I laughed, but it was a sad laugh. It was one of the better moments in my parents' marriage and our life as a family.

The memories always left me tired. Not because it hurt to remember the good times but because it hurt to compare them to the bad times. The more recent times.

I slid the picture back into the envelope and buried it in my shirt drawer. In the hallway, I passed Melina as she was leaving the boys' room. Cooper took naps, and Jackson had what my aunt called "mandatory give-your-poor-mama-a-break time" when he was required to lie quietly for an hour.

"What's up, Sadie?" she said as she yawned.

"You know how you told me to bond with the kids? I think bonding with Trissy is going a little too well. She's been smothering me."

Melina walked down the hall with me. "I can believe it. I wanted to show you something anyway. Come in here." She pushed open her bedroom door.

I'd toured the rest of the house, but this was the first time I'd ever seen inside Kurt and Mel's bedroom. And I must say I was impressed.

A plush red and gold comforter draped over a cherry wood bed, complete with carved posts and headboard. A matching vanity and dresser stood against one wall, and a valance of candles adorned the top of the chest of drawers. A window on the opposite wall overlooked the backyard, flanked by richly colored drapes that matched the bedspread. A small loveseat sat against the window. It was the fanciest room in the house by far.

"Wow, Melina," I said. "This is like a sanctuary or something." My toes sank into the chocolate-brown rug at the foot of the bed.

She smiled. "Thank you. I love this place even more than the kitchen, if you can believe it. It's someplace special, just for the two of us. It's easy to get caught up in the craziness of life, so this is like our own private little retreat. We don't let many guests in—even the kids."

I smiled back. "Then I'm honored. Thank for showing me." And I meant it, although I couldn't figure out why she wanted me to see her room.

"You're welcome. But I actually wanted to show you something I have in here. I've been waiting for the right time." She paused and faced me. "Meaning a time when you're not surrounded by the kids."

She walked over to the closet and grabbed a stepladder that was propped against the wall. "I meant to let Kurt get this down this morning before he left for the church, but you know ..." She handed me the ladder and pointed to a small cabinet above the closet. "Reach up there. There's a box I want you to get down." Her voice was solemn, all traces of laughter gone, like she was afraid of breaking a spell.

I had to stand on my tiptoes on top of the ladder to pull out the large shoebox. It was more bulky than heavy, so I gingerly climbed down the stepladder and set the box on the bed. I crawled up next to my aunt and sat crisscross-applesauce style, like a little girl waiting to open a present.

"Go for it." Melina put a hand on my back, and I only twitched a little at her touch.

I carefully pulled apart the worn flaps. A distinct mothball scent greeted me when I opened the box, causing me to take a moment to cough. I reached into the box and found a stack of journals.

"What are these?" I whispered, my fingers tracing the gold swirls on a brown, leather notebook. Melina took the journal out and handed it to me.

"These are Melody's—your mama's—journals from the time she was little until ... Well, until she moved out. She didn't take much with her when she left, so I kept these safe for her."

Here's what I knew: I knew my mom had left home and run off with my dad right after she turned eighteen. I knew my grandparents disagreed with her decision. I knew my mom got pregnant and got married soon after in an unsuccessful attempt to cover up what she'd done. And that's it. That's all of the family history I had. I hadn't worried about the details much when I was younger, but this, in the box, could contain the answers to some of the questions I'd been asking as I grew up.

"So these are my m-mom's?" I stuttered. I raised my eyes to meet Melina's.

"Mm-hm."

"What's in them?" I stared at the books, caught in a trance, unable to bring myself to touch them. What if I didn't like what was in there? What if they tainted the carefully preserved image of my mom?

But what if they answered the questions?

Melina pushed herself off the bed. "I'm going to put my feet up in the living room before I see about supper. You can stay in here and read them where no one'll bother you. Put them back in the closet when you're done, and you can come back and read some more another time, okay?"

"Wow." The word left my mouth in exhale. "Thanks, Melina."

She smiled in a way that was very gentle, very kind. "No problem, kiddo. Enjoy your visit with your mama."

The door clicked as she left me alone in the sacred room with the journals. For several moments, I just stared at the box. It was almost like I was so hungry I couldn't eat or too tired I couldn't sleep. I desperately wanted to know what Mom wrote, but at the same time, I didn't. She was gone, and she wasn't coming back. Reading the journals wouldn't change that.

Settling against the stack of pillows on the bed, I tucked my legs under me. I took a deep breath and peeled open the worn cover.

I drew in a breath at the sight of her handwriting. It was different from the handwriting she'd used in my birthday cards and lunch box notes—more childish. But I'd recognize the tiny, loopy letters anywhere. I ran my fingers over the thin layer of blue ink, imagining her doing the same thing years ago. Inscribed on the first page were the words "Melody June Carter, age 9."

These were my mom's little girl journals! She was around Trissy's age when she wrote them. She was also around the age I was when she died. How much different was her childhood from mine? I caught myself smiling as I began to read.

> Dear Diary,
> This is the first time I have wrote in you ...

Okay, that was cute. I continued to read all about the woes of elementary school and how my mom thought she was adopted because she couldn't possibly be related to someone like Melina.

> Melina thinks just cause she is the baby she is a princess and makes me get in trouble and me and her fight a lot about that. At supper she told a story and said I kicked her. That is a lie! I have to go do my words list now cause I have a test tomorrow. I hope I do good ...

I kept reading, even after my eyelids became heavy—page after page, entry after entry, month after month ...

Sometime later, I jerked into a sitting position, knowing I'd been caught sleeping in Kurt and Mel's private room.

I rubbed my eyes and my vision cleared enough for me to see Kurt hanging his tie in the closet. He turned around and gave me a lopsided grin. "Nice nap?"

I caught a yawn in my throat. "Yeah, sorry."

He laughed. "I'm sorry I woke you up. Are you hungry?"

"Yeah, I'll just clean this stuff up ..." I trailed off as I set the journal back in the box.

Kurt crossed the room and patted my shoulder. "Take your time, but there's no guarantee the boys and I will leave you any homemade pizza. Our self-control has limits."

I finished packing up the journals and then carefully climbed the stepladder and put them back in their hiding place. The room felt even more like a sanctuary—a safe place—since I'd read some of the entries. I hadn't even finished a whole book yet, but I could already tell my mom and I would've gotten along if we had been kids at the same time.

Chapter 8

"Enjoy!" Melina slid a plate covered by a large slice of hot, cheesy homemade pizza in front of me.

"Looks great, Mel." I inhaled the fresh-baked crust, seasoned meat, and Rotel tomato.

"You've seriously never had homemade pizza?" Trissy asked, her mouth hanging slightly open.

"Nope. Never."

"Well," Melina said as she handed Cooper a cup and took her seat next to Kurt's spot at the head of the table, "this is the best kind to be your first. It's my mother's special secret recipe made with fresh tomatoes from the garden."

"What's the secret?" I poked at the pizza with my fork and it was all I could do not to dive into it, face first. The prayer ritual still cometh.

"It's a secret, duh!" Trissy rolled her eyes. I glanced up at Melina, who shrugged.

The screen door squealed like an unlucky pig at the packinghouse we drove past that afternoon. "Hey, it's the yard man!" Kurt said, waving to whoever entered behind me.

Melina stood and grabbed another plate out of the cabinet.

I heard a laugh that sounded familiar, although I couldn't remember where I'd heard it before, and caught sight of the "yard man." I stifled a groan.

"Hey, y'all." Truitt took the empty seat beside me as Melina set a slice of hot pizza in front of him.

"You're just in time! Tea or water, Truitt?"

"Tea's good." He scooted his chair up to the table, and I looked at him, surprised by the casual outfit he wore. Rather than a dress shirt, bow tie, and slacks, he had on a worn gray T-shirt and an old pair of jeans. Sunglasses hung around his neck, and a crease from a baseball cap circled his thick head of hair.

He must have sensed me looking at him because he turned toward me. "How's it goin', Sadie?" He drawled in that southern way of sliding his words into each other.

"Fine, thanks." I turned back to my pizza, mentally suggesting Kurt hurry up and pray over the food.

Kurt leaned back in his seat. "Truitt, would you ask the blessing?" Close enough.

Truitt nodded and held out his hands. What did he want? He wasn't about to burst out into a rendition of "Kumbaya" while we held hands, was he? The Elliots didn't usually hold hands during prayer. Trissy, who sat at the foot of the table, grabbed Truitt's hand as her cheeks tinged pink. On the other side of her, Jackson stuck out his tongue but grabbed his sister's hand anyway, before reaching for Cooper's. Melina took the toy racecar out of Cooper's other hand and held on to his fist, and then she took Kurt's hand. It came down to me. I couldn't look like a jerk and refuse to hold Truitt's hand, but still …

Before Trissy could say something about how cooties weren't real, I stifled another groan and laid my hand on top of his palm. His skin was tough and calloused. And unlike a heroine in a movie who secretly likes the guy she outwardly despises, let it be known I felt no tingles when he tucked my hand in his.

Truitt bowed his head. "Lord, thank You for Your love, and thank You for the love of these people around me. Thank You, Lord, for this food and the hands that prepared it. In Jesus' name, amen."

Throughout the duration of his prayer, I stared at my plate. Had he forgotten I didn't even know him? I slipped my hand out of his grasp and went after my pizza.

"This is great, Mel," Truitt said around a mouthful of pizza. "I really like the crust."

Melina smiled and sipped her sweet tea. "Thanks, Truitt. I tried adding Parmesan and garlic to the crust like you suggested."

Wait, what? Truitt cooks? I caught myself staring at him. The boy wore bow ties and cooked.

"Hey, did'ja know I'm makin' a ramp for my dirt bikes?" Jackson piped up, sauce dripping from his chin.

Truitt leaned across the table for a fist bump. "That's cool, man! Maybe you can show me after supper, before I start working, huh?" Jackson grinned—something I didn't see very often—his eyes sinking into his cheeks. Around me, Jackson was always a little surly, like the thought of having another woman in the formally male-dominated house was way too much for him.

"I'll show you so you won't cut it up with the mower." More sauce dribbled onto his shirt.

Trissy readjusted her hot-pink hair band, which clashed with her near-orange hair. "Jack, Truitt is a good worker. You don't wanna distract him." She batted her lashes in Truitt's direction. Gag. It seemed little Trissy had a crush on Truitt. I mentally stored this blackmail material away for later.

Truitt smiled. "Nah, don't worry, Tris. I'll have time." He emptied his tea glass, which Melina quickly refilled.

It seemed everyone in this family was enamored with this guy. I still couldn't figure out why, but as I sat there, silently eating, it made me feel like a third wheel. Or rather a seventh wheel.

Truitt pushed back his chair and took his plate to the sink. "Thanks for dinner. I'm gonna head on out and start weed eating. Jack, come on out when you're done, and I'll take a look at that ramp."

After dinner, Melina asked if I would keep an eye on Trissy and Cooper while the others were outside. Jackson went out to show Truitt that BMX ramp, and Melina and Kurt took a walk around the block to, in her words, "prevent pregnancy cankles."

Somehow, I agreed—or didn't protest enough—to load the dishwasher and babysit. The babysitting was a first for me. Trissy brought an art set into the kitchen and set about sketching what looked like a refrigerator. I couldn't confirm that, though, because every time I tried to look, she splayed her hands across the paper and muttered something about losing her inspiration if others saw her unfinished work.

I'd just wedged the last plate into the dishwasher when I heard a crash. I followed the noise into my room, where Cooper stood next to the dresser, a broken picture frame at his feet. Shards of glass surrounded him, and his lower lip quivered as he started to wail. My best guess was he was trying to reach the small, stuffed teddy bear Trissy kept on her dresser and knocked the frame down in the process.

I carefully made my way to the dresser, tiptoeing to avoid the shattered glass. "Shh …" I put my finger to my lips. "You're okay. You're okay." My soothing words had no effect on the toddler, who screamed louder. I wrung my hands. *Um, okay. Think, Sadie!* I saw my purse on the floor by the bed. An idea hit me. Oh yes, this should earn me the babysitter gold medal for sure.

Fishing through the contents, I quickly grabbed at a peppermint. I paused to ponder whether a two-year-old could have a mint, but the screams continued to escalate. I set it on the floor and stomped on it so that it broke into smaller pieces inside the wrapper. I unwrapped it and handed a piece to Cooper.

"Here, want some candy? Stop crying, and I'll give you some candy." I tried to keep my voice soft and soothing like my aunt's, which was just as foreign to me as the act of babysitting.

The bribe worked. Cooper wiped his nose on his bare arm— okay, *ew*—and I handed him the mint.

He popped it into his mouth and smiled ever so slightly. Apparently, he got the same mood-swing genes as his sister.

Relieved, I bent down and carefully picked up the largest chunks of glass.

"See, Cooper? It's okay. Really." I looked up. *Uh-oh.* Something wasn't right. Cooper's face had turned a weird green color. Seriously, his face was *green.* I watched in horror as the kid doubled over and puked—right on top of the glass pieces I had been gathering into a pile. I jumped backward as quickly as possible. Cooper doubled over again and started to cry.

I gagged. *No, I cannot lose it too. Not now.* Not knowing what else to do, I ran out of the room, hoping against anything that Kurt and Melina were back.

I didn't find my aunt or uncle, but Trissy still sat in the kitchen, doodling that stupid fridge picture.

"Trissy, are Kurt and Mel back yet?"

Without so much as glance, she shrugged and continued her sketch. She'd moved on to adding what looked like a large ham flank.

"It's kind of an emergency, Trissy. Are they back?" I raised my voice.

She rolled her eyes and sighed. "They're still on their walk. The cankles require maintenance. Now what can I do for you?"

"I have a problem. It's Cooper."

"Join the club." She added a carton of juice to her fridge.

Losing patience, I drummed my fingers on the table. "No, seriously, Trissy. Something's wrong. How can you ignore his screaming?"

A particularly loud wail reached the kitchen, and I ran back into the bedroom. I heard Trissy slide her chair out from the table.

Entering the room, I was assaulted by the sour smell of vomit. I fought back the urge to gag as Trissy shoved past me.

"Cooper!" she screamed, which only made the little boy cry harder.

"He's really upset!" *You think?* "Sadie, what did you do?"

"Well, he was crying, so I gave him a peppermint, and—"

"You *what*?" Trissy wrapped a comforting arm around her brother, but her eyes shot laser beams at me.

"I gave him a piece of peppermint. He couldn't have choked, though."

"Of course not!" Trissy put her hands on her hips, her face red. "He couldn't keep it down long enough to choke because he's allergic to red food coloring!"

What? "I didn't know, okay? I was just trying to make him happy." Beads of sweat broke out on my forehead. I could practically see smoke coming out of Trissy's ears. I had no idea the kid had such a temper. She stomped her foot like I was a roach beneath her feet, completely ignoring the glass pieces, and then grabbed Cooper by the hand and led him out of the room. "How could you be so … so … so … *ignorant*, Sadie? You're such a clueless freak!" Trissy's face burned redder than her hair, like she'd just used the foulest words she knew, and she was very pleased by it.

Before I could stop myself, I spewed a word I'm sure Trissy would never dare to say. Trissy's mouth dropped open, and she ran out of the room, dragging Cooper and yelling for her father.

Oh no.

***

Truitt made a smart move by declining a trip inside for a glass of water when he finished the yard work. Kurt was washing the puke off Cooper, and Melina was trying to calm a still hysterical Trissy while also putting Jackson to bed. And me? I sat at the kitchen table, drumming my fingers on Cooper's plastic placemat, just hanging around. Inhaling, exhaling. Trying not to freak out.

After what seemed like forever, my aunt and uncle walked in.

"The kids are in bed," Kurt stated, like I needed to know. Actually, that bit of information made me more nervous because my aunt and uncle could now say whatever they wanted without little eavesdroppers.

Kurt sat at the head of the table and ran his fingers through his curly hair. Melina took her time brewing a pot of coffee.

Even after Mel sat at the table, and there was a cup of coffee in front of each of us, no one said anything. I desperately wanted to break the silence, but I wasn't exactly trusting my mouth at the moment.

Kurt took a sip of his coffee. Mine was still way too hot to drink, but Kurt took a second sip before setting the mug on the table.

"Okay, Sadie." He crossed his arms on the table and leaned forward, turning his head slightly so his eyes could meet mine. I didn't let them. Mine were trained on the little bubbles rimming the dark coffee in my mug.

"Trissy will apologize to you for her behavior. She shouldn't have overreacted like that."

He paused for another sip of coffee, and Melina finished his thought. "And we know you didn't know about Cooper's allergy. We're so used to monitoring what he eats that we forget to mention it to people sometimes. Although we'd appreciate it if you cleared it with us before you feed him anything in the future, okay?" Her voice was soft and kind. Kurt's voice? Not so much.

"Now," Kurt said, his voice low, steady, and dead serious, "what we're certainly not okay with is your use of language. You knew we weren't okay with it, and we trusted you to clean up your speech. That has to stop. You need to quit the cussing cold turkey."

"Kurt." Melina tucked her arm in Kurt's, and he stopped talking and looked at her. They had one of their silent conversations before she continued for him, slipping into the tag-team thing they were so good at. "We know our lifestyles are different, and we know you're not used to being around young children. But our children's innocence is the most valuable thing we can protect. Do you understand?"

I nodded. "Yeah. It's just habit, though."

My aunt and uncle nodded in unison. "We'd like for you to apologize to Trissy in the morning, Sadie," Kurt said. "You don't have to make a big deal out of it, just apologize for raising your voice. That way you won't draw attention to what you said."

I swirled my coffee around in the mug. "I get it. Thanks for not going off on me."

Melina nodded and slid out of her seat. "I think I'm going to bed. You kids don't stay up too late, okay?"

Kurt stood too. "I'm coming, honey. Good night, Sadie."

The day had been eternal. It started off kind of fun with the shopping trip, and then I read the journals and felt like I grew closer to my mom. But then the digression began with Mr. Perfect coming over and the incident I affectionately referred to as "Puke in the Glass" and all that was involved with that. Oh, and as icing on the cake, I slept on the sofa. Too much tension in Trissy's room. I'm telling you—people always talk about teenage hormones running rampant, but I'm not entirely convinced eight-year-olds don't have their own set of chemicals controlling them too.

***

The next morning, I woke early when Kurt got up to go to the gym. I snuck into the bedroom, grabbed a change of clothes, and jogged around the backyard. The last thing I needed was to be busted for something else, and I figured they couldn't find fault in me running laps around the house. I even had my phone with me.

By the time I came back inside, the rest of the house was awake.

I headed into the kitchen, relieved the pain in my side had been more like a dull ache while I ran. Maybe it was going away for good. The smell of fresh coffee greeted me. The thought of holding a hot mug of rich, strong coffee calmed me.

I almost turned around when I saw Trissy stirring a tablespoonful of sugar into her coffee, but Melina caught my eye from where she stood pouring juice into cups for the boys. She gave the slightest of nods. I mean it was so slight that if I didn't know any better, I'd think my eye twitched or something. But I did know better, and I also knew I wouldn't give Trissy the satisfaction of receiving an apology in front of her family. It was already bad enough that I even had to apologize to her.

"Uh, Trissy?"

I could tell she was ignoring me, but I tried again. "Trissy, I …"

She began to hum a song—something from church Sunday—and spooned another pile of sugar into her coffee.

Melina reached over and took the sugar pot from her. "Tristan Elise Elliot. Your cousin is talking to you." Melina arched a dark eyebrow.

Trissy twisted her lips, and I could tell she was trying to keep herself from rolling her eyes in front of her mother.

"Trissy, can I speak with you in our room?"

It was the first time I'd referred to that place as *our* room. I didn't like hearing it come out of my mouth, and judging by the sour look on Trissy's face, she didn't like it either.

But Trissy shrugged and slid out of her seat, brushing past me on her way to the bedroom. When we got there, I closed the door. She perched on the edge of the bed, like an innocent little canary or something. Oh, how looks could be deceiving!

I sat on the floor in front of the door and crossed my legs. "Look, Trissy. I want to apologize for last night. I shouldn't have yelled, and I'm sorry."

Trissy fingered a wild ringlet and studied her knees. "I'm sorry too."

Okay, well, that was done. What next? We both looked around the room, avoiding eye contact with each other.

A scream emanated from Trissy, interrupting our moment of awkward silence. I jumped up. "What's wrong?"

She scrambled to her feet and leapt to the head of the bed, where she stood on a pillow—my pillow.

"Trissy, what the—"

"Sadie!" She hopped up and down, pointing at a pair of shorts on the floor.

I rolled my eyes. "Attack of the killer pants, *huh?* Gotta watch those polyester blends. They're vicious."

She shook her head so hard I was afraid her neck would dislocate. "N-n-n-o. No. Look at the pants!"

I walked over to the shorts and kicked at them. A roach scurried out of the pocket and under the dresser. The roach surprised me, but I'd never been a screamer. I grabbed the shorts, dropped to my hands and knees, and crawled over to the dresser.

"Sadie, no! Don't do it. I'll go get Daddy!" Trissy yelled. But by the way Trissy had climbed the headboard, I knew I was our only hope.

I craned my neck and brought a finger to my mouth. "I'm gonna need you to be quiet, Trissy." She gulped loudly enough for me to hear her across the room and nodded. I turned back around and dropped to my stomach, groaning as my gut hit the carpet.

"Oh no! Did he bite you?" Trissy hissed.

Ignoring Diva, I slowly turned my head and lay down on the floor. Yup, he was under there. A nice, big roach too. I slowly wrapped the shorts around my hand and slid it under the dresser, quickly grabbing the bug and clenching my fist.

By this point, Trissy couldn't contain her horror anymore. She screamed and ran from the room. I shook my head and trekked through the house to deposit my captive in the toilet. After sending him to his watery grave, I went on a hunt for Trissy. Hopefully, she wouldn't need comforting, because I was definitely not a comforter.

I found her back in the kitchen, consoling herself with another cup of coffee, her lip in a pout.

"There, there. It was just a bug." I awkwardly patted her on the shoulder while the rest of the family watched us in fascination.

Her lip poked out a little farther. "I had a nightmare about a roach once." *Okay ...*

I offered another pat and finally got my own cup of coffee.

"You don't understand," she said as she gulped. "It was the worst thing that's ever happened to me."

Resisting the desire to top that a thousand times over, I tried my hand at the whole maternal thing and hoped it would win some points with my aunt. "Just don't think about it. It'll get better."

She sniffed. "You're right. But I do need to pray about it." And she bowed her head like she was about to start right there in the middle of breakfast.

Chapter 9

Wednesday morning, I sat at the kitchen table, backpack at my feet and a glass of orange juice between my jittery fingers. We were supposed to leave the house for my first day of classes at eight o'clock.

Melina had promised me a pancake breakfast for the first day of school, but Kurt told me Bean kept her up all night. So instead of pancakes, we broke out the cereal stash. I wasn't really a big breakfast eater, but Kurt said I looked like a beanpole and needed to "beef up." That sounded gross. So maybe I was thin. I knew lots of girls who starved themselves to be skinny, but it'd always come naturally for me. Now my uncle wanted me to get meaty? Southerners were so backward.

After breakfast, Melina came out of her bedroom, makeup perfectly applied so that you'd never know how tired she was. She even had a seemingly inhuman amount of patience as she herded her kids into the minivan, coffee in one hand and car keys in the other. Trissy and Jackson were doing some sort of learning camp with the homeschool group, then getting a head start on their fall assignments before the baby came, and Cooper was tagging along for the ride. I hadn't had a chance to see much of Pecan Creek yet, but the drive took us past stuff we'd already seen, like we were headed in the direction of … church. What?

Sure enough, Melina pulled into the Pecan Creek Baptist parking lot and cut the engine.

Assuming she might just be running (or waddling) inside to get something, I stayed in my seat. But then Trissy climbed out and Melina unbuckled Cooper.

"Come on, Sadie. You don't want to be late." Melina leaned in to look at me, forcing my eyes to meet hers.

She glanced out the front window and pulled back. "Tris, why don't you take the boys inside? I have to fill Sadie in on a few details. I see Mrs. Pam's car here, so just ask her, and she'll tell you what room you're in." Her usually airy voice sounded a little strained.

Trissy nodded her head of curls, took Cooper by the hand, and started skipping toward the door, the little boy struggling to keep up.

"Tristan Elise Elliot! Don't skip!"

Trissy stopped and marched with exaggerated steps toward the door where Jackson already waited.

Melina laughed softly as she sank back into her seat behind the wheel. "I hate squashing her free spirit, but I have a feeling the boys will want to repay her one day. So I call it looking out for her, you know?" The way she said that sounded like she was talking to a friend and not a stubborn niece. Something stirred inside me, and for a moment, it was as if I was looking at my mom, who was telling one of her friends about my own wild tendencies. I blinked away the thought and looked out the window.

"Listen, Sadie," Melina said softly, "I can imagine you're probably hating me right now ..."

"Not hate, Melina." No, not hate. But a synonym, maybe. I looked out the windshield.

I felt her hand loosely cup my shoulder. "Kurt and I are doing the best we can. If you don't do this, you'll be a grade behind with no way of catching up. If you work hard over the next few weeks, you'll have a good shot of staying where you need to be." She tugged my shoulder until I faced her. "Plus we both agree you might need a change of scenery. I don't know everything about your life, of course, but I know some change might be good—a chance to form some new friendships and not have to worry about fitting in at school."

I still looked at her but squirmed until she removed her hand from my shoulder. "Then why are you sending me to classes? I thought homeschool happened at, you know, *home*."

She smiled a little. "I don't think I'm up to schooling a high schooler, given the current stage of my life." She patted her stomach and motioned toward the church building. "I couldn't give you the attention you need with the kids around. Plus I thought you might like to get out of the house as much as possible. I was sixteen once too."

"But not my kind of sixteen," I muttered. Melina opened and closed her mouth like she was about to argue, but thought better of it.

Finally, she slid out of the car. "We'll talk more later. Right now we have to go inside."

I followed Melina like a kid on her first day of school, reminding me of the feeling I got as I waited to meet my relatives at the Atlanta airport.

I felt like I'd lived a lifetime since I arrived, even though I still didn't feel settled. Half of a week in Georgia meant half of a week since I left behind a mess I couldn't fix with people who didn't care about me like I thought they would. But those weren't thoughts a homeschooler entertained on her first day of classes—or co-op, as Melina called it. Nope, I needed to pull it together. Take deep breaths.

A thought hit me. I picked up the pace until I was climbing the steps next to Melina. "Is Becca here?" Hey, I had to ask. Her friendly, welcoming personality, coupled with the fact that she was the preacher's daughter, just seemed to fit.

"No, she goes to public school."

"What about Truitt?"

"Public school. Don't start stereotyping, Sadie."

The top of the stairs led to a long hallway. Melina pointed. "The last door on the right down there is the little kid room. That's where I'll be hanging out most of the time if you need me for anything." She opened a door on her right. "This is your class. Miracle of miracles, we're actually a bit early, but there should be five of y'all. I'm going to make sure the kids are settled in."

I stepped into the room. To my left, a large whiteboard covered a wall with a wooden table in front of it. Two more wooden tables, put together in an L shape, stood in the middle of the room. On the wall directly across from me, windows were set into the beige block walls, facing the parking lot I'd just come from. On the far wall, a mural of a flower garden brought color to the otherwise average room, a Bible verse painted across it. A Sunday school room. Of course.

I set my backpack filled with textbooks Melina gave me the night before on the floor by the table and pulled out a chair. As I adjusted myself on the cold piece of metal and wondered if the scrambled feeling in my gut was nerves or associated with the pain that was becoming more frequent, the door opened. A tall, linebacker-type guy wearing a rusty, orange T-shirt and loose-fitting jeans stepped into the room.

He seemed surprised to see me but pulled out the chair next to me and sat down. "Well, hey."

"Hello." For a brief, just short of awkward, moment, we looked each other over. I felt his eyes on me as they wandered from my ponytail to my yellow T-shirt. His eyes were brown, like pools of dark chocolate, and his wavy hair was kind of caramel mixed with what my aunt would call "dishwater brown." Like a chocolate swirl cone. Not bad.

"I'm Hansen." He bent one long leg so that his foot was propped on the rung of his chair.

"I'm Sadie. Sadie Franklin." I felt my cheeks tinge when he smiled in response, and I self-consciously brushed my bangs off my forehead. That was strange. Sadie didn't get nervous around guys.

"You know what that means, right?"

"Huh?" I forced my thoughts to return to the conversation.

"Your name. Sadie means 'princess.'" His eyes danced.

I hadn't known what my name meant, and I couldn't tell if he was being truthful or trying to flirt. "Oh really? And I guess Hansen means 'handsome,' right?"

"Actually, I don't know, but I'm flattered you think that." He dramatically flipped his hair out of his face. "I just know what your name means because my aunt had a Pekinese named Sadie once. Sadie was spoiled rotten and had thyroid issues. Her kidneys quit workin'."

I scrunched my nose. He had been doing *so* well in the flatter-me department.

"Ooh, Princess has a temper." Hansen leaned away from me, and the scared little boy expression on his face made me laugh.

The other students filed into the room, talking and laughing and already good friends. My shoulders sagged a little, even though I hadn't come to necessarily make friends. The door opened again, letting Willow in.

"Hi, Sadie," she said as she passed my seat and sat on the other side of Hansen.

"I didn't know you were homeschooled," I said, although I really didn't know much about anybody around here yet. "What grade are you in?"

"I'm going to be a senior, but my dad thinks I need some sort of summer activity to keep me out of trouble." She rolled her eyes.

"I hear you," I offered. She smiled at me and started catching up with Hansen.

I turned around as the door opened again. My jaw went slack as Melina walked in, carrying a stack of books. She set her stack on the table in front of the whiteboard and perched on the edge. Even at six months pregnant, she resembled a petite, little bird.

"Oh good," she said as her bright eyes scanned the room. "We're all here! Let's learn some literature."

Melina was my English teacher? I mentally ran through all I'd learned about the woman in the past few days. I knew she had a degree in early childhood education, but I hadn't heard anything about a love of American literature. Would I ever figure out this family?

"Now," Melina said as she crossed her legs at the ankles. She looked adorable in her dark wash jeans and peasant top. "We've got two new students this summer, so let's do some introductions.

Tell us your name, age, and *hmm …* favorite subject, Go." She clapped her hands briskly—her signal to get moving—and pointed to Hansen.

Hansen kicked back in his chair, arms folded across his broad chest, and looked about a thousand times more relaxed about this whole situation than how I felt. He spread his hands in my direction. "Ladies first." *Ooh, southern charm.*

I cleared my throat and glanced at Melina. She would analyze my every word to be used as fodder in her next attempt at a heart-to-heart conversation. "I'm Sadie. I'm sixteen, and I like …" I paused here. I could go for the typical "my favorite subject is lunch" answer, but that would be way too cheesy. The last thing I needed was a class-clown rep. But what was my favorite subject? School was something I did because I had to. Get in, get out, and hopefully end up with a diploma at some point. "I guess I don't really have a favorite subject." I crossed my arms, signaling the end of my sharing time.

Melina looked at Hansen. "Your turn, Hansen." So Melina already knew him? I felt myself deflate a little. I'd been hoping I'd found a friend who wasn't part of my family's close-knit circle of friends. Hansen was probably just like everyone else they hung around: a lot more clean and good and in control of their lives than I'd ever hope to be. An image of Truitt popped into my thoughts, and I shoved it away.

Hansen shrugged casually. "I'm Hansen. Age? Eighteen. Favorite subject? Lunch." He smirked like he'd just created the greatest joke ever. He just lost some cool points.

Willow went next, her eyes flashing against her soft complexion. "I'm Willow Crane, and I'm going into my senior year. My favorite subject is English, actually." I wouldn't have guessed Willow would be a teacher's pet. I hoped Melina could see through her.

The remaining two students were Deni and Autumn, fifteen-year-old twins. They were both friendly and outgoing, and glanced at each other occasionally, no doubt having a silent conversation only people who knew each other inside and out could have. I couldn't help but wonder what it'd be like to have a sister who knew absolutely everything about you but stuck by you and loved you anyway. It was such a foreign concept to me.

After the twins, Melina took her turn introducing herself. "You girls all know me, but Hansen, I probably know more about you than you know about me. My baby's due on Labor Day." She laughed at the irony. Would she ever tire of that joke? "But class will be over before we get to that point." I sank a little lower in my seat. "Until then, let's dive into some literature and start off with a timeline of American lit, then I'll introduce you to our first text: *The Scarlet Letter* by Nathaniel Hawthorne."

I had a feeling it was going to be a long summer.

***

I had to hand it to Melina. She actually handled the class really good. I mean *well*. I hated English, but at least she didn't embarrass me to death. After English we had a ten-minute break, and then it was time for anatomy and physiology. Just the name anatomy and physiology made my skin crawl. That sounded hard.

When I arrived back to the classroom in time for A&P after scouting out the drinking fountain, I slid into my seat next to Hansen. He caught my eye and winked. It wasn't like a super-flirty wink or anything. More like a "here we go again" wink. The tips of my ears warmed, and I busied myself with flipping through my empty notebook.

The teacher, I learned, was none other than Mr. Crane, Willow's dad. He wore khaki slacks and a polo shirt and had dark-like-Willow's hair. He passed out some coloring books and told us to complete page one. Yes, a coloring book. Unfortunately, I hadn't been prepared for a preschool repeat, and I'd left my crayons at home in Seattle … ten years ago. Mr. Crane was prepared with extras, though, and he generously let me use some to color my human body diagram, which was surprisingly intricate for a coloring sheet.

"So," Hansen said after we'd gone over the syllabus, listened to a brief overview of the organ systems we'd study over the next few weeks, and were left to color before the SAT class.

"So what?" I added blue polka dots to my diagram's liver. Hey, Mr. Crane said science should be fun. I glanced over at Hansen and watched him drag his orange pencil through the small intestine.

"What's your favorite organ?" He kept coloring nonchalantly, his voice lacking all traces of emotion.

"My favorite what?"

"You know, your favorite organ in the 'marvelous human body.'" He kept his voice quiet, although Willow was talking to Autumn and Mr. Crane was explaining something to Deni.

"I've never thought about it." Okay, yes I had. But seriously, I wasn't about to tell him eyes were the first thing I noticed about a person. Sadie Franklin was not a romantic by any stretch of the imagination, but if you know how to look, eyes can tell you everything about people—even the things they think they bury deep inside themselves.

"I've thought about it," Hansen whispered.

"Oh yeah? What's your favorite organ?" I was almost scared to ask.

"The heart."

Well, that was unexpected. "The what?" I set my pencil on the table and turned to face him. He shrugged and looked at me. "You know, the heart. Where all of the emotions are and stuff."

I choked on a laugh. This guy was completely serious. "Uh, you do know the emotions and stuff are in the brain, right?" I may have been dumb, but I wasn't that dumb.

He blinked, brushing his hair out of his eyes. "I knew that. Okay, note to self: don't try to impress the princess with your soft side. I'll just be blunt. Want to go to a party with me this weekend? Give me your number, and I'll text you the details."

I knew my aunt and uncle would never go for it. I absolutely knew it. My ears felt hot again, and I knew they looked like I'd just burned them with my hair straightener, but I grabbed a mauve pencil and leaned over to write my cell phone number on his coloring book.

Chapter 10

After a half-hour SAT prep session, I climbed back into the minivan and went back to the house for PB&J sandwiches. Melina cleaned up the lunch supplies and then left to read Jackson a story and put Cooper down for a nap, leaving Trissy and me to work on homework in the kitchen.

While I looked up definitions for English class in an old-fashioned dictionary—meaning an actual book—Trissy bopped around the kitchen, popping popcorn and pulling a bowl of grapes out of the refrigerator.

"Um, Trissy?" I watched her squirt chocolate syrup into two milk glasses. "Is it just me, or are you procrastinating on that map you're supposed to be labeling?"

Trissy stopped squeezing and looked at me. "What makes you think I'm procrastinating? I don't even know what that means." She handed me a glass of milk.

"It means you're putting off doing your homework."

"Oh. Nope, you're the only one procrastinating. I'm just fixing some yummy snacks for us."

Melina entered the kitchen carrying a wide-eyed Cooper. "That's it. No more sugar at co-op for this guy." She set him on the floor and walked over to the pantry. "I'm thinking chicken pot pie for dinner. Sound good?"

Trissy did a fist-pump, head-bob routine. Little Cooper and I just stared at her.

Melina faced us. "Well, Sadie? Cooper? What do y'all think?"

I glanced at Cooper, who was watching me, a finger in his mouth. I still intimidated him for some reason because he had yet to come within a three-foot radius of me.

"I'm game if he is." I offered the little guy a thumbs-up, which he responded to with a smile. He then completely shocked me by walking over to my chair and climbing into my lap.

Melina grinned like she'd just overseen the signing of a world peace treaty. "All right, chicken pot pie it is."

***

Cooper didn't leave my side for the rest of the day, even though he still hadn't spoken to me. One look in those huge, doe eyes, though, and I could tell he had an opinion about everything. I liked that. I think he sensed the same thing about me, and that's why I was his new BFF. Jackson, on the other hand, still tolerated me. I'd take it. At least someone was respecting my desire to not share all my life details this summer.

Kurt announced he had a surprise for me after dinner, so with dishes still on the table, he told me to sit tight while he went into the closet-sized room he somehow used for an office. He returned a few minutes later and set a large, black thing in front of me.

"What's this?" I peered at what seemed to be some sort of electronic device.

"This," he beamed, "is my old laptop! I remembered how you said you shared one with your dad back home, so I knew you'd need one for your school stuff and to keep up with your friends in Seattle. Boo-ya! I've claimed that elusive Uncle of the Year title you've been hanging over my head all week." He placed his hands on his hips and waited for me to check it out.

I pulled open the laptop. It was really heavy and had to be at least six years old. "Wow. Thanks, Kurt." I drew swirls in the dust on the screen and noticed the Y key was missing. Optional vowel, optional letter. Same difference, I guess.

"The battery'll last you about fifteen minutes, but the rest of it works like a dream."

I stood and tucked it under my arm. My very own laptop. Something most kids my age already had or had already traded in for a tablet. But although I'd checked out of social media for self-preservation purposes, I still appreciated the gift. I knew he wasn't very thrilled with some of the choices I'd made since I moved in, but he still cared enough to make sure I had what I needed. "Thank you, Kurt." I offered him a sincere smile, surprised when it wobbled.

***

I used Kurt's geriatric laptop to answer some practice SAT questions, the machine wheezing loud enough to block out any potential distractions.

I guess I was feeling all warm inside from Kurt's gift because I found myself agreeing to play a game of hide-and-seek with my cousins after homework. In the first round, Trissy found Cooper and me under the dining room table and rolled her eyes, saying she expected more of someone my age. When it was my turn to seek—a total disadvantage since I didn't know any of the house's secret hiding spots—I found Cooper and Trissy in the pantry and then spent about ten more minutes looking for Jackson. The house was small, and I had no idea where he could be, but Trissy told me the family rule was that you weren't allowed to quit because then people might be stuck hiding for a long time. It seemed like she knew that from experience. We finally found him in the back of the linen closet, tucked under a down comforter. When I tagged him, he jumped out of the closet, brushing past me, and fist-pumped the air before running down the hall to start counting for his turn as seeker.

This time, I refused to be outdone by a little kid, and I refused to feel inferior to Trissy, so I upped my game. Literally. I figured little kids rarely thought to look above eye level, and I proved myself right. Kurt, for whom I *was* at eye level, happened to walk by while the kids were looking through the linen closet and underestimating my skills. I kept my eyes on Kurt until he turned around and jumped, putting his hand on his heart.

I tried to signal for him not to blow my cover, but I couldn't get over the startled look on his face.

"Sadie." I could tell he was trying desperately to keep his tone serious, but his twitching mouth gave away his amusement. "What are you doing on top of my refrigerator?"

"Just ... chillin'." I covered my mouth in a failed attempt to stay quiet. You have to admit, that was funny.

"Sadie, Sadie, Sadie." Kurt clicked his tongue, recovering from the surprise. "What are we going to do to discourage this type of behavior?"

I adjusted my position to bring the circulation back to my tingling foot. "Well, when I suddenly become a homeschooler living in a small town with cousins a decade younger than me as friends and no way of leaving, I just have to make the best of it."

He opened the refrigerator and removed a can of Coke, muttering, "Sadie, Sadie, Sadie," as he popped the top and walked away.

***

"All right, you're going to share your summaries of *The Scarlet Letter* to see how each of you understood the first part of the novel. Hopefully, these different viewpoints will point out things you may have missed before you move on to the second half and prepare for the test. Sadie, you're up." Melina sat behind her table, her feet propped on a stack of books, and motioned for me to stand in front of our little co-op class Friday.

I had a hard time dealing with the novel, especially since I'd never had to read so quickly before, but Melina said we were in turbo mode since the summer semester was so short. I perched on the edge of Melina's table-turned-teacher's-desk, focused my attention on my paper, and took a deep breath.

"My summary of *The Scarlet Letter* by Nathaniel Hawthorne," I began. "So Hester Prynne is married to this creepy old guy named Chillingworth." I turned around to glance at Melina. "I'm pretty sure that name means something. You told us to look for that." Facing the class again, I continued. "But Hester wasn't really into creepy old guys, so she cheated on him. She got pregnant and it got obvious, so all of the other Puritans put her in jail. Dimmesdale— the guy she'd committed adultery with—was actually a preacher, so he didn't want anyone to know about what he'd done. I think the reason is obvious. So Hester was like, 'You're such a wimp. I've been dodging mudslinging from the village kids and wearing this huge A on my chest'—scarlet-colored, obviously—'living in this little hut for years with our kid, and you'll only admit it when no one can see you.' Now, their kid was named Pearl, but she was, like, really wild, and—"

"Thank you, Sadie, but because we've got a lot to do today, let's move on to Willow's summary." Melina's voice was serious, but her mouth threatened to spread into a smile. "I will say you certainly stayed true to yourself on this assignment. Go ahead, Willow."

I didn't know what that meant, but I had worked hard on my summary. I really did want to pass this class, if only because I didn't want to read these books again next year.

Hansen clapped as I returned to my seat. Willow rolled her eyes at him but smiled in my direction as she grabbed her paper off the table. When I sat next to Hansen, he whispered, "That's pretty much the best book report I've ever heard." Such high standards he had.

And then later, in A&P, he leaned over and whispered, "It's still cool if I text you sometime, right?"

His text came that evening during dinner. My phone beeped in my pocket, and I felt a flutter in my chest, thinking Reese was finally trying to contact me after I'd reached his voice mail. My heart dipped—but only a little bit—when I saw the name: *Hansen.*

I slipped my phone out of my pocket and glanced at the message. *Hey, Princess. Party Saturday night? I'll pick you up.*

I started to reply with an enthusiastic *Yes!* but stopped myself. It'd been so long since I'd been to a good party, and I bet Hansen knew a good one when he saw it. But how would Kurt and Melina respond to that? I could ask, but …

"Who you talkin' to?" Trissy leaned over to look at my phone before I had a chance to close the text. "Oh, a *par-tay!* Whose birthday is it?" I glanced up and saw my aunt and uncle watching me.

"Whose party, Sadie?" Melina asked.

I bit the inside of my lip. *Might as well go for it.* "Hansen's."

"Hansen Avery?" Melina's eyebrows slanted toward her nose.

I didn't know his last name yet, but how many other Hansens could there be in Pecan Creek? I nodded. "Can I go?"

Melina glanced at Kurt before responding. "Let's talk about this later, okay?" And that was that. I picked up my phone and replied to Hansen's text with "I'll have to get back to you on that."

We talked about it later that night. All of the pieces of their argument seemed to blur together in a big blob of overbearingness. It didn't help that the pain in my side had intensified again after dinner, making me both clammy and irritable.

"He has a rough background," Melina said.

"I thought Christians weren't supposed to judge," I said in response.

"We're not judging, Sadie." Kurt tapped his fingers on the table. "We just know he makes decisions we don't want you to be a part of. And we have no idea what kind of party this is."

"I've been to parties before," I admitted. "All the time, actually. I know how to take care of myself."

Melina sighed and leaned back in her chair, hands on her swollen abdomen. "I don't doubt that, but ..." She turned to Kurt, who finished her thought.

"But not this party, okay?" And, once again, that was that. I thought about sneaking out, but I had a feeling they'd ship me back to Seattle before I even had a chance to tell Hansen good-bye.

Chapter 11

Saturday morning, I rode to the church with Kurt to fill up the ice chests for a day at the lake with the youth group. Thankfully, the pains had settled down a bit, even though I was starting to think there was something wrong.

On the ride to the lake, I blocked out the girly giggles coming from the backseat of the van and focused my attention on watching all of the trees fly by, pieces of a wide-awake summer sky peeking through the pine trees.

Kurt had asked me if I'd ever been to the lake before. "Of course," I'd replied. Although I had to admit I'd never been tubing or water skiing, two things Kurt had promised I'd get to experience. That did have me excited.

When we arrived at the lake, a couple of guys came over to the van.

"Sadie, these are some of our college students. They agreed to fix the food for us today if we gave them a turn on the boats." He slapped a brown-haired, tan guy on the shoulder. "This is Brant, Kari Taylor's brother …"

He went on with the introductions, but my attention had focused on Truitt and Becca climbing out of his truck. Hopefully, he'd be so preoccupied with her that he wouldn't have time to harass me. I wished for not the first time that day that Hansen had come. Since there was no way on the planet Kurt and Mel would ever let me go anywhere with Hansen, I'd invited him to the lake, realizing the irony of me of all people inviting someone to a church event. I'd made sure to pepper plenty of "It'll be really lame if you're not there" phrases into my invitation, but he'd still refused. Willow had gone to see her grandparents over the weekend or something, so it was just me and all of the ones who'd grown up together.

Becca slung her bag over her shoulder and walked up to me. "Hey, Sadie!" She gave me a quick side hug. "Let me help."

We carried a cooler of cans between us, down a short trail, until we reached a covered pavilion surrounded by pine trees. The beach was a few yards beyond the pavilion, complete with boat dock.

Kurt came up behind us, sharing a cooler with Brant, and rallied the troops. "We'll have a late lunch because I want us to go out in the boats before we eat. Pete and Logan are at the marina filling them up, but they should be back soon. In the meantime, let's open with prayer."

After doing the handholding "Kumbaya" prayer thing, Kurt told us to "Grease up" and meet down at the docks.

"Do you want to borrow some sunscreen?" Becca asked as she slid her T-shirt over her head. That left her in a mint-green one-piece swimsuit and a pair of board shorts.

"No, thanks. I'm behind on my tan this summer." I slid off my swimsuit cover-up, revealing my purple halter bikini top and bottoms.

Becca briefly glanced at my stomach, and I knew she was probably biting back a modesty speech. "You'll be out on the water, though. The sun'll reflect off the lake. At least put some on your shoulders and face?" She said it so sweetly that I obliged.

Kurt stopped and looked at me on his way back to the van. I braced myself for a lecture about my swimsuit. But he surprised me when he said, "Have fun today, all right? Enjoy being a kid."

And thirty minutes later, I really was having fun. I sat on the boat, wedged between Becca and Kari, whose boyfriend had to work and couldn't make it. Lena and four other girls were also piled in. At first, I'd thought the girls and guys were required to be separate or something crazy like that, but then Becca informed me that Kurt had a wild reputation when driving a boat. All of the guys loved it, but the girls would rather stick with Pete, a tall man about my dad's age. Pete was fun too.

I leaned back, feeling the spray of the water tingle my hot skin, closing my eyes and breathing in the fresh, clean air. This was the kind of summer I'd hoped for.

"Who's first?" Pete called over the roar of the boat. A strawberry-blonde named Krissa passed me a life vest. *Me?* I mouthed. She nodded. Once the boat came to a stop, I slipped on the life vest and turned to face Becca. "I'm not doing this alone."

She giggled and slipped on her vest. "Of course not. You've gotta have someone knock you off the tube." Becca opened the door on the back of the pontoon boat and helped Krissa toss the large float into the water. The red tube was the size of a large truck tire and had a trampoline-like tarp on top of it. I shivered in anticipation.

"I'll get on first, okay?" Without waiting for an answer, Becca gracefully leaped onto the tube, only creating a few ripples on the surface of the water. Easy enough.

I stepped onto the little, wooden platform at the back of the boat and jumped. I landed with a belly flop on the tube, and the girls on the boat applauded me.

"Whoa!" Becca laughed. "Now pull yourself up toward the top so your feet don't drag. No, down a little. You don't want the nose to dip under and flip us. Good."

I lay on my stomach as Krissa kicked us away from the back of the boat. Becca's side pushed up against mine, and she looped her right arm through my left before grabbing onto the handle. "So you can't shove me off," she told me. She gave Pete a thumbs-up, and the motor churned to life.

"Hold on tight," she instructed. "If you wanna go faster, it's thumbs-up. Slower, thumbs-down. If you wanna stop, holler."

The rope connecting us to the boat slowly snaked around until we faced forward. As the boat began to move, the line pulled taut and yanked us. Our tube took off with a bounce, and a spray of water shot into my eyes and mouth.

Becca nudged me with her shoulder and grinned. "You good?"

I returned her smile.

"Sometimes, I sing when I'm out here, but Pete said he's gonna 'break in the newbie,' so we need to focus," Becca said. The boat turned sharply to the right. "Uh-oh. He's goin' for a doughnut. *He's goin' for a doughnut!*" Becca shrieked in my ear. I'd never heard her say anything that wasn't in her gentle voice. Before I had time to ask what in the world a "doughnut" was, the tube shot out to the side of the boat.

"Lean!" Becca screamed, and I pressed into her side. Next to me, the water appeared as smooth as glass, and I reached out a hand. My fingers skittered across the surface, and I felt like I was flying. I grabbed the handle again right as the tube jerked the other way.

"He's gonna hit our wake now. Hold on!" Becca's twang deepened in her excitement. I turned to look at her and noticed she totally had the natural beauty thing going for her, even more so than I'd first realized. Her long, brown ponytail swung out behind her, and her thick lashes sparkled with droplets of water. A constellation of freckles was splashed across the bridge of her nose, and her eyes glimmered. She was gorgeous, and I caught myself wishing I could be that pretty without even trying.

The tube suddenly jumped at least two feet in the air and crashed down with a thump. I tightened my screaming arm muscles and yelled for all I was worth alongside Becca. I'd be hoarse in the morning, for sure. The guys' boat passed us and everyone waved. Becca flung her arm out to wave, but I didn't trust Pete enough to let go. We sailed into their wake and went airborne again. The tube bounced hard, and for a moment, I really *was* flying. I dropped into the water, and the force made me flip. I went down, down, down before my life vest bobbed me back to the surface. I came up coughing and sputtering.

A couple of yards to my right, Becca grinned at me before flagging down Pete. "Awesome, right?"

"Oh yeah!" I didn't even care the guys had observed my epic dismount. Kurt turned off his boat's engine, and the boat bobbed a safe distance away.

Becca and I laughed until I was afraid I would choke. Our boat circled back to us, and I swam to the ladder behind Becca.

She climbed out first, her life jacket dripping on my face, and then turned to give me a hand. I reached for her, but froze.

"What's wrong?" Lena's head popped over the side of the boat.

"I, *uh*, don't have my swim bottoms," I whispered.

Lena hooted with laughter, and I scowled. What was I supposed to do?

"Here." Becca quickly shimmied out of her board shorts and passed them to me. "You know," she said softly, "one-piece swimsuits aren't just a modesty thing when you're tubing."

"Good to know," I said as I took the shorts from her. She was a little bigger than I was, but I was able to tie the drawstring tight enough to hold them in place. Of course, they completely clashed with my top, but what choice did I have? I climbed into the boat and Krissa passed my towel to me. My muscles felt like noodles, and I'd left my dignity swimming with the fishes, just like my swimsuit, but I still found myself laughing with the girls on the boat.

Until I saw Truitt belly laughing from his tube a few feet away.

***

"I bet you made some lady catfish's day with a new swimsuit, huh?" Truitt elbowed me as I put a hot dog on my plate at lunch. He leaned close and reached for the coleslaw. "Oh, come on. That was great!"

"Moving on …" I said under my breath. I shook the mustard bottle and considered squirting Truitt's smirking face.

"I can't win with you, can I?" he asked, his voice loud enough for just me to hear. "I try to joke, and you get mad. I try to be serious, and you get mad. I'm trying to be your friend."

He sauntered toward a picnic table, and I noticed a large, purple bruise on his side. "Truitt," I said as I clutched my towel with one hand and balanced my plate in the other, "you get that bruise tubing?" I smirked.

He glanced down at the area just above his hip. "Baseball bat, actually." He walked away before I could point out his lack of coordination.

After lunch, we lounged around for a bit, played a game of badminton, and then went back out on the boats. I attempted to water ski but could never get the hang of it. Instead, I went back to tubing with Becca. Becca let me wear her shorts the rest of the day. I'd have a weird tan line on my legs from sitting out in the sun, but it was better than the alternative.

By the time I got back to the house after having a dinner of leftovers at the lake with the youth group, the sun was beginning to set.

I was hot and dirty and my bangs were plastered to my face like stringy spider webs. I gathered my things for a shower while I waited for my turn in the bathroom. After Kurt cleaned up, he took Cooper from Melina and went to bathe him, since Melina said she could no longer bend over the tub.

I pulled off my cover-up on the way to the bathroom, more than ready to scrub the contents of the lake off my tired arms.

"Sadie!" Behind me, Melina gasped, and I braced myself for another modesty moment. "You're blistered!"

"I'm what?" I rested a hand on my warm hip and felt the tightness of the skin on my back when I moved.

"Did you use sunscreen?"

I nodded because, technically, I did use sunscreen. On my shoulders and nose. While Melina waddled closer and began inspecting my skin, I did the same. My stomach was tanned with just a hint of pink, and so were the fronts of my legs. But Melina was fussing over my back half.

"I don't mean to sound naggy, but you should've reapplied back here. You were on a boat with the sun reflecting off the water and hitting you plumb on the back." Her thumb pressed into the space between my shoulder blades. "Oh, you poor piece of bacon. You're fried. You need an oatmeal bath."

A bath? I hadn't had a bath in years. I wasn't one of those girls who liked to relax with a good book and a tub full of bubbles. No, showers worked out just fine for me. Then there was the oatmeal part.

"Melina, oatmeal is for eating."

She laughed. "It's also for soothing the skin. Go on into the bathroom, and I'll fix it for you. Kurt'll get my other kids ready for bed."

I reluctantly followed her into the bathroom, although a part of me felt warmed by the fact that she'd grouped me in with the rest of her family. I blamed being out in the sun too long.

I turned on the water and rinsed out the tub, and then I put the plug in. I couldn't imagine a cold bath, but the thought of hot water on my skin made me cringe.

Melina came up behind me and adjusted the faucet. "You don't want it too hot, or you'll blister your blisters." She dumped a pack of oatmeal bath into the water. Once the tub was full, she told me, "Stay in until your teeth chatter."

"Now," she said as she turned off the faucet, "I'm washing the swimsuits, so give me yours once you get it off."

I stepped into the tub and closed the curtain. After carefully untying my top and removing Becca's shorts, I handed the clothing out to Melina. If she noticed my lack of swim bottoms, she didn't say anything.

I slowly sank into the tub, hissing as the lukewarm water made contact with the back of my legs. I managed to hold back a whimper until I heard Melina leave the room.

She really was a good mom, and even a good aunt, if I were being completely honest. I swirled my hands in the water and blinked away a sudden wave of emotion. Where did that come from? One moment I was thinking of how gentle Melina was, and the next my mind shifted to memories of my own mom. Oh, how far I'd come since I was eight. Since that horrible, horrible day that changed everything.

For years, I'd sworn I'd never drive a car, never get behind a wheel out of sheer terror. Once I did start driving, I'd think of her—of us—and the car wreck that changed everything.

"It should've been me," I whispered to the air as a blanket of sadness pressed against me. "I shouldn't have made it out." But life wasn't meant to be fair; my mom had told me that plenty of times. And if God actually had compassion, He'd never let an eight-year-old witness her mom's death and have to live with a father who didn't know how to handle his own grief.

Okay, breathe, I ordered myself. *That's enough. You're okay.* I took deep breaths to steady my shaking limbs. I hadn't let myself think like that in a while, and that was why. Once I let the memories flow, the hole in my heart only grew bigger. I slid further into the water until my head was submerged.

After dressing in gym shorts and a tank top, I found Melina on the couch in the living room, waiting with a bottle of blue aloe vera gel.

"Sit on the floor," she said. I obeyed. "Now it may be a little chilly—"

"Whoa!" I yelped and clamped a hand over my mouth. "Why is that so frigid?"

Melina smoothed the goop onto the back of my shoulders. "I just took it out of the fridge."

"Is refrigeration necessary?" I tensed beneath her touch. It must've been pretty red back there. She didn't reply, just kept massaging the gel onto my back. Again, I thought of my mom. So similar yet so different from Melina.

When she finished, I sat on the other side of the couch, a hand on my stomach, careful not to smear aloe on the furniture. "Um, Melina?"

"Mm-hm?" She rubbed the extra gel into her hands.

"I think something's wrong with me. Those muscle pains, you know, have bothered me for a while."

She turned to face me and leaned against the arm of the couch. "How long?"

I shrugged. "Off and on for a few months, but more intense once I got here. And when I run. And tube, apparently."

I scooted next to her on the couch. "Feel this."

Her brow creased as I guided her hand to my abdomen. Sure, it was a little awkward, but I'd spent plenty of time feeling her stomach recently. I brought her hand to my side and pressed lightly. "Feel that?"

She nodded. "Is it a tight muscle, you think?"

I shook my head. "I don't know. All I know is it hurts so much I feel like yelling. And it's been like this, so I know my abs aren't just sore from tubing like the rest of me or anything."

"Hmmm." She removed her hand from my stomach and rubbed the back of her neck. "I'm calling to get you an appointment with my doctor."

I snorted. "*Your* doctor?"

My aunt rolled her eyes. "She does more than just take care of expectant mothers. She's really good." She smoothed a piece of damp hair off my cheek, and the gesture felt too familiar. "We'll just get her opinion, okay? You should probably get some sleep." I nodded and silently left to brush my teeth. I hadn't been to the doctor in years, but if she could help me, it'd be worth the inconvenience.

Chapter 12

The stained-glass windows inside Pecan Creek Baptist Church splashed colored prisms of light onto the padded pews and burgundy carpet as the sun filtered through the biblical scenes. As I sat and waited for the service to start, I studied those windows for the first time. My first time in here, last Sunday night, had been some sort of quarterly conference meeting, so this was my first time in the regular service. Becca's dad, a fortysomething guy with fading brown hair and a navy suit, stood up and introduced himself to people who might be visiting. He talked for a minute and then prayed before a guy came up to lead music. I guess I don't know what I expected, but not all of the songs were filled with *thee* and *thou* and *thy*. Actually, a couple of them sounded pretty modern.

About three songs in, the music guy led everyone in an old song I remembered my mom singing to me when I was a little kid.

> Great is Thy faithfulness, O God my Father,
> There is no shadow of turning with Thee;
> Thou changest not, Thy compassions, they fail not
> As Thou hast been Thou forever wilt be.

I'll admit I'd never really paid attention to the words, and I wasn't even sure what half of them meant anyway, but something about hearing that familiar tune got to me.

I stared at the projected words on the wall, letting my mind go back to the days when I sat in church. When Mom would dress me in little, floral sundresses and braid my long, silky hair. When the preaching started, I'd lie down on her lap and she'd stroke my hair, tucking the loose strands behind my ears over and over. I'd kept my hair long ever since.

I didn't realize my eyes were cloudy until Melina reached over and squeezed my arm. I glanced at her, startled, and she smiled a soft, sad, knowing smile. I looked away and my eyes caught the windowpane of Jesus and the children. Where was Jesus when *I* was a child? Where was He when I was an eight-year-old little girl whose world completely fell out from under her? What was I even doing in church? I didn't belong there.

I didn't hear much of the sermon. I didn't let myself. Instead, I focused on bubbling in all of the letters on the church program. God obviously didn't want very much to do with me, so why would I sit there and listen to someone tell me all the reasons why I should trust Him?

***

The Old Man and the Sea, my next reading assignment, took an eternity to read, but Melina had decided we wouldn't give individual summaries of the story. Clearly, she didn't want the others students feeling inferior to my report. I was actually starting to get into anatomy, though. Who would've thought coloring could actually help you learn? My first test was on Friday.

I was still trying to figure out the mysterious Willow. She seemed nice enough, but her smile seemed to harden just slightly whenever I talked to Hansen. She'd said hello to me at church Sunday, but when I told Hansen about my tubing adventure, I caught her rolling her eyes. How did I get myself in the middle of these things?

After co-op Monday, Becca came over to bake a surprise cake for her dad's birthday. She arrived with ingredients stacked in a picnic-type basket and made herself at home in the kitchen. I hopped up on the counter, dying to do something other than quiz myself using the SAT flash cards I kept in my back pocket at all times.

"So what kind of cake is this?" I asked as Becca cracked an egg on the side of the bowl. I stirred the egg into the mixture of sugar, butter, and cocoa with a rubber spatula while Becca cracked another egg, I didn't know the first thing about cooking, but I sure was good at winging stuff.

"It's actually just devil's food cake with espresso and a few extra ingredients added, but Dad loves it." Becca concentrated on measuring a teaspoon of vanilla.

I reached around her and grabbed the old church recipe book. The page was crusted by dark batter, and a few added ingredients were scribbled in the margins.

"The pastor's favorite cake is devil's food? That's ironic."

"Everyone has their weakness." Becca measured a second teaspoon of vanilla, attempting to be as precise as possible.

I took the spoon from her and dumped it into the mix. "Perfectionist." She snatched the spoon back, and the overhead light reflected off the silver band around her finger.

"So what's with the ring on your wedding band finger?" I handed her a can of condensed milk for the chocolate frosting.

"It's a purity ring. It shows my promise to wait for the guy God has picked out for me. I'm already his, even if I don't know him yet."

I slid off the counter and pulled a pot out of the cabinet. "And you expect whoever he is to do the same for you? Chastity died with chivalry."

She shrugged. "Sadly, that's true for some people, but I have to disagree with you. I believe the whole marriage thing is sacred." She hooked the teeth of a can opener into the rim of the condensed milk and gave the handle a twist. The appliance popped off the can. "Ugh. The pains of a lefty living in a right-handed world." She switched the can opener to her other hand and tried again.

I was still tossing her words around in my mind. "What do you mean, 'sacred'?" I asked, dipping my finger into the thick, sweet milk. "Isn't that a religious word?"

"Yeah, like holy, pure, consecrated—"

I raised my hand. "Hold up. You lost me with your preacher's kid terms."

She laughed. "Sorry. Indoctrination comes with the title. I basically meant that when I meet the guy I'll spend forever with, I want to be able to say I've practiced loving him before I even knew his name."

"Hmm" was all I could say. Maybe I wasn't completely sold on Becca's ideas, but she seemed to have thought through a lot of things for herself rather than just doing something because someone else told her to. She had depth, and despite our differences, I liked that about her.

***

After dinner that night, Melina recruited me to help with the dishes. "I made you a doctor's appointment for Friday after co-op," she suddenly announced.

I took the plate she held out and stacked it in the dishwasher. "Already?"

She scrubbed a scorched pot. "I'm a frequent customer," she joked. "No, actually, Dr. Summers is an old family friend, so I was able to get you in."

"I don't think—"

"It doesn't matter, Sadie. I don't like to see you in so much pain. Something's going on."

"It's been a while since I've been to the doctor, Melina. I think last time was when I got my twelve-year-old shots or something."

Melina gave up on the pot and handed it to me. I fit it into the nearly full dishwasher like a piece of a jigsaw puzzle.

"All the more reason you should go, my dear."

"Go where?" Kurt walked over to the now-empty sink and set a dirty cup in it. Melina shot him a look.

"Nowhere, Kurt. I'm basically stranded." I ran his cup under warm water and wedged it into the dishwasher.

My uncle leaned against the counter, crossing his arms over his chest. "You have a driver's license, right?"

"Lot of good that's doing me."

He tilted his head and looked over to Melina and then back to me. "We know about the suspension, Sadie. Your dad sent your license to us when they reinstated it."

Ooh, that was an awkward subject. Although, in my defense, I had left my license at home and passed through a license check. After curfew, but nothing major. If Kurt had my license, it meant

I could at least have some of my freedom, provided I had a vehicle to actually *drive*.

"Why don't we go for a ride tomorrow?" Kurt asked.

"No offense or anything, but I don't think driving a minivan is going to help my cause." I tossed the dishrag at Kurt.

"Then we'll take my truck!" he said, referring to his '85 pickup. Because that was so much better. "Can you drive a stick shift?"

"You're funny, Kurt." *What teenager knows how to drive stick shift anymore?* "Guess I'm stranded."

"Nonsense!" He grabbed a new cup out of the cabinet and filled it at the sink. "We'll have a lesson tomorrow. Meet me out back at ten o'clock sharp." He sounded like he was making some sort of shady exchange. I told him so. He drained the cup and left the kitchen, calling over his shoulder, "Just don't be late!"

***

The next morning dawned bright and dewy. After going for a run around the backyard, which was beginning to make me feel like a hamster running around its cage because I'd yet to learn to navigate the neighborhood, I showered, slathered aloe on my hot, pink skin, ate some of Melina's buttermilk french toast, then went out to Kurt's truck to await my lesson.

I squinted and watched my uncle come out the back door, a leftover piece of french toast hanging out of his mouth. Even though it was still morning, it was already like an oven in the cab of his truck. Sweat had passed the point of beading on my forehead and gone to all-out drippage. I shoved my braid over my shoulder.

"Sorry, Sadie, but I've gotta run." He held his french toast with one hand and swiped his forehead with the other. Please. He'd been outside for all of five seconds, and I'd been waiting around for like ten minutes. "One of our elderly church members was rushed to the hospital from her nursing home in Augusta. Possible heart attack. Pastor Shepherd's in Atlanta, so I'm on call and need to get down there."

I took a second to decide if I was disappointed or not. I mean freedom—relatively speaking—was within my grasp if I could tame this gas-guzzling beast, but at the same time, an hour or two of uncle-niece bonding time didn't exactly stir up the warm, fuzzy feelings. The last thing I needed was some sort of sermon while I tried to figure out what to do with the extra pedal.

I snapped my fingers, swinging my hand in front of me. "Oh rats."

He bit his french toast. "Never fear!" he said in a cheesy superhero voice. "I've called in backup."

"Huh?"

A smug look shadowed his face.

What ...

"Listen, I've gotta run. Stay put. Your lesson'll start in about ten minutes." He traded places with me and peeled out of the driveway before I could respond. Not knowing what else to do, I started walking back toward the house, keeping an eye on the driveway for any signs of Kurt's "backup."

A strange puttering sound announced my instructor's presence. *Oh no. You're kidding ...* I instantly knew by the yard equipment piled in the back that this day could only go downhill.

"Mornin', Sadie!" Truitt called out his truck's open window as he killed the engine. I mean it literally sounded like he killed it. That gurgle couldn't be normal.

I rolled my eyes, muttered something along the lines of "Why me?" and stepped over to the truck.

"Shouldn't you be whacking weeds or something?" The sun created such a glare on his rusty red truck that I had to flip my large sunglasses down over my eyes.

"I prefer the phrase 'grooming the landscape,' and no, this is my job."

"My uncle paid you to babysit me?"

He shrugged, and something—amusement?—flicked in his eyes. "Your ability to intimidate the kids is too great. Kurt and Mel feel threatened by your influence."

I examined a mosquito bite on my arm. "Your services will not be needed. Although," I said as I gestured toward the backyard, "the lawn is looking a bit patchy." He climbed out of the truck and walked over to me. I stiffened when he grabbed me by the elbow and escorted me to the passenger side of the truck.

"Don't touch me with those grungy nails. What? Were you raised in a dump?"

He pushed me in and shut the door. Then opened it and slammed it. Then repeated the process a few more times.

"Hey, don't blame me for your bad hygiene, yard man."

He chuckled as he slid into his side of the cab. "Nah, Beulah's door sticks. Might wanna go ahead and crank that window down too. She gets a little ripe."

"Wait. *Beulah?*" I couldn't get past the name.

"It's Hebrew."

"Ah." Because that answered all my questions.

"All right." He fastened his seat belt. "Let's go, Joe. Watch my every move as I demonstrate, and then I'll let you take a shot."

I grunted in response and reached for the radio knob.

He shooed my hand away. "No. No music. Just the gentle purrs of ol' Beulah. You've gotta listen to her closely so you know when she's ready to shift gears."

I tilted my head and clicked my seat belt. "Do you have to make everything awkward?"

He replied with a crooked grin. "Just watch. Now, before I turn Beulah on—"

"Stop it."

"What? You're the one with your mind in the gutter. As I was saying, before I start the truck"—he cut his eyes over to me—"I push the clutch down with my left foot and the brake with my right. Like so ..." He demonstrated his instructions. "Then you release the parking break—mine happens to be right here by the clutch—and crank the truck. Got it?"

I scratched my head. "Which one's the clutch again?"

Truitt knocked his head against the back of his seat. "Oh wow. I see we need to start at the beginning. This is a truck. This is a key. This is—"

"Knock it off, jerk. I asked a legitimate question." I pulled deep breaths through my nose.

"You're right. I'm sorry. Let's start over."

I watched Truitt's every move like he was a Hollywood A-lister and I was an obsessed fangirl. Which, obviously, couldn't be any more of a stretch from how it actually was, but the point was I paid rapt attention. Truitt showed me how to release the parking break—"Pull up a little first; it's a little rusty"—and shift the truck into first gear. Then he made me crouch down in the floorboard, so I had an eagle-eye view of his old, rotten-smelling tennis shoes as he slowly eased off the clutch and depressed the gas.

He circled around the backyard, during which time he told me to release the gas, push down on the clutch, and shift to second gear. Finally, when we got back to the driveway, he released the gas, let the truck cruise a bit while he pushed the clutch in, and then slowly brought the truck to a stop. Easy peasy.

"Now," Truitt said as he slapped his knee and unfastened his seat belt, "your turn."

Believe it or not, I was actually itching to get behind the wheel. I was used to driving my dad's car since he worked nights and didn't need it during the day. But this? Now this just looked fun.

Truitt walked around to the passenger side of the truck, and I slid over behind the wheel. I rubbed my hands together maniacally. "Let's do this." I stared at the wheel.

"Left on clutch, right on break, crank the ignition ..." Truitt turned his hand in a circle. "Good. Now push the gearshift over and up to the left." I did as I was told. Truitt dropped his voice to a whisper. "Now ease off the clutch while pressing increasingly on the gas." I nodded, realizing I was holding my breath.

I released the clutch and pushed the gas. A distinct revving and grinding came from the belly of the truck. Beulah began to shake violently, and I stomped the brake. The truck went still and very, very silent.

"Whoa, Nellie!" Truitt exclaimed as he gripped the door of the truck.

I hit the steering wheel and vented my frustrations under my breath.

"Sadie!" I jumped at Truitt's raised voice. I hadn't heard that before. "I get that you're frustrated, but that was your first try. And those words you just said ... As a Christian, it hurts me to hear them."

"Oh, like you've never cussed before." I returned the gearshift to neutral and then to first.

Truitt exhaled. "Look," he said, more quietly this time. "I'm sorry I yelled. You're right. I'm not perfect. Let's start over. Again."

I nodded. Truitt closed his eyes and whispered something. I couldn't make out all the words, but I caught a couple of "Please" phrases. Was he praying?

I took a few more breaths and focused my attention on the truck. My second attempt ended much like the first. Truitt just rubbed the back of his neck and nodded for me to try again. After the third failed attempt, Truitt tried manning the gearshift so I could focus on the pedals, but that ended with me biting my tongue so hard my mouth tasted metallic.

I decided to give it one more shot. Sadie Franklin was many things, but she was not a quitter. I peeled my sweat-soaked bangs out of my eyes and ignored Truitt's conversation with Beulah. I put the truck in first, inhaled, eased off the clutch, exhaled, depressed the gas, and moved forward.

"Beulah, I love you!" I yelled. "Whoo-hoo!"

We circled the backyard at a snail's pace, and then Truitt told me to shift into second gear. It happened without a hitch—literally. We looped around the backyard several times, even though we didn't have enough room to gain enough speed for third gear.

"Yes!" Truitt fist-pumped. "Now home, James!"

I turned toward the driveway. "What's with all of the names you keep using? Joe, Nellie, James? What are you doing? Summoning the help of your ancestors?"

Truitt laughed and turned his ball cap backward. I pulled back into the driveway and pressed on the brakes. Unfortunately, I forgot about the clutch, so we lurched forward, catching ourselves on the dash. I pulled the key from the ignition and turned to look at Truitt. He gave me a full-on, dimple-engaging grin. Then we high-fived.

"Well," Truitt said as he pulled off his cap and mopped his forehead with the back of his hand. "We made it back alive."

I pressed my hand to my stomach. All the jerking hadn't exactly helped my pains.

"You okay?" Truitt asked.

I dropped my hands in my lap. "Um, yeah. I'm fine."

He peered at me for a minute, like he was trying to read my face.

"Seriously, I'm good." I gave him a thumbs-up. "Okay, well, bye." I started to climb out of Beulah's cab. *This could be awkward if I don't leave now.* "I hope they paid you enough to make this lesson worth your while." I closed the door a few times—good for the biceps—and leaned in the open window as Truitt slid over.

"Paid me?" Truitt shook his head. "Nah, I volunteered. See you later, Sadie."

I took a step back as Beulah grasped at life and watched Truitt pull out of the driveway, one arm on the steering wheel and the other propped in the open window.

***

Trissy was jealous. Oh, she didn't actually *say* she was jealous. She just kind of flipped her hair over her shoulders and stuck her nose in the air whenever we interacted the rest of the day.

"What's up with you?" I asked as we crawled beneath the covers that night, both staying as close to our edge as possible. But that was nothing new.

"What are you talking about?" she asked.

I clicked off the bedside lamp. "Don't play innocent. I saw you watching Truitt and me out the window this afternoon, and you've snubbed me all day."

"Whatever, Sadie. I'm tired. Good night." She flopped over so she was facing away from me.

"Fine. Good night." I flipped onto my stomach and sighed. "Besides, if you're worried about me liking Truitt, you're wasting your life. That guy is self-righteous."

I heard no response other than Trissy's quick, jealous breaths. As if being a teenage girl doesn't sound tough enough for you, try adding adversity with an eight-year-old to the mix.

Just as I was falling into that wonderfully fuzzy twilight zone between awake and asleep, I felt a sharp poke in my ribs.

"Owww," I moaned into the pillow. I rolled onto my side and propped my head up with my elbow. Trissy's shadowy form sat facing me, the moonlight reflecting off her eyes. "What do you want, Trissy?"

"I'm sorry, okay?"

"Okay." I flipped onto my other side.

"Whenever I make out with someone, we usually hug it out."

I bit the edge of the comforter to keep from bursting into obnoxious laughter. Trissy was so annoying, yet she constantly made me laugh. "You mean make *up*? Make *out* means major kissing."

I heard something smack, most likely Trissy's palm on her forehead. "Ew, nasty! That's not what happens! Anyway, we should hug it out."

"I'd love to, Trissy," I lied, "but I'm really comfortable right now, and I don't want to risk losing my cozy spot. You know how it is."

"Yeah, I guess," she said softly, and I wondered if I'd hurt her feelings.

"Are you—*oomph*!" Trissy landed on me and wrapped her arms around my waist. "Trissy, what are you doing? Get off!"

After an uncomfortable pat on my shoulder, she crawled back to her side of the bed. "We needed to hug for closure, and I didn't want you losing your comfy spot. *Duh*."

"I see." I yawned and snuggled beneath the covers.

"Hey, Sadie?"

"What?"

"Have you ever made out with a boy?"

"Good night, Trissy."

She sighed. "Okay. G'night."

Chapter 13

"I don't understand what happened." Melina sat next to me in the waiting room of her doctor's office in Augusta, flipping through a parenting magazine. "Oh, please. My eight-year-old does not need a cell phone." She glanced over at me. "You completely dropped the ball this week."

It took me a moment to realize she was talking to both me and her magazine. I shifted on the uncomfortable chair, peeling my tender, sunburned legs off the vinyl and crossing them. "I don't know what happened. I tried."

And I had, really. Somehow I'd made a C on my English test … and in A&P. But in my defense, the respiratory system was way too complex for such a short time to learn it. On top of that, I'd blanked out in the middle of a practice SAT essay and ended up with a lousy grade on that too. The worst part of all was the look on my aunt's face when she saw my exams. Somewhere along the way, I'd begun to try to please her, at least a little bit, but now she was back to viewing me as a loser.

I picked up a cooking magazine and looked at pictures of summer cobbler recipes until a nurse called my name. "Sadie Franklin?"

I stood. Beside me, my aunt stood too. Was she really thinking she would go in there with me? "It's okay, Melina. I've got this."

"Oh, okay. I just thought …" She fidgeted with her necklace. "Never mind."

Maybe it was the hormones talking, or maybe she really wanted to go in with me, but she looked a little emotional. I remembered how much she'd done for me since I'd come to Georgia; how much she'd put up with; how much restraint she'd practiced when I showed her my wimpy test grades. I closed my eyes for a second while the nurse waited.

"You know what?" I said slowly. "I'd like for you to come with me."

"Really?" She reminded me of Trissy with her wide green eyes.

"Really, but if they have to do anything like …" I trailed off.

She waved to the nurse to signal we were coming eventually. "No, no. I get it. You say the word, and I'll step out, okay?"

After the nurse weighed me and took my blood pressure—turns out I really was alive, if anyone had doubts—Melina and I followed the nurse to a room where we waited. And waited. I sat on the paper covering the examination table and picked at what I could reach of my peeling shoulders while Melina sat on a chair in the corner and read the magazine she'd brought from the waiting room. Every now and then, she'd use her phone to snap a picture of a recipe or mutter under her breath about how society was forcing kids to grow up too fast these days.

We were about fifteen minutes into the waiting process when I realized I really was glad Melina was in the room with me. Otherwise, the small, sterile space would make me go crazy. I held my hand over my stomach, trying to put so much pressure on the pain that it would stop, but it didn't work. Melina, meanwhile, also had her hand on her stomach due to pain, except she had a baby kicking her ribs.

The clock on the wall above the door ticked off each second as it passed, and I grew more and more anxious. My fears grew from "It's probably just sore muscles" to "I think I'm dying." I was beyond relieved when the door finally opened and a middle-aged woman came in.

"Miss Franklin? I'm Dr. Summers." The doctor's cool, smooth hand enveloped mine, and we shook. She had pretty, gray hair and wire-rimmed glasses and seemed to be in her late fifties. "How are you?"

"I'm okay." My voice was raspy. Honestly, she should've known that if I were really okay, I wouldn't be there in the first place.

Dr. Summers turned to my aunt. "How are you and Baby Elliot, Melina?"

My aunt beamed. "So far, so good. This is an active one. That's for sure."

"And we're still keeping the sex a mystery, yes?"

Melina nodded. "I have a theory, but no, we don't know for sure."

Dr. Summers rolled a stool out from under the counter and sat. "Okay, Sadie. Let's start with some questions." She pulled a pen from her white doctor's coat pocket and retrieved a clipboard from a drawer. "How old are you?"

"I'll turn seventeen August fourteenth." I crossed my legs at the ankles and swung them, feeling like a little kid and hoping doctors rewarded sixteen-year-olds with lollipops.

"Are you on any medications?"

"Well, my lovely aunt has me on a daily multivitamin." I smiled sweetly at Melina, who rolled her eyes and went back to studying her magazine.

Oblivious, Dr. Summers made a note on her clipboard. "And what is the date of your last menstrual cycle?"

I stopped swinging my legs and pulled one of them up, tucking it under me and leaning against the wall. "I'm not sure."

Dr. Summers nodded while she jotted something down. "That's okay. Just give me a ballpark guess."

I used my fingers to count. "Um, well." I counted inside my head. *One, two, three.* "March, I guess."

Dr. Summers looked up from her notes and Melina's magazine fluttered closed.

"March?" They asked in unison.

I swallowed, suddenly uncomfortable. I knew that wasn't exactly normal. "Well, yeah. Or possibly February? It's always been weird."

"Do you know why that is, Sadie?" Dr. Summers asked casually, as if we were chatting about why the sky is blue.

"No. I just figured I've had a lot of stress—like, a *lot* of stress— in my life recently, so I didn't think it was that big of a deal." I glanced at my aunt, who looked a little pale. "It's probably not that big of a deal," I repeated in an attempt to reassure myself.

Dr. Summers rolled her stool to my exam table and set her clipboard beside me. "We'll come back to that. Explain to me why you're here today."

I pulled my knees to my chest and wrapped my arms around my legs. Shorts had been a bad idea. It was freezing in the tiny room, and I was shivering. Resting my chin on my knees, I said, "I've had really bad stomachaches recently. Really bad. I just moved here a couple weeks ago, and before I came, I thought it was just from … Well …" I paused, considering the wisdom of telling a healthcare professional how often I, a minor, consumed alcohol, even though I hadn't been in a five-mile radius of the stuff since coming to Georgia. "I didn't think much of it, like maybe it was just muscle cramps that wouldn't go away because I run a lot and probably don't drink enough water or eat enough bananas or whatever it is. I've also been really tired, but not able to sleep at night, which is probably because I have a ton on my mind." I slid an arm between my legs and my stomach.

Dr. Summers put her hand on my knee. "You couldn't be pregnant, could you?"

Melina's face shot from pale to green. I looked back and forth between the two women. I know I wasn't exactly the poster child for purity, but nothing that serious happened … I thought back to my last week in Seattle. Back when I knew I was leaving and getting a fresh start and anything that happened in Seattle would stay in Seattle and … That wasn't something to broadcast to the world, but there was no way … Reese and I didn't …

I had trouble finishing a complete thought. "That's not possible."

Neither woman looked too convinced. I quietly pleaded for Melina to believe me. "What kind of person do you think I am? I'd never bring a kid into my crazy life. You have to believe me, Melina." My voice sounded like nails on sandpaper.

Melina rubbed her hand over her face slowly, stilling her hand over her eyes for a moment. Sighing, she said, "Okay. I believe you."

"I actually believe you too," Dr. Summers added. "I just wanted to rule out all other possibilities before we run those tests to verify what's wrong. I can send you to the lab for blood work today, then we'll schedule a follow-up appointment, all right?"

"Okay," I said, like everything really was okay. Dr. Summers patted my shoulder and entered some notes on the computer in the corner while she chatted with Melina, but I couldn't make myself join the conversation.

***

"I can't believe you think so little of me." I sat at the table and watched Melina spoon leftover lasagna into a plastic container.

Melina stopped scooping and drooped her shoulders. "I don't think little of you, Sadie. I just want answers as much as you do. I'm sorry I hurt you."

I slid my cup back and forth on the table, watching the contents slosh against the sides of the glass. "Maybe some fresh air will help." Melina answered my silence. "We're leaving for Jackson's game in about ten minutes."

During those next ten minutes and the ride to the ballpark, I thought about how it wasn't just Melina thinking I could be pregnant that hurt, although it did. It was also the uncertainty of the whole ordeal—not knowing what was wrong and why it was wrong and how I could fix it. That's what hurt the worst.

At the park, I sat on the bleachers between Melina and Trissy. Cooper sat on my lap, his eyes fixed on his brother, who was taking his turn at bat.

"Come on, Jack! You can do it!" Trissy yelled as Jackson approached the tee at home plate.

Kurt stood at first base, bent forward, hands on his knees, silently encouraging his son. Jackson adjusted his helmet and tapped the bat on home plate.

"Go, Jack!" Cooper yelled, catching me completely off guard. *He speaks!*

We faced the early evening sun, so even though I wore sunglasses, I still had to squint to see the field.

My mind was foggy, and I tried to make myself focus on the game. I pushed my glasses farther up the bridge of my nose and leaned to the right so I could see past Cooper's head. After his bat-tapping routine, Jackson stood to the left of the plate and took a swing. And missed. Seriously? The kid couldn't even hit what was right in front of his face?

"Strike one!" the umpire called, and I wondered for not the first time why they needed a pitcher's mound and umps for a six-year-olds' T-ball game.

Undaunted, Jackson tapped his bat against the plate again and kicked at the dirt with his little cleats.

"Atta boy, Jack! You got this!" I stiffened at the sound of Truitt's voice and groaned. What was he doing there? Had I not dealt with enough today?

This time, Jackson swung and made contact. The ball rolled toward the pitcher's mound and Jackson took off, chugging toward first base. Even though the first base kid ran to get the ball from the kid at the mound, Jackson slid dramatically into first base, where he promptly fist-bumped his dad.

"I hate dirt stains," Melina muttered to herself before cheering for her son. I looked over at Truitt, who stood at the bottom of the bleachers with his fingers hooked on the chain-linked fence, a ball cap tucked into his white baseball pants pocket. He stuck two fingers in his mouth and let out a shrill whistle.

Ouch.

I slid Cooper off my lap and grabbed my purse. "I'm gonna go get a snack," I told Melina. I thought Trissy might tag along, but she'd noticed Truitt and was doing her best to preen the fountain of ringlets spilling out of her ponytail.

Rolling my eyes, I hopped down the bleachers and slipped past Truitt before he could turn around. The driving lesson had ended on a surprisingly good note, but I was not in the mood to handle him picking on me or waving his "perfection" in my face after the day I'd had.

I walked across Pecan Creek Recreational Park, wondering what was with all of the pecan names and the whole creek thing when I'd yet to see a creek. I found the snack hut and got in line. I desperately needed some sugar and caffeine.

"What can I get you?" the girl on the other side of the window asked when I stepped up to order.

I glanced at the chalkboard menu and drummed my fingers on the window's ledge. "I'll take a pack of blue sour straws and a Coke."

The girl handed me the candy. "And what kind of Coke do you want?"

I furrowed my brow, not sure what she was asking.

"Add a bottle of water to that," a voice said from over my shoulder. I turned and found myself face-to-face—well, technically face-to-pectoral muscles, to apply my anatomy knowledge—with Hansen. "Hey, Princess."

I took a step back and my backside hit the wall. He wore a baseball uniform and a backward baseball cap, his sandy hair sticking out beneath. "Um, hi."

He reached around me and passed the snack girl a ten-dollar bill. I pulled out my wallet. "No, I've got mine."

He smiled. "Somehow, I'm always treating my teammates to a drink, but it's rare I get to buy for someone who's doesn't smell like an old gym bag."

Lovely. I could only stare at him and marvel at how he could manage to be so charming yet so disgusting at the same time.

"Um," Snack Girl interrupted, "you didn't say what kind of Coke you want."

I gave her a puzzled look. "What are you talking about?"

Hansen gently pushed me aside and leaned into the window. "She wants regular Coke."

The girl nodded and went to grab my drink. I turned to Hansen, whose elbows were still propped in the window. "I didn't know they had different flavors here."

"Oh, they don't. But you're in the South, Princess. What do you call soda back home?"

"It's pop."

He motioned to the menu. "Where you say pop, we just call it Coke. So you could ask for a Coke and really be asking for Pepsi, even though that's Coke's rival. See?"

"This place is so backward," I huffed. "You're actually the first person to explain this stuff to me without looking at me like I've grown a third eye."

Hansen took my cup from the snack girl, handed it to me, and then took his own water bottle and change. "Stick with me, Princess. I've got your back. You gonna watch me play?"

I sipped my Coke. "When? I'm watching my cousin play, then my aunt and uncle wanted to hang around and watch another game."

Hansen took my candy from me and opened the package. "Who're they watching?" He helped himself to a sugarcoated gummy straw.

"This guy named Truitt Peyton."

Hansen swallowed. "You know ol' Truitt, huh?"

I refused to let my face answer for me. "Sort of."

Hansen handed me my sour straws and flipped his cap around to the front. "Let me tell you something. Truitt acts like he's some saint or whatever, but don't buy into all that."

I nodded slowly, not sure what to say. I knew there had to be more to Truitt Peyton than what was on the surface.

"My team's playing against his tonight, but I know who you want to root for." He took a step back. "Oh hey, are you going to the party tonight?"

In the craziness of my week, I'd completely forgotten about Hansen's latest invite. Man, I wanted to go. But I knew it was impossible. I shook my head. "I don't think I can tonight. But thanks for inviting me."

He tipped his cap and jogged off toward his team. I went back to Jackson's game, slowing my pace as I approached the bleachers and noticed Melina had joined Truitt at the fence. They seemed to be engaged in some sort of intense conversation. It would be easy for me to sneak past them and back to my seat.

"I honestly don't know, Truitt," Melina said as I snuck behind them, "but I know she's not a believer. She's been through a lot, and

Sadie—" I heard my name right before a crowd at the adjacent field let out a cheer that drowned out the rest of her sentence.

They were talking about me? And not only that, but my thoughts about religion? I stopped and strained my ears to listen.

"That's what I thought," Truitt said. "I've been trying to talk to her, though. I understand what she must be going through, and I want to—"

"Excuse me," I said, startling myself as much as I startled Truitt and Melina.

Truitt whipped around, his cap falling out of his pocket, and Melina hurried off to attend to an imagined call from her kids on the bleachers.

"Is that what you think of me, really?" I asked Truitt through clenched teeth. "That I'm just some charity case headed for hell?" I realized a split-second too late how loud I'd shouted that last part. It earned me some looks, one of which was from Trissy. *Oh, perfect.*

I'd shocked Truitt too. I could tell by the way he took a step back, crunching his hat. "No, Sadie, of course not. I was just telling Mel how I understand what you're—"

"Stop it." I leaned forward and lowered my voice. It came out as a growl. "You don't know the first thing about my life. Neither does my aunt, for that matter. You don't know what I'm going through. Besides, I can handle whatever I've got going on. I don't need you to get caught up in saving Sadie. I get enough of that living with the Elliots."

He reached down and picked up his hat. He twisted it in his hands. "You're absolutely right. Sadie, I—"

I didn't give him a chance to finish his thought. Just took my snack and marched over to Hansen's field.

Chapter 14

In an effort to not think about what I just witnessed and risk exploding, I thought about Hansen's party invitation. That could be the distraction I desperately needed. But how could I get there? By the time I could sneak out, it would be too late to go, but there was zero chance my aunt and uncle would let me out of the house.

On the silent ride back to the Elliots' house after Truitt and Hansen's game, an idea formed in my head. It was a terrible, terrible idea, but I couldn't shake it. Because as terrible as it was, it was terribly perfect. Before I could stop myself—since when did I grow a conscience anyway?—I texted Hansen, "Does the party invite still stand?"

He immediately replied, "What's your address? I'll pick you up in twenty."

I answered Hansen and then went searching for Melina. I found her getting the boys ready for bed. I hadn't spoken to her since *the incident* at the ball field, but she knew how stressful my day had been, so if I wanted the plan to work, she was my best bet.

"Mel?"

She turned from where she sat on the floor stacking a pile of Lego blocks. "What's up, Sadie?"

"Well," I said as I sat next to her and took the block Cooper handed me. "Would it be okay if I hung out with Becca tonight? She offered to help me memorize the bones for A&P." As soon as the fib slipped my lips, I wished I could take it back. Until today, Melina had been so supportive of me, and look at what I was doing. But she'd never let me go out with Hansen, and the stress of the whole thing certainly couldn't be good for her current condition. We had the baby to consider, after all.

Oblivious to my conniving, Melina smiled. "Becca is such a sweetheart, but it's already getting late. Are you spending the night?"

"No. But I'll probably be back really late. She's picking me up and dropping me back off." I chewed the inside of my lip while I waited for the verdict.

"I'll let Kurt know, but it shouldn't be a problem. And I know the whole curfew thing hasn't really come up yet, but …"

Here we go … Of course the curfew thing hadn't come up yet. I hadn't had anywhere to actually go.

Melina placed a tiny little knight figure on top of the blocks, which Jackson promptly knocked down with his comb. "Son, please!" Melina gave up and shoved the blocks into the corner. "How about we just say before midnight? Becca has a driving curfew, so as long as she's able to be back at her house by then, you'll be good. Okay?"

That wasn't very much time for a party, but I'd take what I could get. I thanked Melina and then headed to the room I shared with Trissy. Now that one hurdle had been jumped, the bigger one stood in front of me: deciding what to wear.

When I entered the room, I stepped on something sharp. I stifled a choice word and hopped over to the bed, where I located a Barbie stiletto stuck to my heel. Lego blocks may be the number one torture weapon in a kid's toy box, but Barbie shoes come in at a close second.

"Trissy, what are you doing?" I massaged my heel and took in the spread of dolls who all looked like silver mummies.

Trissy brushed the curls out of her face. "I'm making duck tape togas. We're learning about the Romans at co-op, so I wanna put that into my hobbies. See here." She held up a male doll. "This is Caesar Augustus."

"Is he the father of Little Caesar?"

"No, silly." She rolled her eyes. "That's a pizza place. And the cartoon is not a real man either. Caesar Augustus *was* real. He's the one that did that thing when Baby Jesus was born where he

counted everybody. You know, 'In those days, Caesar Augustus ...'"
I recognized Trissy's quote as part of the Christmas story but tuned her out as I sorted through the shirts in my closet.

Twelve minutes later, I stood a few yards away from the house, waiting on Hansen and flagging him down when he turned onto Magnolia Street.

Hansen's truck was at least ten years old, but it was in better shape than Truitt's. The door was tougher to open than I anticipated. I ended up with a flip-flopped foot pushed against the side of the truck and both hands on the handle. It was a struggle until Hansen decided to be all chivalrous and open the door from the inside. I promptly fell backward. I picked myself up and dusted the dirt off my legs.

"Hey, Princess." Hansen looked at me with a half smile, playing it cool like I didn't just wipe out on the ground. I slid into the cab of the truck.

Hansen shifted the truck into drive and took off down the street. Ugh, stick shift. Old trucks and manual transmissions in Pecan Creek were becoming a bit of a cliché for me.

"Does your car have a name?" I asked, thinking of Truitt's Beulah.

"Do what?"

I turned my head to look out the window. "Never mind." I fastened my seat belt. "So where are we going?"

"Clark Green's parents are out for the weekend, and he's having some friends over for a bonfire."

"Will there be food?" I placed a hand over my growling stomach, regretting my decision to eat sour straws at the park instead of something more filling, like nachos.

He nodded and turned onto the main road. "S'mores, drinks. As much as your heart desires."

I nodded my approval. "I've had the worst week ever. I could really use a drink."

Hansen laughed. "Youth pastor doesn't keep a secret stash of beverages? I lost that bet."

Surprisingly, Hansen's joke offended me. If anything, Kurt was authentic. He would never keep that kind of a secret from people.

We drove the rest of the way in silence, the evening air slipping through the cracks in the windows of the truck. It was a good night for a bonfire, since it hadn't been sweltering that day.

After a couple of miles, we passed the church and Becca's house. I looked away and shoved a bit of conscience to the back of my brain. When we turned on a dirt road, I rolled up my window so a cloud of red dust wouldn't stain my shirt. After a few more minutes, we turned onto another dirt road and then a gravel driveway. Passing a wooden, two-story house, we drove through an open gate and into a pasture.

Some guys were just getting the fire started as the last light of the day dipped below the horizon. A couple of older teens and college students sat on coolers and camp chairs while a truck's tailgate held a spread of marshmallows, chocolate, and graham crackers. I felt my stomach growl again as Hansen parked the truck. He hopped out, walked around the front of the cab, and opened my door for me. I smiled in response.

Reaching into the back of the truck, he pulled out a large black garbage bag. "Blankets."

"Classy."

I allowed Hansen to take my fingers in his and mingle with some of his friends. One of whom was Willow.

"Hi, Willow." I was cautious until I could gauge her mood, but I forced my voice to be chipper anyway.

"Hey, Sadie." Her greeting sounded like a question, and her eyes didn't leave Hansen. If I'd had any doubts before, I now knew for sure. Willow would accept me as a friend, but not competition. I thought about telling her envy green was so not her color, but Hansen dragged me to another group of people.

Despite Ice Queen Willow, after being introduced to about fifteen people, I felt myself begin to relax. This felt familiar to me, like summers past when my friends and I hung out. I'd intentionally left my phone in the truck so I wouldn't be tempted to try to reach Reese—just one more time—but I still felt pangs of homesickness.

As I roasted a marshmallow, I enjoyed the heat of the fire against my legs and the carefree sound of the voices behind me. I smiled to myself when I realized no one out here would quote a Bible verse or tell me my shorts were too short—although tonight they actually weren't. No one would care what I said or how I said it. I'd finally found a place I belonged.

"Where's Hansen?" Willow came up behind me, a red, plastic cup in her hands. You could tell she was from the South, but she still didn't have that lazy-sounding accent I was growing so used to hearing.

"He went to the house for some paper towels or something."

"You know," Willow said as she leaned toward me, "I've liked Hansen for five years." Well, that came out of nowhere.

"Uh, thanks for sharing?" I squinted at her and flames swallowed my marshmallow while I wasn't paying attention. I quickly pulled it out of the fire and blew on it.

"No." Willow said the word so forcefully her slick black ponytail swished. "You don't get it. Hansen and I are in a relationship."

"Really?" He must have been more superficial than I thought, because he sure couldn't be swept away by her social graces.

The fire sparked in Willow's dark eyes. "We're taking a break for the summer, but yeah. So he's taken."

I laughed. The whole thing was like some cliquey high school drama saga I'd seen on TV shows and movies about a million times. Willow didn't appreciate my laughter. "I just wanted you to know it's in your best interest if you don't get too attached. I like you, Sadie, really, so I just wanted you to know."

I leaned back to avoid her alcohol breath. "I think half a cup's your limit." The very last thing I needed was drama. I pulled my charred marshmallow off the stick and popped it into my mouth. Wincing at the taste of ash, I walked away.

Chapter 15

At some point during my little chat with Willow, Hansen rejoined the group and fixed us drinks. He pulled me up beside him on the hood of the truck and handed me a cup. I took a sip of my drink, then another, savoring the coolness as it rushed down my throat, enjoying a slight summer breeze as it rustled my hair.

"So," I said, not realizing my eyes were closed until Hansen spoke, "Seattle, huh?"

"Yeah."

"Have you been to that what's-it-called place? The Space Needle?" Clearly, the rest of the country had a clichéd view of what Seattle had to offer. But then again, I'd had a few ideas about the South ...

I wiped my mouth with the back of my hand, wondering where Hansen had put his paper towels. "Of course. But when you've lived near something your whole life, it's not really that big a deal anymore."

Hansen set his cup between us and leaned back on his palms. "You like to hit the nontouristy places, then?"

I shrugged. "My boy—my *friend's* brother owns a pool hall."

"Got a boyfriend out there?" Ugh. So he had picked up on my little slip.

"Actually, no. We ... we broke up." I swallowed back a sea of memories. Good memories, bad memories, all mixed together, just like our relationship. Reese and I definitely had a history, but I missed him. He'd been one of my truest friends. So why hadn't he returned my calls and texts?

117

"So you're over him, right?" Hansen reached out and fingered the wisps of my hair that were too short to pull into my ponytail.

"I could use a refill." I might or might not have been completely over Reese, but I was definitely over this conversation.

Hansen took my cup and slid off the truck. I knew I'd be going back to Kurt and Melina's house before too long, so I wouldn't get sloppy drunk or anything. But my angst was finally beginning to settle. One more drink would be perfect. When I got back to the house, I could hop in the shower before they smelled beer or bonfire.

Hansen returned a moment later, drinks in hand. "Let's go sit in the back. These fools are killing my mood," he said, referencing the loud joking and music blaring from some portable iPod speakers. I agreed, scanning the area for signs of Willow. I found her fully engrossed in a conversation with another girl, so I quickly followed behind Hansen.

The music changed to a country ballad about lost love and found faith or something as we spread the blankets and climbed into the back of the truck. I leaned against the cab, tucking my knees under my chin. The sky was clear, and the stars were abundant. Not something a girl from the city saw very often. They looked like little twinkle lights from far off, but I knew many of them were even bigger than the sun. Mom used to tell me that anyway. I couldn't see the moon.

"Are you having a good time?" Hansen sat close, his voice a whisper just loud enough to be heard over the noise of the night.

"Mm-hm." I closed my eyes and tilted my head farther back. "You have no idea how much I needed this."

"Try me."

I took a sip of my drink. What would it hurt to tell him just a little? Not much, of course, because I knew the danger of giving someone an edge over you. But just enough so I could have *someone* to empathize with. I wouldn't tell him about my doctor's appointment. That would be too awkward and too much to deal with.

"I don't know where to start." I spread my hands out on my lap.

"You said you lived with your dad. Where's your mom?"

"She died. In a … in a car accident," I whispered.

"Oh, Sadie. I'm sorry." His words were warm in my ear. "My mom died too. When I was really little."

I felt an invisible cord tie us together, if only just a little bit. So he *could* relate. I'd sensed something familiar about him ever since I met him. I'm sure it'd be different for a guy to grow up without a mom, but still, it had to be unimaginably difficult. "I'm so sorry, Hansen."

And then it happened. I opened my mouth and let out the story of Sadie Gray Franklin. I whispered about growing up with only my dad, who was clueless when it came to parenthood or love. Hansen sat quietly, taking it all in, as I told him of how my dad had worked nights, leaving me home alone ever since I was ten. I told him how I was queen of the parties, how I had friends over at least one night a week so the constant flicker of loneliness wouldn't flare up and engulf me. I even told him about learning my "friends" only hung around me because of my house and lack of parental supervision. Except for Reese. He accepted me. On nights when I starved for a true friend, he'd come over and watch a movie, usually falling asleep on the couch. Then I would leave him and head off to bed, and he'd be gone by the time I woke up the next morning. He was my constant. For a while.

I was on a roll, but I stopped just short of that last night before coming to Georgia. The night that made my dad's decision to ship me off irrevocable. The night I had to break up with Reese despite all we'd been through. My chest hurt just thinking about it. As it was, I was still trying to swallow it all without choking. I stopped talking. Despite the loud music, it was so peaceful out in the country. Out in the open air where it was impossible to feel cluttered with emotions.

"Thanks for listening." I yawned, exhausted from my confessions.

Hansen shrugged and put an arm around me. "No problem. I know I have a bit of a rep, but you look past that."

"Willow told me you're dating." The words slipped between my lips before I stopped to evaluate the wisdom of spilling that information. I had been having such a good time.

Hansen snorted. "Willow's like a bitter old lady. We dated for a while, but her dad made us break up when I got kicked out of school. One little mistake," he said as he snapped his fingers, "and you're out. Then you end up a grade behind all because you were trying to defend your girl. But did Crane understand? No."

"I'm sorry, Hansen," I said. And I was. I knew the sting of a breakup, even though I didn't allow myself to feel it very often.

"Willow hasn't moved on, but I have." Hansen's words tickled my ear and warmed my chilled heart just a little.

He leaned closer to me, and I allowed him to kiss me. It was a heart-stuttering kiss, and I pulled back after a moment to make sure he understood I'd be in control—and to be sure I'd have the will power. Satisfied, I leaned back into him. The blood pounding in my ears as he pulled me even closer drowned out the other partiers, drowned out the music, drowned out the pain.

***

I woke up in a fog, not sure of what I was. It was dark, but an orange glow came from behind me. I felt a gentle breeze, and it all started to come back to me. What time was it? Panicking, I shook my head to clear it but stopped when a pain shot through my temples. Placing a hand on my forehead, I groaned and sat up, shivering a little even though my legs were under a blanket. *Blanket. Hansen. What did I do?* I quickly wracked my brain. I hadn't been so drunk I was completely oblivious to my actions, but the lines were still blurred. Kissing. Plenty of it, sure. But no more.

What I really had to worry about was how long I'd been gone.

As my eyes adjusted to the campfire light, my ears tried to listen for other sounds of life. Beside me, Hansen stirred in his sleep. I patted my pocket to find my phone and then realized it was in the cab of the truck.

"Hansen," I hissed. Man, my head hurt. "Hansen!"

He sat up slowly, moaning and rubbing his head.

I put my hands on his shoulders and made him focus on me. "Hansen, what time is it?"

He shrugged dramatically and pulled his phone out of his pocket. The screen illuminated a giant crease on the side of his face. "One forty-five."

My breath caught in my throat. I was so dead. I smoothed my T-shirt and fidgeted with my ponytail as I tried to stand. I took a step to the edge of the truck on wobbly legs.

"Where're you goin', Princess?" Hansen slurred as I climbed out of the truck bed.

"I have to get back. Can you—" I stopped, realizing Hansen would not be a good designated driver. But it was too far to walk back. "Can I take your truck?"

Hansen scooted to the edge of the truck and took my face in his hands. His hot, sour breath burned the inside of my nose, and I pulled back before he could kiss me.

"What's wrong?"

"I really need to go. Let me use your truck?" I begged. He reached into a pocket, and then another pocket, until he fished out his keys. He dropped them into my palm before rolling out of the truck with his blanket.

"It's too late," he murmured. "Come inside and stay with me. Go home in the mornin'."

Ignoring him and the unpleasant shiver than ran up my spine, I walked to the driver side of the truck. A few people were still huddled up in groups around the fire, but most had moved to a second bonfire someone had built a few yards away. That was disaster waiting to happen. "I'll leave this up the street from the house with the keys in it, 'kay?" My head still hurt and my stomach churned. Hansen nodded and took a seat in front of the fire.

Anger swelled inside me. I knew he shouldn't drive, but he didn't even offer to find a ride for me. I jerked open the door, dreading the thought of navigating the stick-shift transmission. I located my phone and stuck it in pocket, not even stopping to see the inevitable string of voice mails and texts Melina had probably sent me.

"Umm," I muttered to myself, biting my lip and putting my feet on the clutch and gas. No, that wasn't right. Clutch and break.

I started the truck, exhaling only once it actually started up. I jerkily shifted into reverse, making about an eight-and-a-half point turn before I faced the driveway. Or at least, the general direction of the driveway. I didn't remember so many trees on the way in. Come to think of it, I didn't remember them swaying, either. Hm. That was pretty interesting.

Once I heard the crunch of the gravel driveway, I shifted into second, only to have the truck stall out on the hill. I mumbled to myself and tried again, finally making my way back to the dirt road but still completely unsure of which way to go.

"You're doing good, Sadie," I encouraged myself. I took a shot in the dark—literally—and turned left.

A moment later, I saw lights up ahead, which hopefully meant I was headed toward the paved road. The texture of the road changed, and I saw the lights came from a house. Other than that, it was still really, really scary dark out in the country. I turned onto another dirt road, narrowly missing the ditch. I jerked hard on the wheel, and the truck died. I hit the steering wheel with my fist and tried again. It worked, but when I hit the pedal, the truck shot backward into the ditch. I had a clear view of the stars through the truck's dash by that point.

I pushed open the door, leaning into it and stumbling out into the ditch. A wave of nausea hit me, and I steadied myself against the truck so I wouldn't be sick. I slowly climbed out of the ditch and began walking.

The night was louder than I expected. You'd think it'd be quiet in the middle of nowhere, but frogs croaked and crickets chirped, and the tall pine trees rustled. My fear of deer had never felt more justified than in that moment.

Headlights came over the hill, and I froze. I gulped and waited for the car to pass, turning my head slightly so my eyes wouldn't catch the light.

Before I had time to consider which side of the fight-or-flight spectrum I'd fall on, the car pulled off the side of the road and stopped a few yards away from me. I wanted to run, but my head and abdomen hurt so badly. Dread pounded in my temples and throbbed in my throat.

The car door opened and a flashlight clicked on, its beam a harsh white against the darkness. I focused on breathing—not to avoid thinking, which I really needed to be doing, but to kill the spots that danced in front of my vision.

"Don't move!" a deep male voice called out. My mind started flipping through worst-case scenarios, but somehow I knew I needed to obey and stay still.

The large figure ambled toward me, averting the flashlight to light his path. I bent my knees slightly so I wouldn't fall over and tried not to puke when the light hit my face.

"Well, I'll be … Aren't you Kurt's niece?"

"Y-yes, sir."

Something about the man's voice was familiar … *Pete!* The man who drove our boat at the lake!

"What are you doing out here?" Pete's voice was stern and thick, the opposite of his laughter at the lake party.

"I'm going home," I told him.

Pete reached me and shined the light on Hansen's truck. "Sadie, it's past legal curfew for minors."

"I'm s-s-sorry," I stuttered. "I didn't know."

Pete brought the light to my face, and I covered my eyes. "Well, Sadie, I was going to give you the Breathalyzer, but after one look at your eyes, I have my answer."

I wondered why he had a Breathalyzer and why he thought my business was any of his business. I just really wanted to lie down under a pile of thick, dark blankets.

He finally pointed the light back toward the ground. "I'm going to go out on a limb and assume your aunt and uncle don't know where you are."

I gulped as big, warm tears began to roll down my cheeks. I couldn't stop crying, and the tears only came harder when Pete put an arm around me and told me to walk to his car with him. He was so stern, but his actions were gentle.

"I'm sorry," I whimpered over and over. "I've had the worst week ever. It's been the worst day ever."

When we reached the car, I noticed the distinct blue lights on top and the familiar emblem on the door. I doubled over and threw up next to the cop car.

Pete opened the back door, and I slid in. I dropped my head into my hands, fighting another wave of nausea and gritting my teeth against the sharp pangs coming from my stomach. Pete silently cranked the car and drove me in the opposite direction I'd been heading. He called Kurt, keeping his voice just low enough I could only make out a few words of the conversation. "Niece ... ditch ... intoxicated."

My head throbbed, and I put my head in my hands. When we reached the house, Pete motioned for me to stay in the car and went to the door where Kurt already waited. I sank down in the seat so my uncle couldn't meet my gaze.

Pete slid back into his seat a minute later. "Get out, Sadie." He sounded tired. "Your uncle will discuss this with you."

"Are you gonna take me to juvenile hall or something?"

"Get out, Sadie," he said, his voice the exact same tone as before. "Your uncle will discuss this with you."

I slid out of the car, hand over my stomach, although I'd rather cover my eyes. I sniffed as I stepped up to the door and hoped the tears weren't noticeable, although my eyes were so puffy I could barely see. That wasn't a good sign.

I ducked under Kurt's arm and walked straight to the kitchen. The clock on the stove blinked, "2:15," the same color of the cop lights. Kurt pulled a cup of coffee out of the microwave and Melina sat at the table. Even from across the room, the bags under her eyes were so dark they looked like bruises. Her brow was wrinkled, and her eyes held none of their usual sparkle. Instead, they were red-rimmed, and the tears trailing down her cheeks put mine to shame.

She opened her mouth like she was about to say something but caught herself. I couldn't read her expression.

Kurt spoke for her. "Sit."

I obeyed. I slid into a chair and put my head in my shaking hands. I thought I would suffocate from inhaling my own breath.

Melina cleared her throat. "Sadie, I—" Her voice broke, and she coughed.

Once again, Kurt picked up where she left off. "Explain yourself." I sensed no kindness, no compassion whatsoever in his expression. Just cold, hard disappointment and anger. When I said nothing, he added, "Have you been drinking?"

I nodded, but it was probably hard to decipher over the shaking.

"Talk, Sadie!" Kurt barked.

"Kurt ..." Melina warned.

"Not now, Melina." I'd never heard him be anything other than gentle with her. "Sadie, answer me."

I opened my mouth to speak but quickly covered it. I jumped from my seat and ran to the bathroom.

I barely made it in time before I lost what I was sure had to be the last of everything I'd eaten that week. Trembling, I sank down onto my knees and dropped my head in my hands. I heard voices echo down the hall, angry and gradually increasing in volume.

"It's out of control," my uncle said.

"She's my sister's *baby*, Kurt!" Melina said. "And who knows *where* she'd be if—"

"We can't let these things keep happening."

"But what if she ..." Melina lowered her voice again, and I couldn't hear anything else.

Kurt and Melina were fighting. Because of me. Tears dripped off my chin again, although I didn't even feel like I was crying. I just felt really, really numb.

A few minutes later, the door creaked open and I heard footsteps. A warm hand touched my back.

"Sadie." It was Melina, and her voice was more solemn than I'd ever heard it before. "Go to bed. We'll deal with this in the morning." I nodded and stood, turning to face her.

I certainly wasn't one for affection, but I half-wanted her to wrap me in her arms and make me feel safe, like my mom used to do. Instead, she turned and left the bathroom without another word.

I decided to take a shower before bed. Not only was the scent of alcohol on my clothes, but also the smell of campfire and cigarettes. I silently retrieved my clothes from the bedroom and climbed into the shower. Once the water ran hot and hard, I sank down against the wall of the shower, the water pounding on top of my head, streaming down my back, washing away the outward evidence of my night. I pulled my head out from under the stream and tried to take some deep, cleansing breaths to help calm my racing heart.

I don't know how long I stayed in the shower, but it was long enough for my fingers and toes to shrivel like raisins. By the time I finished dressing and brushing my teeth, I was lightheaded and my stomach ached. I slipped back into the bedroom and crawled into bed next to the little girl I was convinced could sleep through an apocalypse.

I fell asleep envying her intensely. Trissy was so innocent—so sheltered from so many parts of the world. A couple of which I'd found myself in the middle of tonight. Lying and sneaking out and kissing Hansen seemed ridiculous now, in light of Trissy's innocence, and I regretted it. It all brought me a sense of peace while it lasted, but now I didn't even know how I'd face Hansen again. Or if I'd even have the opportunity.

Chapter 16

When I woke the next morning, my head felt like a brick and it took me a good ten minutes to lift it off my pillow. My temples pounded when I opened my eyes, but I kept my eyes open long enough to note Trissy's side of the bed was empty. The light streaming in from the window made me cringe. I looked at the clock. It was afternoon. I fought the urge to just finish the rest of the day by sleeping, and slid to a sitting position.

I climbed out of bed and grabbed some clothes before slipping into the bathroom unnoticed. I turned the water as hot as I could stand it, and the room quickly filled with steam. The shower made me feel a little better, and almost ready to face my aunt and uncle. But when I came out of the bathroom, there was still no sign of them. When I returned to the bedroom, I noticed a note taped to the door that was written in Melina's precise, slanted print.

> Sadie,
> Took kids to the park. Kurt is in the garden.
> Breakfast is on the table. Be back soon.
> —Melina

I ran a comb through my hair and fastened it into a loose braid. I had neither the desire nor energy for makeup, and chances were good I wouldn't be seeing anyone beyond these walls until I went back to Seattle.

I headed into the kitchen to scout out the promised breakfast and found a plate of cold waffles, a bowl of sliced fruit, and some turkey bacon on the table. As I stuck a strawberry in my mouth, I heard the back door open. I held my breath.

Kurt entered the kitchen wearing an old pair of jeans with threadbare knees and a tattered T-shirt. He pulled a ball cap off his head, set it on the counter, and then pulled out a chair for Melina, who followed behind carrying Cooper. She sent the kids into the living room and promised she'd call them back for lunch soon.

"Sadie, let's talk," Kurt said, folding his grungy arms on the table and leaning forward. I could practically see Melina trying to hold herself back from telling him to wash his hands before touching her table. "Where were you last night?"

I swallowed. "I went out with a friend."

"Who?" Kurt leaned forward even more. If he kept that up, he'd be spread out on the table in a minute. Melina definitely wouldn't tolerate that.

"A friend from co-op."

Across the table, Melina reached for Kurt's hand and inspected his stained nail beds. She still hadn't looked at me.

"Tell the truth, Sadie." Kurt had yet to even fix a mug of coffee. This was really serious.

"Okay," I said as I swallowed back a wave of nausea that had everything to do with dreading this conversation. "I went to a party with Hansen. It was at his friend's house. I got ready to leave, and he couldn't drive, so he let me use his truck to come back. But it was stick shift, and I drove it into a ditch and started walking. Then Pete, who I found out is a cop, found me and brought me here."

Melina winced and put a hand on her stomach. Kurt and I watched her for a minute until she released a breath and started breathing normally again. "Tell us about the party," she said.

"What do you want to know?"

My aunt's and uncle's eyes narrowed to the exact same degree. It was creepy.

"How much did you drink?" Kurt asked.

"Um, I didn't drink ..."

Kurt slapped the table with the palm of his hand, and I jumped. "Sadie, you were so under the influence last night you could barely walk!"

"Kurt, please." Melina put her hand on his shoulder, but he leaned away.

"Okay, okay!" I tossed my hands up in surrender. "I had a couple of beers. Not that many. But I stopped drinking before I lost complete control, especially since Hansen ..." I trailed off as I realized I was getting into some territory I didn't want to reveal.

"Hansen what?" Melina's eyebrows bunched together, but she looked more concerned than angry.

"He's a guy. That explains it."

Kurt said, "I'm a guy." Melina and I blinked at him. "Tell us. Now."

"Nothing like that happened, if that's what you're wondering. I'm not stupid, you know."

"Oh, we know." Kurt's face was so intense it looked like he was restraining himself so he wouldn't jump across the table and shake me. "You're smart enough to try to pull the wool over our eyes even though we've gone out of our way to provide a safe place for you. But one thing you're not is trustworthy. How do we know you're telling the truth about what went on with Hansen in the middle of the night at a keg party?"

"It wasn't a keg party," I said through gritted teeth. Then louder, I said, "This is the second time in two days I've been accused of sleeping around like some sort of—"

"No one's accusing you." Melina's voice was low, but I heard it waver. "But we have given you the benefit of the doubt so many times, and how are we to know you're not—"

"I'm a virgin, okay?" I yelled, my eyes flashing frustration. "I know I don't meet your standards for purity, and I don't claim to be some saint, but I've never been that far. I'd never risk getting pregnant and bringing a kid into this world. I know better than anybody what the choices of parents can do to a kid. You don't know how bad it hurts to be accused of that." I realized I'd been squeezing the table so hard my fingers were purple. I didn't care. Let them fall off. Let one more piece of me break. Just one more piece.

Melina's resolve seemed to crumble, her expression changing from one of confrontation to one of defeat. "I'm sorry, Sadie. I shouldn't have said that. But there's much more to purity than technical virginity."

"Oh, I am not having this conversation right now. I've got a hangover—yes, I said a hangover—the doctor doesn't have answers for why I've been hurting so badly, and honestly? You two are the last people I feel like talking to right now. I'm going outside." I stood, slamming my knee against the table, and stormed out the back door.

Once outside, I pulled my phone out of my pocket. *Reese.* I needed to try again.

Surprisingly, he answered the phone.

"Hello?"

"Reese." I whispered his name and blinked back tears, anticipating his response.

"Sadie." His voice, smooth as always, sounded detached. I imagined those dark eyes, set off by his white-blonde hair, staring at something that wasn't really there. He always did that when he wasn't fully invested in what was going on. But he'd never done that to me.

"Happy belated birthday," I said, almost like it was a question.

"Um, thanks," he said slowly, cautiously.

"Did you have a good day?"

"It wasn't bad."

I pulled in a sharp breath and began pacing the backyard. "I had to go, Reese. My dad made me leave, but I couldn't stay there anyway. I couldn't stay there anymore. Too much drama. And Gavin … He has anger issues. I was scared." I whispered the confession, using a word I never used. *Scared.*

"You don't think I could've handled him?" Reese's voice remained expressionless, and I couldn't gauge his reaction.

"Could you have handled him? Reese, he would've destroyed you!"

Static flavored the phone connection, and I held the phone closer to my ear so I wouldn't miss what Reese said next.

"We could've left."

"You know that wasn't an option. But you were there for me for so long. I needed you." There. I'd said it. The reason I was with him in the first place, because I actually felt wanted. Desirable. Happy. But it was also the reason I'd found Gavin while Reese went to visit colleges over spring break, and when I felt Reese slipping away from me. From us.

But then Reese came back, and I knew we had too many years, he held too many of my secrets, for me to turn to Gavin. Gavin had taken the breakup way too hard and threatened Reese. *Chemically imbalanced* was the phrase he'd admitted to me while Reese was away, but I thought if he loved me he'd never let me see that side of him.

"Dad sent me to Georgia, but I also needed to leave so you wouldn't be hurt." I was also scared of myself and what could happen if I didn't step back from all of the confusion.

From the other side of the country, Reese sighed. "I would've been fine, Sadie."

"Anyway," I said, my voice sounding tired, "I just wanted to tell you happy birthday."

"You told me. And you'll probably hear this soon enough anyway, so I'll go ahead and tell you. I'm with Lori now. I've moved on."

Moved on? I didn't know what else to say. In less than half a summer, he'd turned away from all that we were—or all that I thought we were—and turned toward someone else. I didn't know who Lori was, and I didn't want to know. The conversation I'd needed was over; there was nothing left to say. I ran a hand through my hair. "I guess it's good-bye."

"Yeah, I guess so."

And then I hung up. No "How is your summer?" No "Let's talk more later" or "See you in August." No "I love you." Because I knew now that I didn't love him. All of those times I'd whispered it back to him had been empty, hollow. Like the heart-sized cavity in my chest.

Like the fist-shaped hole in my living room wall back in Seattle. Like all the empty bottles and vacant eyes that last night when things got loud and a neighbor called the police and the cops found Gavin restrained in a closet, Reese with a bleeding face, and fourteen underage drinkers just trying to be happy but failing hard.

My next phone call went to Becca. I knew she wouldn't answer even before I placed the call, and I didn't know what I'd have said if she'd answered. There was no doubt Kurt and Melina had called her house looking for me. Probably asking her why she had kept me out so late. I absolutely hated myself for what I'd done to her. She'd been so nice and nonjudgmental toward me. No, she didn't know anything about my past, but she'd been … kind. I really only knew a handful of kind people, and I'd crushed them all at the same time. Broken trust, broken stem of a friendship just beginning to bud.

The word *broken* reminded me of Hansen's truck. I had to tell him where it was. Plus he was the only one not furious with me. Not furious yet, at least. Hansen's phone rang seven times before his voice mail clicked on. "It's Hansen. Leave a message." I quickly explained where I thought his truck was and that if there was damage, I'd pay for it. I didn't know how I'd pay for it, but I knew I at least needed to offer.

After my phone calls, it was time go back inside and face the inevitable.

Cooper and Jackson were in their room napping, and Trissy was on the phone with a friend in the kitchen. I knew she was exchanging secrets because her voice turned slightly gruff whenever she tried to speak quietly. I'd heard it on nights she refused to go to sleep before we had "cousin bonding time."

"Yeah. Daddy said she was drunker than a fish." She giggled obnoxiously before her voice turned solemn. "Tell her I hope she still comes to babysit us, even though my dumb cousin—*oh!*" Trissy gasped when I reached from behind her and snatched the phone. I ended the call and shoved it at her.

"Who was that?" I demanded. My face was hot.

"Hope." Becca's little sister.

"Why were you telling her those things?"

Trissy took a step back and ran into the counter. Her eyes were wide. "She's my friend. And Becca is my most favorite babysitter."

"What else did *Daddy*," I said as I spit the word out like it was dirty, "tell you about me?"

"He didn't tell me anything. I heard him and Mama yelling."

"That's none of your business." I seethed, trying to maintain control of my temper. There's no telling what Kurt would do if I hurt his darling princess.

"Yeah? Well you made Mama and Daddy fight. Stop ruining my life with your business!" Trissy stomped out of the room.

I felt like my head was on fire. I was so angry-hot, so frustrated I didn't know what to do next. So I just stood there, watching out the window as an ugly little bird tried to peck the dry, sandy dirt.

"My sister is a weirdo."

I jumped and turned to find Jackson standing in the kitchen, clutching a handful of little plastic dirt bikes. His presence wasn't what surprised me, but rather the fact that he actually initiated a conversation with me. I'd been here for weeks, but he'd always been frosty around me for reasons I couldn't figure out.

"What did you do? Everybody hates you." He looked at me with sleepy brown eyes, and I couldn't help but soften my expression.

"You mad at me too, Jackson?"

"Should I be?" The way he phrased the question reminded me of his older sister.

I leaned against the counter. "Well, Jackson, you never talk to me. I feel like you've been angry at me ever since I got here, and you never gave me much of a chance."

He shoved his dirt bikes into his pockets and stared at me, analyzing me with the surprisingly deep perception of a six-year-old.

"Wanna play dirt bikes?"

At the moment, I wanted to do anything that would get me out of the house. I followed Jackson out to his little dirt bike ramp.

"Are you sure this isn't an ant hill, Jack?"

He furrowed his brow in concentration while he lined up the bikes, waiting for their turn to be flung off the little mound of soil. "You can be the purple one. His name is Bob." Jackson handed me a bike, and I noticed for the first time that it had a little plastic rider on it.

"Bob?" I inspected the tiny, fierce expression on the biker's face. "That's not exactly a tough-sounding name."

"Truitt named him. I like it," Jackson snapped.

I set down the biker and put my hands up in surrender. I decided to come out and ask Jackson exactly why he refused to like me. "How come you've been annoyed by me ever since I got here?"

He pushed a bike back and forth over the hill until it made little ruts. He furrowed his brow and poked out his round cheeks a bit. "Because everybody always ignores me anyway. I'm not the baby, and I'm not the girl. I'm just Jack. Or Jackson Nathaniel Elliot if I'm being bad."

I stretched my legs out in front of me and drove Bob's bike up and over my calves. "So you thought if I came you'd get even less attention, huh?"

"Well, that's what happened." Jackson sniffed, and I felt my heart tear.

"Trust me, Jack. I'm not trying to get all of this attention. This life you have here is way different from mine. You have a mommy and a daddy who love you so much. I knew that before I even met you." I paused and doodled a stick figure in the dirt, thinking back to when Kurt and Melina first told me about their kids. "You know what they said when I met them?"

He shook his head, his gaze skeptical.

"Your mom said, 'I'm pretty sure that boy could take his father out in wrestling.'"

"She did not either say that!" Jackson insisted, but I saw the timid grin he tried to hide behind his dirt-stained hand.

"Oh yes she did. They're proud of you, Jack."

He scratched his forehead, leaving a trail of dirt across his face. "I bet your daddy is proud of you too."

I bit the inside of my cheek, knowing for a fact no one was proud of me. I wasn't even proud of me. I hated myself, actually. Melina had told me after my doctor's appointment how proud she was of how I'd handled myself. But after last night, I could guarantee I'd never hear that again.

I sighed. "I don't know about that, buddy. But I do know your family thinks you're awesome."

He was quiet for a minute, aimlessly pushing his dirt bike over the mound. "You're right. God gave me a good mommy and daddy. Watch this one fly over the other guys!"

And like that, Jackson decided our conversation had gone as deep as a conversation between a six-year-old boy and a troubled sixteen-year-old girl could go. But in that moment, I actually felt a little bit good about myself. I'd singlehandedly pulled Jackson out of a slump and made some headway in our relationship.

As I finished playing with Jackson and went inside to clean up for dinner, I realized how when I first got here, I wanted to avoid close relationships, but now I was trying to find just one person to accept me. And it turned out the only person to do that was a little boy who didn't know anything about who his cousin really was.

***

Sunday morning, I felt like a piece of road kill. Like one of those opossums I saw all over the place in Pecan Creek. When I told Melina that, she murmured something along the lines of "Bless your poor heart" and agreed to let me stay home from church, provided I watch a sermon on TV with her.

At ten o'clock, we sat on opposite sides of the sofa.

"That's Drew Roberts," she said, pointing at the thirtysomething pastor speaking on the stage of a large church. "He went to seminary with Kurt."

Rather than wearing a suit like Becca's dad, Drew wore khaki pants and an untucked button-down shirt. He welcomed the Texas audience with a joke about the weather. It was actually pretty funny, and I laughed. Across from me, Melina groaned like it was painful to hear.

"I thought that was pretty good," I admitted. It was only the second time I'd addressed her directly that day. Things were still very tense at the Elliot house, and even little Cooper picked up on it and didn't come near me. I'd been told I wasn't allowed to leave the house unless I was with Kurt or Melina because if I couldn't grow my relationships with the people who loved me most, I wasn't ready for new ones. Or something similar.

"No, no, it was good." Melina waved her hand, dismissing the idea that Drew's joke wasn't funny. "It's just—*oww*." She groaned again. I tucked my legs beneath me and leaned toward her, watching as she placed a hand on her stomach and took deep breaths. Finally, she exhaled. "I've been having these pangs since yesterday morning. It's just Braxton Hicks, but still."

Braxton Hicks. It sounded like she was talking about some sort of backwoods redneck. "Huh?"

"Braxton Hicks are false contractions. They're uncomfortable, but nothing to worry about."

"Is the baby moving?" Angry or not, I still thought it was way cool to feel my little cousin kick my hand. Besides, Bean was the only person I hadn't let down.

"No, not much today, but it's okay because there's not as much room in there anymore, so Bean has to get creative ..." She looked distracted, her eyes glazed over, the sermon completely forgotten even though she was staring at the TV. She began poking herself in the side, trying to get her baby to move. "Oh! Okay, there we go. Come here, Sadie."

I slid across the couch and allowed her to guide my hand. Melina silenced the TV, and we waited. My hand jumped without my permission.

"What was that?" I laughed.

"Bean's got hiccups." Melina smiled.

"You're kidding. They can actually do that?" My hand popped up again. "What does it feel like to you?" I put my other hand on my own stomach. "It makes me feel a little nauseated."

"It definitely feels a little weird. Like a little twitch. Sometimes accompanied by a kick." I looked up and returned her smile. "You know I love you, Sadie Grey."

The corners of my mouth eased back down, and I looked at my knees, nodding slightly. I knew it was her way of saying she wasn't going to kick me out of the house anytime soon. I couldn't respond, because it felt strange to even say thank-you. I mean yes, I was glad she loved me, but the phrase had been cheapened for me, watered down by guys who tossed the expression around casually like it was the thing to say when you dated. Or Reese, who promised he'd love me forever only to move on soon after I left for a few short months.

Still, when she said it, it was different. It wasn't like she said it because it was the right thing for an aunt to say or because she wanted something from me or anything like that. It was the opposite, really. She was saying she really loved me, even after I'd broken her trust and lashed out at her. But returning those words to her? I'd been hurt too many times, taken too many failed chances, made too many mistakes to take that risk again. Besides, I'd always heard you had to love yourself before you could love others. I'd never been farther away.

Chapter 17

"Well, that was ... interesting," I admitted as we waited to see Dr. Summers again later that week.

Melina propped her swollen feet on the bottom shelf of the exam table. "At least the sonogram goop was warm. When it's cold, it's like getting smacked in the gut with a raw fish."

"Seriously, Melina, you're way too poetic."

She winked at me as Dr. Summers entered the room.

"Okay, I think we've finally found a couple answers." She sat on her stool and flipped through some printouts. The anticipation built inside me, and I drummed my fingers on the table. After an eternity, she said, "We compared the results of the ultrasound to your blood work results. All of your symptoms add up—especially those ovarian cysts we found during the ultrasound."

My mind went back to the ultrasound. The number of little cysts that filled the screen made my insides look like a piece of Swiss cheese. And definitely explained the pain.

"How do we fix those?" I chewed on a thumbnail.

"Well, that's the tricky part," Dr. Summers said. "You can't simply get rid of them, but you can try to manage them. Unfortunately, in your case, they're part of a bigger issue." She rubbed the back of her neck as she spoke. "Sadie, I believe you have a condition called PCOS, or polycystic ovarian syndrome."

Melina groaned from her spot in the corner, and I raised my eyebrows. "Huh?"

"For this type of condition, we try to rule out all other possibilities before reaching a conclusion. Simply put, it's a hormonal imbalance that can also lead to diabetes if you don't monitor your diet pretty carefully. I'll send you home with some brochures on what's good for you to eat. You don't have to worry about this for a while, of course, but it's also one of the leading causes of infertility, although if a woman does get pregnant, her chances of having multiples are greatly increased." She smiled like she thought I'd appreciate that fact.

"When will it go away?" I abandoned my nubby thumbnail and started on the other. I was sixteen, so of course I wasn't concerned with the infertility part. I was, however, concerned with life going back to normal ... or some semblance of normal.

Dr. Summers set her clipboard on the table and folded her hands in her lap. "Since we found this while you're still pretty young, there's a possibility you can outgrow it. And if you follow all of the guidelines for living with the syndrome, it won't be debilitating."

I had no idea what debilitating meant, but my ears still rang with the word "syndrome." I gulped and my eyes clouded over. Wasn't that like a disease? I had a *disease?* I ran a hand through my hair and reminded myself to breathe. "How did I get this—this—" I couldn't get the word out of my mouth.

She gently settled her hand on my knee and looked directly at me, her eyes compassionate. "That's not entirely clear to us medical people, Sadie. But we do know it can be genetic. Does anyone in your family have this condition?"

I shrugged. "I don't think so. I've never heard of it."

"Her mother had PCOS," Melina said softly.

I bolted upright, knocking Dr. Summers' hand off my knee. "What did you say?"

"Your mama had this." Melina's voice wavered.

I repeated her words to myself over and over, trying to make sense of them. They collided with that one word Dr. Summers had said: *infertility.* "Then I shouldn't even be here. I shouldn't have been possible," I whispered. The realization made my chin quiver, and I averted my eyes so Melina and Dr. Summers wouldn't see the tears that threatened to spill onto my cheeks.

Everything, including my mind, went numb as Dr. Summers gave Melina and me more information. My aunt nodded at all the right times, adding in "Uh-huh" and "That makes sense" when necessary. At some point during the same blur, I shook Dr. Summers's hand, followed Melina out to the parking lot, and climbed into the minivan.

***

Melina let me sleep in and miss classes Friday morning. I guess she took pity on me because I'd just learned I was broken. When Melina and the kids left for co-op, she left me sitting on the couch to read over the information packet from Dr. Summers. "Insulin, a hormone produced in the pancreas, plays an essential role in glucose absorption ..."

I read all about the pancreas, the liver, and how normally insulin pulls glucose—sugar—out of the blood and converts it into energy for different functions in the body. Some of the terms on the pamphlet were hard to understand, so I grabbed my A&P textbook and flipped to the glossary every time I needed to know what words like *glycogen* or *polysaccharide* meant. The strange part was that I enjoyed reading about all of that. Weird, huh? The girl who usually hated science liked reading about complicated stuff like insulin functions.

But then I got to the part about the importance of a moderated diet and exercise routine and my palms started to sweat again. "The most important component of polycystic ovarian syndrome management is a positive outlook. Living with PCOS requires adjustment, but does not ..."

I continued to read the pep talk, but somehow, all I could focus on was the fact that this was real, and this was my life. Possibly forever.

I walked into my room and found a notebook and pen in my backpack. I took it back to the couch and flipped to the section of the packet that talked about what I could and couldn't eat. A lot of tables and math equations supposedly showed me how I should balance everything, but then I found a page with pictures. *Bingo.*

I startled scribbling basic rules: low carbs, low glycemic (I'd look that one up later), more protein, more leafy vegetables. I tried to create a rough shopping list for Melina's next grocery trip. I'd written down almonds, sweet potatoes, and something called kale when Melina walked in.

"I picked up your prescriptions on the way home." She dropped her purse on the recliner and held out a pharmacy bag. I'd managed to hold it together all morning, but looking down into that bag, something shifted. Suddenly, despite feeling pain for months, skipping periods, having my blood drawn, and having an ultrasound the day before, it all became real. Like a car crash, everything collided in my head at once, and my throat felt like I'd swallowed cotton.

Melina pulled out a bottle of pink pills. "Ironically, these are birth control pills, but they're supposed to help regulate the hormone stuff. So you basically have an excuse for mood swings until we get all of this figured out." Her lips twitched, but I looked down at the pill she held out. "You might want to take this one with food. I think I have some saltine crackers."

I coughed, and she furrowed her brows. "Oh. Right. Limited carbs and salts, so no crackers. How about some carrot sticks?"

I curled my fingers around the small pill and walked into the kitchen. "I just want water."

Cooper followed me, a plastic racecar in his hands. He smiled at me, unaware of syndromes and deficiencies and drastically altered lives. He was just a baby. I thought of what Dr. Summers had said about babies and how a PCOS pregnancy had increased chances of multiple babies.

"Have I always been an only child?" I blurted, making Melina jump as she stepped into the kitchen. For some unexplainable reason, I just needed to know.

Melina told Cooper to go pick up his toys before lunch. As he toddled out of the room, she stepped toward me. In a voice barely above a whisper, she said, "Melody was carrying twins."

The pill slipped out of my hand and bounced on the floor and into the air vent. Medicine forgotten, I brought a hand to my throat. I felt like I was being strangled. "With me? How long did it live?"

Melina shifted her gaze out the window, where the sky was perfectly bright, the birds chirped, and two squirrels chased each other around the yard. It was too cheerful out there. I looked down at the floor. "The baby died early on," my aunt said. "We don't know why."

Somehow, I nodded. And somehow, I stammered, "I-I'm going to the bathroom." And somehow I managed to walk down the hall, close the bathroom door, and sink down against the wall before I completely lost it.

I sobbed. Loud, soul-wracking sobs that shook my entire body. The tears came, and I couldn't stop them. Tears for a life turned upside down. Tears for a life lost and a life I shouldn't be living. Tears for finding out my mom had a disease. Tears for finding out I was a mistake.

I'd always known that my mom got pregnant and then married my dad to somehow fix things. Only now had I learned she never even worried about the possibility of getting pregnant because she never thought I was possible.

I felt like I was drowning. Like water was rising from the ground, mixing with my tears, choking me. The realization hurt worse than any cyst ever could. And then I clenched my fists in anger. Anger at God for letting my twin die. Anger at God for letting my mom die. Anger at God for letting me be the one to live.

Chapter 18

Ever since I'd come to Pecan Creek nearly a month ago, I'd never missed my mom as much as I did that afternoon. It had been weeks since I'd first read Mom's old journals, but I desperately craved her nearness. After saying hello to my grandparents over video chat Sunday afternoon, I found the stepladder and retrieved the box of journals.

I carried them to the backyard, where I spread a blanket under a tall pecan tree. I flipped through the journals until I came to the most recent ones. These were written the year before my mom ran off with my dad.

This most recent book was a deep burgundy color, with a silver flower pattern running along the spine. I pulled the book open, inhaled, and dove into a world I never knew.

> My sister is driving me crazy. She's so afraid I'll die if I don't follow her strict diet program. It's smothering. I don't think a twelve-year-old has any business telling me what to do. She's always hanging around me, making sure I'm taking medicine, like I'm her terminally ill patient! Ugh! She drives me crazy!
>
> Mike understands, though. Mike gets it. He knows I refuse to let this limit my life. Mark my words, the moment I turn eighteen, I'm done with this place. Mike loves me and accepts me for who I am, and my parents would realize that if they'd stop

telling me what a bad influence he is. How could someone who makes me feel so good, so alive, be a bad influence?

It surprised me how much I could relate to Mom. The Melina thing? Yeah, totally felt the same way. And Dad sounded like Mom's Hansen, even if their relationship was rocky at best. And it's not like I planned to marry Hansen. The next few entries said more of the same, and included plans for where Mom and Dad would live and how they'd earn money.

And then the entries stopped. No more. Her last entry said she was turning eighteen in two weeks and then she was gone. Literally gone. I double-checked the box, but there were no more journals. A piece of me felt like I'd lost my mom all over again.

I hugged the book against me. I'd seen all I could of my mother, and even that was slipping away from me. My grandparents were practically on the other side of the world, so I couldn't even fill in the missing parts of my life they'd been involved in.

I couldn't do it. I tried to focus on breathing, but that didn't even seem to help. My breaths came faster and more rapid. I couldn't be by myself another moment, or my thoughts would consume me. Suffocate me.

***

"Let's just take a couple deep breaths and resolve to have a good day." Melina leaned her head against the car seat and inhaled. Our relationship was more complicated than ever. Half the time I was angry at her, and the rest of the time, I wanted to just be her niece and let her comfort me.

I sat in the passenger seat, bracing myself against whatever heart-to-heart conversation she'd try to start this time. I didn't think my emotions could handle it if she tried to bridge the distance between us.

"Let's just go inside," I said, my jaw stiff.

My aunt put her hand on her stomach and a shadow of discomfort crossed her face. "Why don't you go on in, and I'll wait out here?" I realized she was trying to give me some space. Even though she was disappointed in me, and I was technically grounded, she was letting me have this time to myself. She silently handed me her debit card, and I climbed out of the car.

No sooner had I entered the grocery store and started the hunt for almond flour, when I heard a voice I recognized.

"Hey." *Truitt.* I froze. What was he doing? Did he really think stalking was necessary to convert me? He had an extra lawn job and didn't make it to church Wednesday night, so I hadn't seen him since the ballpark. I stepped into the nearest aisle, hoping he would move on. I wasn't ready to face him yet.

"What are you doing?" He eyed me and my list suspiciously.

"Shopping. What does it look like?" My words dripped venom, and I didn't try to hide it.

Truitt wasn't fazed. "For men's deodorant? I didn't take you for the masculine type, but hey, if you got stink ..." I rolled my eyes, not just at Truitt, but at myself for "shopping" in the men's deodorant section.

"I kinda hate you, you know," I said. I also kinda needed him to leave before we had a showdown in the middle of the store. I clutched my list tighter, felt it crumple in my grip. "Well, bye." I turned to leave, hoping he'd take the hint.

"Sadie, wait." He jogged to catch up to me and reached for my arm.

"Don't touch me, Truitt," I growled. "I'm not interested in your proselytizing, or your pity, or whatever else you think I need."

Over Truitt's shoulder, I saw an older woman glance nervously in the direction of our deodorant aisle. I didn't care.

"No, Sadie. Listen." His hand gripped my forearm. I shrugged it off. "I'm sorry, okay? I know I can't force anyone to become a Christian. Believe me, I know." Something dark filled his eyes, but he blinked it away. "I also know you don't have many friends yet, and I wanted to make sure you had some good people to hang around."

"You're so stuck up, you know that?" Truitt's face twisted into an amused expression, and I'm pretty sure he smirked. "I've made plenty of friends so far." *If Hansen and his bitter ex-girlfriend count as friends.* "The preacher's daughter of all people is less judgmental than you," I hissed, even though I hadn't faced Becca since the night of the party. But if it'd jilt him just a little ...

He put both hands up in surrender. "Fine. But I'm sorry, okay? For what I said at the game." He turned and walked away, leaving me with an empty shopping basket and a cluttered mind.

***

All I have to do is pass. All I have to do is pass. All I have to do is pass. That became my mantra as I stared down at my English test grade: 77. That was a C. In the past—less than two months ago, actually—I couldn't have cared less about my grades. In fact, my carelessness was the reason I was stuck in summer classes. But I thought I had a shot at making something of myself this summer. I really did. I wanted to prove myself—show my aunt and uncle I wasn't a total failure. Yet there it was, staring me in the face with Melina's bright-purple pen. It wasn't a failing grade, but it was a falling grade. I was glad Hansen was absent because it was getting hard to avoid him in such a small classroom each day, although the fact that I now sat with Autumn and Deni instead probably thrilled Willow.

I stuffed my paper into my backpack and swallowed the sting in my throat as Mr. Crane began passing out our A&P grades after class. I'd been up until two thirty the night before my English and anatomy tests, trying my best to memorize enough facts about the integumentary system to scrape by on the exam. I guessed it would be a harder test than English, so I'd studied for it more. But after seeing that English grade, I was on the verge of hyperventilation.

It would be really great if I had one of those movie moments where the teacher says he's super disappointed in the class with the exception of one student. Then he hands me my paper and it has a big red A (red, not scarlet) and a smiley face on it. That would be cool.

But Mr. Crane was all business as he passed out our tests, face down. He returned to his seat behind the table and began packing up his things. I took a deep breath, released it, and repeated the process. I didn't realize my eyes were closed until I heard someone's bag zip. They'd already seen their grades and were moving on with their lives.

I slowly reached out and traced the edges of my paper with my index finger. Sliding my finger under the edge of the page, I turned it over, took another breath, and looked down. I saw the number 91. That was an A.

A ninety-one? I looked at the grade again, just to be sure it really was a nine and not a sloppy seven. It was! My fingers trembled as I carefully folded the paper and stuck it in my back pocket, trying to remain calm before I completely lost it and hugged Mr. Crane or something.

I waited until that evening before I showed my grade to Kurt and Melina. As much as I wanted to make the announcement opera style, complete with dancing, I played it cool and slid the paper across the dinner table. I watched their faces as they looked at the grade and then my test answers. Melina's eyes widened, and she promptly waddled over to my chair and gave me a hug. Kurt leaned across the table and high-fived me. Then Melina told me some rules were meant to be broken every now and then and that a good test grade was an acceptable reason to break my "modified diet" and go out for ice cream.

As I walked down historic Main Street with the Elliots, licking my double-fudge, double-scoop waffle cone, I realized I actually felt happy. Maybe I could make up for last year's grades this summer after all. And if I worked hard, I still had another round of tests I could use to pull up my grades even more.

I sighed to myself and watched the sun set behind the tall brick storefronts. The sun seemed to try its best to make the day last just one moment more as its golden arms stretched out from behind the buildings. I wanted to hold on to this feeling of something finally going right in my life.

I wished someone from my life in Seattle cared enough to keep up with me this summer, but I couldn't blame them for not caring, even if it would be nice to know I was cared about by the people

I'd known forever. I shoved those unhappy thoughts aside and focused on catching the sticky ice cream drips before they landed on my hand.

***

After dinner one night, Kurt decided to let me drive him to the gas station. I'd spent so much time with my textbooks and people to whom I was trying to prove myself recently that I jumped at the opportunity. Besides, Truitt was on his way over to mow the lawn, and I still couldn't face him again. It was easy enough to avoid him at church, where I could dissolve into another group of people, but I wasn't ready for a one-on-one conversation with him just yet.

The drive over in Kurt's stick shift was relatively uneventful. We only stalled out twice on the way there: once at the stoplight and once in the middle of the road. I couldn't figure that second one out.

I slowly pulled the truck up next to a gas pump and breathed a sigh of relief. *Made it!*

But then my eyes landed on the person at the pump across from me. *Hansen.* How could I hide this time? I sank low in my seat until I was nearly sitting on the floorboard.

"What are you doing?" Kurt peered down at me.

"I think I dropped the keys," I fibbed. "I'm just looking for them."

Kurt poked at the keys still dangling from the ignition. "Found them. Now get out and pump me some gas."

"You don't understand, Kurt." My voice took on a pleading tone. "That's, you know … *Hansen.*" I pointed across the line of gas pumps.

"Ah, I see. But unfortunately, I still need gas. Go for it."

Mumbling under my breath, I opened the door of the cab. It creaked like some sort of animal getting run over in slow motion. A dolphin, maybe, if one of those ever tried to cross the road.

I slowly swung my legs around and slid out of the truck as discreetly as possible. Kurt also climbed out of the truck— slamming the door, of course—to key in his debit card information.

He climbed back in the truck, and I selected my fuel preference and began pumping gas.

"Hey, Sadie!" Kurt called through the open window. "Come here a second."

Gritting my teeth, I secured the gas nozzle. I stepped toward the cab … and promptly tripped on the gas hose. I smashed against the side of the truck, catching myself but managing to sound like a gong in the process. I didn't dare look to see if Hansen noticed, although the noise was so loud I was pretty sure people in Seattle noticed.

I recovered my dignity, sort of, and rubbed my elbow.

"Yes, sir?" I leaned into the truck, pleased with how I remembered some good ol' southern manners.

"I just wanted to tell you that you might want to fix your hair." He pointed at my ponytail, and I flipped down the sun visor. Using the tiny mirror for reference, I tried to find the issue. That took about two hundredths of a second. A huge clump of hair had pulled loose when I slid down to the floorboard and stuck up and on top of my head like a rooster's wobbly comb. Perfect. There was no way Hansen could've missed that.

I released my hair from the band, ran my fingers through it, and pulled it up into a messy bun. The gas pump clicked, and I pressed "Yes" for the receipt. "Please wait," the screen read. So I waited. And waited. A moment later the screen flashed with "Please see cashier for receipt."

"Kurt, how badly do you need the receipt?"

"Mel will withhold my rations if I don't bring one home again. She likes to balance the checkbook the old-fashioned way."

Shaking my head, I walked into the convenience store and got in line. I recognized the caramel-swirl hair in front of me. I could still feel its texture on my fingertips from the night of the party. I shoved my hands into my pockets and pretended to be completely engrossed by the tabloid stand.

Hansen bought a root beer and chips from the cashier, who looked like she'd worked one too many nightshifts, and then turned around. His eyes widened just slightly so that the yellowy whites showed. He quickly composed himself and returned to that Mr.

Cool persona he'd won me over with at the party. If I was being honest, he was still winning me over, whether I liked it or not. He hadn't gone off on me about his truck. He hadn't forced me to talk when we saw each other at co-op. The sight of him standing directly in front of me for the first time since the party sent chills down my arms.

"Hey, Princess," he said casually, as if this was not on the list of most awkward encounters of all time.

"I, *um*, saw you got your truck back."

"Yep."

Silence.

"Okay. You weren't in class today."

"Nope."

"Oh. Everything okay?"

"Dentist appointment."

"Oh."

More silence. I blinked and coughed simultaneously, which came across as a spastic tick. "Okay, well, I've gotta get my receipt. My uncle is waiting in the car for me." Oh why did I say that? That practically screamed, "I'm grounded!"

He nodded and looked down at my lips. I couldn't tell what he was thinking, but I had a couple of ideas. I couldn't move. What would I do if he tried to kiss me again? I'd take charge and shove him away, right? Oh, who was I kidding? I'd kiss him back.

But I didn't have to decide what happened next, because Kurt broke our spell for us. "There you are!" He turned to Hansen. "Hey, son. How are you?"

"I'm pretty good, sir." Hansen kept his eyes on mine.

"Good, good." Kurt grinned, and I felt my face heat up. "Sadie, now that we've made sure Hansen's doing all right, we should go. Have a good one, Hansen."

Kurt turned toward the door, and I glared at the back of his head, hoping some of the heat from my face would travel to his obnoxious head and ignite a spark.

***

149

"Your husband is insufferable!" I stormed into the living room, nearly tripping over a plastic fire truck.

Melina sat on the couch with her feet propped on an exercise ball while the boys played with their trucks. "What's wrong?"

"Where do I start?" I was too annoyed to sit down, so I paced back and forth in front of her, sidestepping toys and little boys. "First, he made me pump gas, even though Hansen was at the station. He was the reason Hansen saw me! Then when I was innocently talking to Hansen with, like, two feet of space between us, Kurt came storming into the store and reminded me I'm on restriction! Like I didn't know! I'm just so, so—"

"Can you help the kids get ready for bed?"

I stopped midrant and clamped my jaw. "Can that wait, like, five seconds? I'm trying to talk to you."

Melina shifted her weight. "I know you're frustrated, but can I listen to you rip at my kids' daddy when they aren't present? And to answer your question, yes, it can wait, but I'm going to need some help tonight."

"Okay. But why?"

"Because," she said as she lowered her voice and I leaned closer so the boys couldn't hear our conversation, "I don't feel very good. I haven't all week, but I should feel fine once I get some rest."

"Backstabbing Hicks again?"

"Ah, no," she said as she smiled a little, still looking uncomfortable. "Those were Braxton Hicks, and I've got some other issues going on. A terrible headache, for one."

I realized how badly it must've hurt when I came in, slamming the door and yelling. "Okay. I'll help with the kids."

Chapter 19

"Sadie, wake up! Sadie, wake up! Wake *up*, Sadie!"

I moaned into my pillow and opened one eye. Trissy stood beside the bed in her silky princess nightgown, her hair sprouting off her head like streamers. I started to close my eye, but the look of terror on her face made me jump to a sitting position.

"What's wrong, Tris?"

"Mama's gotta go to the hospital and Daddy's taking her. You have to watch us. Get up! Hurry!" She ran out of the room before I had a chance to respond.

Hospital? Was Melina in labor? The baby wasn't supposed to come until the end of summer.

I changed into a T-shirt and shorts and ran into the living room. Melina sat on the couch, sliding her feet into her trendy white sandals.

"Is the baby coming?" I panted.

She looked up at me, her short hair already styled in the purposefully tussled way that always looked so cute on her. Her eyes drooped, though, and deep circles showed through her carefully applied foundation.

"Good morning, Sadie. No, Bean isn't coming, but something's up. I was so sick last night, and my abdomen hurt, and the headache—my purse! Kurt, can you bring my purse?" She yelled down the hall. I helped her stand. "Sadie, we need you to watch the kids, okay? Feed them, get them dressed, teeth brushed, you know. Marigold's probably hungry too."

I took a step back. "All three kids? Plus Marigold? While you're in Augusta?"

Melina nodded, her hand wrapped protectively around her stomach. "Yes to all of those. But it's okay because Becca and Hope will be here in about half an hour."

Becca? Oh, this day kept getting better and better, and I'd been awake less than ten minutes.

"I don't think Becca—"

"You're just gonna have to put aside your differences. Please, Sadie. We don't have any other options." Her eyes pleaded with me. "Hope will entertain Trissy and Becca knows our house inside and out, so you'll still be able to take care of your homework." I must've still looked skeptical, because she put a hand on my shoulder. "Please?"

I sighed. As much as I didn't want to see Becca, she had to want to see me even less. So maybe it was a good sign if she was willing to come. "Okay. I'll help."

"Thank you, Sadie baby." She pulled me close and kissed my cheek. The gesture was warm and comfortable and reminded me of home when Mom used to hold me tight and reassure me whenever I faced something scary. She released me as Kurt entered the room.

"Thanks, Sadie!" my uncle called over his shoulder as he escorted his wife out the door.

Before I knew what was happening, I found myself alone in a house full of kids and a demonic cat.

"Well, *um,* I'm gonna go feed Marigold before he comes out of hiding. Trissy, can you go get the cereal out of the cabinet?"

Trissy nodded as a big tear slipped out from under her lowered lashes. In the laundry room, I filled Marigold's water dish and then dumped some food in the bowl. Marigold meowed from behind me and scared me so badly I spilled some of the kibble in the water dish.

"Well, Marigold, looks like you're having cereal for breakfast too." I set down the bag of food and jogged into the kitchen, where I found Trissy pouring milk into three bowls.

"Here, Sadie. I gave you the new cereal that'll make your tummy feel better." She slid a bowl my way. A hurting tummy was the explanation Melina had given her children when I came home from the doctor, and I was beyond okay with that.

"Thanks, Trissy." I set Cooper in his booster seat. "Where's your bowl?"

"I don't think I can eat with all of this going on. I think I'm just gonna have my coffee."

Trissy ran a hand under her nose and shakily poured coffee into her mug before loading it with milk and sugar. Sitting in her seat at the table, she said, "I'll say the blessing."

We all held hands, and I watched the kids—even little Cooper—close their eyes. "Dear Jesus," Trissy began, her voice uncharacteristically soft. "Thank You for this cereal and this coffee. Please be with Mama and Daddy and our baby. Please don't let Bean die because that's our brother or sister. In Jesus' name, amen."

Okay, that one had even me sniffing. But I had to keep it together and be the levelheaded adult in the situation. "Bean isn't going to die, Trissy." I kept my voice even.

"We don't know that, Sadie. You don't have to be old to die. You can die before you're born."

Her words pricked my heart. I thought of my mom first and then my twin I'd recently learned about. "I know, Trissy. But that doesn't mean it'll happen to Bean. Maybe your mom just needs some more vitamins. We just have to think positive thoughts, okay?"

"Like thinking good things about something will make it turn good." Trissy rolled her eyes. She had me there. My statement really did seem hollow. Positive thoughts, luck, well wishes—what did those ever accomplish? They were just something nice you said when you tried to cheer someone up.

"We'll pray a lot," Jackson piped up, his mouth full of soggy Fruit Loops.

Trissy nodded and took a sip of coffee. "Sometimes you're all right, Jack."

He shrugged and ate another mouthful as the screen door creaked open.

"Good morning!" Becca called.

153

"Becca!" Cooper yelled in response. I was his own cousin and he barely talked to me, but he ate up the attention from his babysitter.

Hope came in first, her pretty, blonde hair french-braided and tied with a bright-blue ribbon that matched her eyes. Her tan little face lit up when she saw Trissy, and the two girls immediately took off in the direction of the living room. Jackson followed closely behind. I expected to hear squeals of protest any minute. Poor little guy.

"Sadie?" Becca stood in the doorway, frowning. *Uh-oh.* "What are you doing here?"

I looked around the kitchen. "I kinda live here."

Becca took Cooper out of his seat and set him on the floor. "Go find Jack, Coop. I'll come play with you in a second, okay, buddy?" She turned back to me and shook her head. "That's not what I meant. I was expecting Truitt to help me. I didn't think you'd be here. But I don't know ..." She trailed off and turned to set her purse on the counter, but not before I caught the look of disappointment in her eyes.

"You don't have to be here, you know. I've got this," I told her. Okay, so that was a pretty big lie, but if she was going to give me the cold shoulder, we'd be in for a long day.

"No." She shook her head. "I love Kurt and Mel and their kids." She shrugged. "And I love you, Sadie. I want to help."

Wait, did she just say she loved me? These Christian people sure believed in telling people how they felt. I couldn't think of a time my closest girl friends ever told me that. Sure, they'd text a "luv u" or even a "love ya," but never an all-out "I love you" in face-to-face conversations. Especially if I'd hurt them. I couldn't figure it out. If she'd loved me at all, it would've been before I used her as a pawn in my game of deception, right?

"You just met me a month ago, Becca. And I ... Look, I shouldn't have used you to go behind Kurt and Melina's back, okay?"

Becca sat in the seat next to me. "First, no, you shouldn't have done that. I was so angry, Sadie. I thought we were friends." She splayed her hands on the table and stared at an abandoned bowl of cereal. "And second, love isn't like a carton of milk. It doesn't last for so long then expire. Real love doesn't turn sour. Jesus loved us enough to die for us, for Pete's sake, so the least I can do is love and forgive my friends when they hurt me. I forgive you, Sadie."

"Wow." That was all I could say. Becca took the whole forgiveness thing seriously. I would be so bent on revenge if I were her. And there would be plenty of ways for her to get back at me. "Do you think Melina and the baby will be okay?" I asked because she was being so open with me. I felt as young as Trissy.

Becca twisted the end of her long ponytail and chewed on the corner of her lip. "I think we have to trust God."

"That doesn't answer my question." Especially since this notion of a loving God was still so far-fetched. Even Jesus dying. I'd heard that story when I was little, of course, and I knew historians didn't deny a man named Jesus who went around teaching people back in the day, but there was no way anyone could die for someone they'd never met.

Becca released her hair and turned big, honest eyes on me. "I honestly don't know, Sadie. But I do know Mel's gotta be remembering Bailey."

I sat up straight. "Who's Bailey?"

Becca's eyes looked sad. "You didn't know?"

When I shook my head, she sighed. "Melina was pregnant between Jackson and Cooper. She lost the baby, and they don't know why. They went in for an appointment to find out the baby's gender, and she was gone."

I swallowed a lump in my throat. "Bailey would've been Trissy's sister."

"Yeah, she would've been," Becca whispered. "Trissy was young, but she remembers. If she seems worried, that's probably why, although she'd never admit it."

"Oh, man." I leaned back in my seat and rubbed my head. "I had no idea. I mean I know how much Kurt and Melina love their kids, so that must've been hard."

Becca looked like she was about to say more, but the girls came into the kitchen looking for Play-Doh.

While Becca pulled out the Play-Doh for the kids, I stacked the cereal bowls in the sink and thought about what Becca had said. Just by looking at Kurt and Melina, you'd never be able to tell they'd experienced that kind of tragedy. On top of the tragedy of my mom's death. They just seemed too happy and full of life.

My throat thickened, and I cleared it. I just needed to breathe. That would help. *In and out, in and out.* There was so much I didn't know about the people whose blood ran through my veins.

Chapter 20

Becca and I tag-teamed the day. I mopped spilled juice, she wiped leaked tears when Cooper tripped on a doll. She made tuna sandwiches while I made lemonade … and a salad for myself. While I'd barely gotten into my new diet, it was already making me weary. I hadn't told Becca about it yet because "Hey, did you know I've got defective ovaries?" isn't exactly a casual conversation starter.

After lunch, Becca laid Cooper down for a nap and read Jackson a story for his down time. I collapsed on the couch and watched Trissy and Hope style each other's hair. I couldn't remember ever being so exhausted.

After braiding each other's hair, the girls decided they wanted to play dress-up and took off in the direction of my room. I quickly ran in there to tell them my stuff was off-limits and then returned to the couch.

Becca joined me a few minutes later, plopping down next to me and yawning.

"I don't know how you do this babysitting thing, Becca," I admitted, my eyes at half-mast.

"Ha. Sometimes I don't know either. I just know I love little kids."

I nudged her. "You'll make a good mother one day."

She laughed at that. "Thanks, but it'll be a long time before that point."

"Becca!" I turned to face her before I lost my gumption.

"Sadie!" She laughed and faced me too, her knees bumping against mine.

"What's the deal with you and Truitt?" I said casually, doodling a picture with my finger on the suede sofa cushion.

"What deal?"

"Oh, you know …" I added petals to my flower, pretending the question wasn't gnawing at me. "How serious are you two?"

Becca grabbed my hand and used it to erase my flower. "What do you mean 'serious'? We're friends. Really good friends."

"I see." My voice was singsongy. Becca's face was tomato red.

"No, seriously." Becca shook her head hard, her long ponytail swinging. "We've known each other forever, so he's like a brother to me. It's not like that. Plus Truitt likes to keep to himself. He's not one for heart-to-heart talks or anything like that."

I pondered her response but couldn't help wondering if her stance had anything to do with her dad's job. My guess was—

"Do you like him?" she asked.

"What?" I sputtered. Becca swiped at her cheek and grimaced.

"No. In fact, I was hoping you'd be able to tell me why he's so self-righteous. I mean you're both Christians, but he seems intent on trying to convert me. I honestly have a hard time being around him, but my family is obsessed with the guy. They treat him like he's some sort of celebrity."

"I see. Well, I can't talk freely about Truitt's private life, but that's kind of his personality, I guess. He doesn't see it as trying to convert you, but just … *hm* … he has a heart for seeing souls saved."

"Same thing."

My back pocket buzzed, and I jumped. Ignoring Becca's stifled laughter, I answered the phone. "Hello?"

"Sadie? It's Kurt."

"Kurt!" I jumped off the couch and paced, barely giving my feet a chance to sink into the carpet. "What's going on?"

"Mel has pregnancy-induced hypertension, or PIH for short."

"She has what?" Becca stood and started pacing with me, her ear pressed against the other side of the phone.

"Basically, it's high-blood pressure that comes from big amounts of stress."

I stopped pacing. "So she had an anxiety attack?"

A rustling sound came through the speakers, and then Kurt said something in a muffled voice. "No." He came back on the line. "It's actually very serious and can develop into something worse if she doesn't take care of herself. We're talking about possible problems with her liver, kidneys, and blood flow to the baby among other things." His voice sounded pinched. "It could even lead to seizures and preeclampsia."

I didn't know what preeclampsia was, but I felt the color drain from my face. I glanced over at Becca, who stared back at me with wide eyes. I sank down to the floor. "Does she have to stay in the hospital?"

"Thankfully, no. But she is being put on bed rest until things calm down some, and she'll need to lay off the southern fried food. Y'all can be accountability partners. We'll talk more about that when we get home, but for now, just know that we need to keep her environment as calm as possible."

"Easier said than done."

"Maybe so, but we have to try. The alternative is to deliver the baby, but it's way too early for that. We're checking out of the hospital now, so we'll be home in a little while."

After getting thorough updates on the kids—for Mel's sake, I was sure—Kurt hung up and left Becca and me staring at each other.

"Poor Mel," Becca said as she sighed.

I nodded and tossed the phone on the couch. "I should go check on the girls."

***

When Kurt said Melina wanted a moment with me, my brain went into spaz mode. As I said good-bye to Becca and Hope, waited for the kids to visit with their mom, and threw a mini-tantrum when I saw the disastrous state of my bedroom, I tried to think of what would cause Melina to be so stressed out. She didn't work; just stayed home with the kids all day. That in itself would be enough to send me to the nuthouse, but she insisted it brought her joy or whatever. I'd had a couple of run-ins with her, and then that Friday night I—

Friday night. I snuck out and came back with a hangover and a big attitude. Me.

Oh no. It was all my fault.

I slipped into Kurt and Melina's bedroom, pulling the door shut behind me. The overhead light was off, but a lamp glowed soft yellow next to the bed. Melina reclined against a stack of pillows in her pajamas and silky robe. She patted the bed when she saw me, so I perched at the foot of the bed.

"How's it going, Melina?" I gave her a chummy smile.

"I hate this."

"What?"

"I hate this." She grabbed a glass of water from the bedside table and took a sip. "No fried foods, no sweet tea, no playtime with my babies. Most moms would probably love to have an excuse to lie around, but not Melina Elliot. No, ma'am. The sedentary life is not for me."

I covered my mouth to hide my smile. Only Melina would be irritated about relaxing. She looked at me and blew her bangs off her forehead.

"You know what the ironic thing is?" she asked.

"No, what?"

"They tell you to stay in bed, but they also tell you to drink like five gallons of water a day. I'll be doing more walking just going to the bathroom than I would on a normal day." She flopped her hands on the bedspread. "I'm sorry, Sadie. This pregnancy was just going so well, and this stress thing is stressing me out. I mean Cooper was a textbook pregnancy. As close to perfect as it could be. But this," she said as she spread her hands over her middle, "hopefully will be temporary. Then I'll be up and at 'em until Bean arrives."

I knew what that meant. I was the stressor. She'd never admit that, maybe even to herself, but I knew I was the reason she'd wound up on bed rest.

"This must stink for you, Melina."

She shrugged. "It does, but as long as my baby's still healthy, that's all I care about. I'll have plenty of time to be the perfect homemaker later. Truitt's coming over to help with dinner before he mows. Would you mind helping him? I would, but ..." She turned a pair of puppy eyes on me, and like that, she was back to her old self.

I walked into the kitchen and found Truitt already tossing a salad. Trissy stood beside him, handing him one grape tomato at a time. Oh, brother.

I accidentally kicked a toy racecar, sending it sliding into the table leg. Truitt turned around and smiled. I didn't. "Well, hey, stranger. It's been a while."

I took a tomato out of Trissy's hand—those were okay for me to eat, right?—and popped it in my mouth. "What're we eating?"

Truitt dumped some shredded cheese into the salad and shot me a sly grin. "Trissy greeted me with 'What's cookin', good lookin'?' You could try being a little sweeter."

Trissy's mouth dropped open, and her face matched the color of the tomatoes in her hands. "Truitt! I did not!"

Truitt winked at her and stole a tomato. "I'm just messin' with your cousin." He leaned closer to her and stage-whispered, "She could use some friends."

Trissy nodded.

It was my turn for my mouth to drop open. Truitt shoved the tomato in my mouth before I could respond and then went back to tossing the greens. I chewed and swallowed. "Where are the three men?"

Truitt glanced down at Melina's pink apron he wore around his hips. "What are you trying to say?" I reached for a cucumber slice, but he slapped my hand lightly with his wooden spoon. "They're outside. By the way, I'm taking the mower and stuff over to the church after I do the yard, since the one I keep over there is broken. Kurt said you wouldn't mind going with me, especially since you were cooped up with the kids all day."

Ooh ... I fumed, trying to think of a response that wouldn't get me in deeper trouble with my uncle. I rolled my eyes. Kurt was using my punishment to make me do things he knew I didn't want to do. He was a sneaky one.

Chapter 21

"Aw, rats." Truitt ran a hand through his sweaty hair. I leaned against the opposite window to avoid the splash zone.

"What's wrong?"

Truitt rested his left arm in the open window of the truck. The eight o'clock sunshine was pleasant, casting long shadows on the road, hinting at the impending darkness. "Nothing really. I just left the church shed keys at my house. I guess we have time to run by there before it gets dark."

"Where do you live?" So far, this was the most uninsulting, noncondescending conversation I'd ever had with the guy. But if he mentioned a Bible verse ...

"I live in Cobblestone Estates. It's a couple miles beyond the church."

He turned on the radio, surprising me with his country music station. I'd expected hymns or a sermon or something. About five minutes on the other side of Pecan Creek Baptist, he slowed Beulah down and turned by a wooden sign for Cobblestone Estates. If the owner of this place wanted to be more accurate, it should've been named Gravel Estates. The road was ribbed from rainfall, and gravel had been seemingly tossed across the road to fill in some of the gaps. It made for a rough ride.

What surprised me most was that we had entered a trailer park. Not that there weren't nice trailer parks. It's just that this one ... wasn't.

The mobile homes lined the road in clusters, close enough that if you sneezed out your window, you'd hit your neighbor's house.

Clotheslines hung behind the houses and chain-link fences claimed each house's territory. A dog barked nearby, and I fought the urge to roll up my window.

I glanced at Truitt, who kept his eyes focused on the road. After a minute of tailbone-bending bumps, he pulled off at a white singlewide. The paint looked fresh, especially compared to the peeling homes flanking it. The grass behind the fence was evenly trimmed, and the shrubs by the door were shaped to perfection. Truitt definitely lived here.

I heard Truitt exhale and followed his line of vision to an old green Oldsmobile parked beside the house. I looked back at the trailer, dark except for the throbbing glow of a television.

Truitt shut off the truck and opened his door. I followed suit.

"Sadie, wait." Truitt held up a hand. "I'm going to grab a drink and find the key. I'll just be a second. Wait out here."

"I don't want to stay out here by myself." I winced, hoping he didn't think I thought his neighborhood was sketchy. Although I kinda did.

"Nah, it's okay." His voice was casual, but he glanced at the house again. "I'll be back." He closed his door.

I leaned out my window. "Oh, are you scared to be alone in a house with a girl who doesn't—"

"Fine. You can come in, just give me a second. I have no idea how messy I left the place. I'll stick my head out when it's clear."

Satisfied, I sank back into my seat and crossed my arms over my chest to wait. After locking the door, of course.

I watched a light flicker on inside and saw Truitt cross in front of the window. The blue light from the TV disappeared. Truitt ducked occasionally in front of the window as he picked things up. I couldn't imagine Truitt living in a messy house and wondered for the first time if he lived alone, even though he was only seventeen. That would explain the bachelor pad vibe I was picking up on. Truitt disappeared from view. I'd had enough waiting.

I climbed out of the truck, looking both ways to make sure the barking dog wasn't hiding in the bushes, and walked up to the door. I put my hand on the knob and twisted right as Truitt pulled the door open.

"Sadie!" He took a step backward. "I was coming to get you."

"Truitt, I live with my dad. I can handle a man cave."

"I know, but I—"

"What happened to your face?" Fresh red scratches traced his right jawbone. I allowed my hand to hover over the wounds before pulling it away. I could almost feel their sting.

Truitt rubbed the scratches and winced. "Cat claws. I tried to put him in the bedroom, but he mauled me."

I stood on my tiptoes and peered around Truitt's shoulder but didn't see a cat. Marigold may have been a psycho pain in the neck, but he hadn't attacked me. Yet.

"What's your cat's name?" I saw a sofa littered with candy bar wrappers.

"Bob."

I pulled myself back to look at him. "Bob? Your cat's name is *Bob?* Isn't that the name you gave one of Jackson's bikers?"

Truitt shrugged. "Creativity is not my strong point. Let me change. I'll be right out."

Ignoring him, I pushed past Truitt and stepped into the house. I inhaled tobacco smoke, along with something else I couldn't quite put my finger on. *What ...*

I had friends who smoked all kinds of stuff, but I'd never been able to tolerate it. Neither could Truitt's floral wallpaper, apparently. Where it wasn't peeling off the wall, the paper had a yellow hue, although I could safely bet it was supposed to be white. I raised my eyebrows at the liquor bottles that sat on the coffee table in front of the sofa.

Truitt was already in the back of the house, so I sat on the edge of the sofa's arm, trying to absorb what I saw. A picture of baby Truitt stared at me from on top of the TV. The eyes and dimple gave his identity away. The picture next to it displayed a dark-haired girl holding a newborn in a hospital bed. Truitt's mom?

I turned to face Truitt, who emerged from the back of the hazy house wearing a fresh T-shirt. Something clear and gloopy was smeared across his scratches.

"Are you ready to get out of here?"

I nodded, not sure of what to say and not wanting to inhale so much secondhand smoke at the same time. When we got outside, I gulped air like I'd just run ten miles. Truitt noticed me behaving like a beached whale.

"You okay?" he asked.

"Truitt, wh—" *Inhale. Exhale. Gasp. Inhale.* "You've been lying to me."

"I tried to make you stay in the truck. I didn't want you to see that."

"Even worse, you've been lying to my aunt and uncle. They *trust* you, Truitt!" Okay, so yes, maybe I was being hypocritical, but I never claimed to walk the straight and narrow.

"It's not like that, Sadie. I just—"

"Drink and smoke? And I know I smelled more than tobacco in there, Truitt. Don't try to convince me otherwise."

Truitt pushed me into the truck, midrant, and shut the door.

"Let's just go," he mumbled once he'd climbed into his side.

"No." I snatched the keys from the ignition. "You tell me the truth, or so help me, I'll put these keys down my shirt. *Then* let's see you drive off."

Truitt gritted his teeth so loud, my own teeth screamed for mercy. "Fine. I'll tell you. Let's get to the church first, okay?"

"Fine by me. Let's see you lie at church."

***

"First of all, let me say I really do have a cat named Bob who really should've been declawed." Truitt leaned against the back of his truck, watching the sun sink behind the church building.

"And?" I wiped my greasy hands on my shorts. We'd put the yard equipment in the storage shed, and now I refused to move until I heard an explanation.

"And I don't drink. Or smoke. Never tried either."

"Oh, that's rich." My sarcasm oozed thicker than the ointment on Truitt's face.

"I live with my mom, Sadie. My dad ran off with another woman when I was thirteen. She's misguided in how she handles her bitterness."

"So the liquor and stuff are you mom's?"

Truitt nodded slowly. "They are."

"How can you live with that?" I thought of my dad. When he wasn't working nights, he sometimes went out drinking. But we didn't live in the filth of his habits. He was convinced by some delusion that if he didn't drink at home, I wouldn't be tempted to be like him. It was laughable, really.

"She's my mother, Sadie. She has trouble holding down a job, so if I left her, there's no telling what would happen." Truitt studied his ratty tennis shoes.

"That's why you work so much?"

Again, a nod. "That's why your uncle let's me cut your grass. They don't exactly have loads of money either, but they're awesome people with huge hearts."

I looked at my own feet. "Yeah."

"I meant what I said about never having a drop to drink in my life. You know how tempted I've been on days when I'm beyond the point of exhaustion? Just one drink, and the world would never know. But God would know."

"The rules. I get it."

Truitt crossed his arms and stared at the white steeple offset by the pink sky. "No, you don't. I don't choose not to drink because it's a rule or something. I don't drink because I love God and want to be as close to Him as possible. Getting drunk when I'm stressed out could only pull me farther away from God when I should turn to Him for strength. My mom's an alcoholic, so I know that does nothing but destroy you. Slowly at first—so slowly you can hardly tell—but it does destroy you. You forfeit a full life for an empty bottle."

I scratched my chin with the back of my hand. *Huh.* I'd never heard someone give that sort of reasoning before. "You really don't have to explain that to me. It's your life, your choices."

"But our own choices ultimately affect others too. Look at my mom. Look at your dad." He stopped, most likely sensing he'd hit a nerve. He didn't know anything about my dad. If he did, he'd know that I was worse. I bit my lip to keep quiet. "See, Sadie? I do understand at least a small part of where you're coming from. Not all of it, I know. But we have some similar experiences."

We stood in silence together, both of us lost in thought. The cotton-candy clouds gradually dissolved into gray streaks as the sun disappeared for the night.

I stood up straight and rolled my tired neck. "Speaking of experiences, I should get back to make sure Kurt gave Trissy decaf coffee after dinner."

One side of Truitt's lips turned up in a smile, but not enough for his dimple to appear. "You're right. Tris on extra caffeine would be an experience."

Chapter 22

I'd never been so exhausted in my life. I spent the next week juggling homework, co-op classes, babysitting, cleaning the house, and learning to cook while Melina was on bed rest. Oh, and trying to make my body adjust to my medicines and new diet. It was a battle of what I knew I needed to eat versus what I wanted to eat. Dr. Summers had called to check in so we wouldn't have to drive all the way back to the doctor's office and told me that once I adjusted, I'd be able to sneak in what I wanted to eat as long as I controlled the portions. The difficulty was actually making it to that point without throwing my PCOS packet out the window of a moving vehicle.

The good news was Melina's blood pressure started heading toward normal, but she was still on bed rest and spent her days alternating between her bed and the sofa. I hadn't known she was capable of being grumpy until someone told her she couldn't do something. I didn't take the time to let the familiarity of that personality trait sink in.

Late at night, after everyone was asleep, I'd pull out the box of journals Melina now let me keep in my closet and read, hungrily searching for clues of how my mom handled her PCOS. But for once, the journals lacked details.

Ironically, the final chapter of my A&P book was on the reproductive system. And while it was kind of awkward reading about those details while my aunt lived it out, it flipped a switch in me. I'd been fascinated by Bean's progress ever since I felt that first kick, and now I had the opportunity to chart the baby's progress. I also had the opportunity to see how my own organs should be working, rather than how they'd decided to shun insulin and cause me pain.

Despite my Internet research, I still had questions about my condition, but I didn't know who to ask. Melina knew some things, but she wasn't an expert. After anatomy Friday, three weeks after my diagnosis, I cornered Mr. Crane in the empty teacher's room before SAT prep class.

"What can I help you with, Sadie?" Mr. Crane's dark eyes looked at me over his wire-rimmed glasses. Willow definitely had his eyes, but his were softer, kinder. Not evil.

I swallowed, realizing it was the first time I'd discussed my diagnosis with anyone. "Well, I recently found out I have this, this … condition." Mr. Crane's nod prompted me to continue. "Okay, so it's PCOS. Have you heard of it?"

He nodded again. "I work pediatrics, so I don't really see that, but yes, I've heard of it."

"My body is resistant to insulin because of that, so I could get diabetes if I'm not careful. Now I know I got a B on the endocrine system chapter, but isn't the liver in charge of insulin? Why would my, well, my other organs keep my body from processing it?"

I realized I'd been braiding a strand of hair the whole time I talked. I untangled my locks and shoved my hands behind my back.

"I've been trying to figure it out, and I can't, so please don't tell me to go look it up."

"Hmm …" Mr. Crane rubbed the side of his neck. "You know, I'm not really sure. Consider this a homework assignment for your teacher. I'll bring you an answer next time, okay? Congrats on stumping me." He smiled and patted my shoulder. I took off to join the SAT prep class already in session. If my aunt heard I was late … I was finally off restriction, so I didn't want to think about that.

Truitt came over to help with dinner again that night. For reasons beyond my understanding, the family was tired of salad and canned tuna. I thought I'd been creative with my salads, using various meat and veggie combos, but no. Trissy said she feared turning into a rabbit, Jackson said he was sick of eating weeds, and Kurt started holding "counseling sessions" with members of the youth group during dinner time. At McDonald's. Right.

"So what are we making?" I cut open a thawed package of pork chops.

Truitt grabbed an apple from the fruit bowl and ran it under the tap. "Honey apple pork chops, fresh snap peas, and dark chocolate chip cookies."

My jaw dropped, and I pushed my chin back into place with the back of my hand. "Can I—I mean can *Mel*—eat that?"

"Oh sure." He smiled. "She gave me a list of stuff to look for. Plus we'll be using the sugar substitute for the cookies your aunt said you bought." Just thinking about the hour I'd spent shopping for more healthy foods earlier that day exhausted me.

Truitt tossed me an apple. "I'll get the meat started. Why don't you slice up these apples into thin strips, okay?"

I found a knife and cutting board and went to work on the apple. This was humiliating, getting schooled on the culinary arts by a guy. And not only that, but getting schooled on low-glycemic culinary arts by a guy. A guy who, thankfully, didn't know why I needed to modify my diet and had the good sense not to ask.

After the apples were sliced, I followed the recipe to mix apple cider vinegar, lemon juice, and soy sauce into a glaze. Truitt, who had been cooking the peas from the garden Melina shelled in her abundant down time, spread the chops in the pan and instructed me to pour the glaze over them. We spread the apple slices over the meat and drizzled more honey over the top before sliding the concoction into the oven. I had to admit it smelled wonderful.

"All righty. Where are those dark chocolate chips?" Truitt wiped his hands on a dishrag and then swatted me with it.

"Melina told me to put them in the top of the china cabinet so no one would be tempted."

"Was she talking about herself?" Truitt winked, and I yanked the towel from him before he could hit me again.

"Just get them," I said, feigning impatience. He turned to walk toward the china cabinet, and I walloped the gullible guy on the back of his leg.

He shrieked, sounding a bit like Trissy, and I laughed. It felt good, so I kept laughing as he stood on his tiptoes to reach the chips, stopping only when his shirt rode up. The exposed skin was a greenish color—a bruise.

"Truitt?"

"Yeah?" He grunted as he pulled the bag of chips out of a crystal bowl. His shirt went back to its normal place.

"Your back. Where'd you get that green bruise?"

He set the chips on the counter and furrowed his brow, reaching a hand behind him to feel the bruise. "Oh." Realization dawned on his face. "Baseball."

"You got hit in the back with a baseball?"

He shrugged. "Can't protect everything. It's over a week old, though. I don't even feel it anymore." He shrugged again and ripped open the bag. He motioned for me to open my mouth and tossed a bittersweet morsel into my mouth. I swallowed and then reached for the bag to do the same to him.

Thus commenced a ten-minute contest to see who had the better aim. I allowed myself to enjoy this small pleasure, but I couldn't force that bruise out of my mind. I knew Truitt liked to play ball even though his season was over. But then I remembered the baseball bat bruise from the lake and shuddered. Either Truitt was the South's biggest spaz or he held secrets beyond his home life.

***

"I don't know." That wasn't the answer I expected Mr. Crane to bring me.

"How come?" I felt my heart rate speed up at the knowledge of how there was something else I couldn't understand—one more thing I couldn't control—about my body.

Mr. Crane spoke softly, even though we were the only two in the teachers' room. Under any other circumstances, I'd be weirded out by this. "There are a lot of unknowns about this condition, as I'm sure you know. But I do know professionals say insulin resistance can lead to PCOS, Sadie. When the body doesn't process insulin, it builds up, causing different systems to attempt to counteract that resistance. I could tell you more, but—"

"No, that's okay. I appreciate you looking up the answer for me, though." Mr. Crane smiled and went back to grading our homework assignments while I slipped into the in-progress SAT session late again, no closer to understanding my condition than when I started this journey.

I sat in the empty seat next to Hansen, who slid me a scrap of paper. "Are they sneaking you snacks in the break room or something?" I glanced at the teacher, the twins' mom, who was busy writing a list of reminders on the board. "I wish!" I scribbled back. "I had another A&P question for Mr. Crane."

Hansen rolled his eyes as if to say, "Yeah, right." Willow glanced over at us, her dark eyebrows pinched together, but her pencil never stopped copying down the list.

After class, Hansen held out my backpack while I stood from my seat. "So there's this party, and—"

"No, thanks. I'd rather not be busted again and risk being grounded until my flight back to Seattle."

Hansen's eyes widened. "You're still planning to go home?"

In my peripherals, I saw Willow take her sweet time packing her bag. "Well, yeah. Senior year is coming up, and I want a chance to buy supplies, learn my schedule," *find new friends* … "That kind of thing."

"Well, that's even more of a reason for you to come out to Willow's lake house."

"Willow's lake house?" I glanced over at her. She pretended to be oblivious to the conversation.

"Hey, Will!" Hansen said over his shoulder.

"Don't call me Will." She stepped into our conversation. "I wanted to invite you myself, but Hansen has this theory that girls don't trust each other." *I wonder why.* "So yeah. You can come if you want. It'll be our last chance to hang out. I'll text you the address."

Although the idea of willingly hanging out with Willow didn't sound all that appealing, I knew Melina and Kurt thought a lot of her parents and might actually let me go. One last hurrah before I left Pecan Creek.

"I'll think about it," I told Hansen and Willow, although honestly, I'd already made up my mind.

Chapter 23

Sadie Franklin had never been a screamer, yet my scream made Marigold jump off the couch and run out of the room. The cat passed Kurt, who frantically ran into the room carrying a pile of socks he'd been matching in preparation for the church mission trip to Chicago he was leaving on the next day.

"What's wrong?" he panted, first looking at me and then Melina. I pointed at the paper in my hand. He set his socks on the sofa and took the paper from my shaking fingers, silently reading the words I'd already memorized. "Anatomy and Physiology final grade: A."

Realization that I was screaming out of happiness dawned on him, and he started laughing. "Sadie, you're awesome!" He scooped me into a hug and spun me around the room. "I knew you could do it!"

I gulped for air when he set me down, my face beaming despite the lack of oxygen from the giant hug.

"If I weren't pregnant and short, I'd do the same thing to you." Melina grinned at me.

I'd made a B in literature (which had been taken over by the twins' mom when Melina went out of commission), an A in SAT prep (simply because I'd shown up to class and taken the practice tests), and an A in A&P. My grades hadn't been that good since kindergarten.

Melina clapped her hands, signaling she had an important proclamation to make. "We'll celebrate."

"Ice cream?" My mind immediately fixated on a giant ice cream sundae. Then depression hit at record-breaking speed as I realized that was off limits. I frowned.

"What could possibly be wrong in the middle of this miracle?" Melina reach out her hands and Kurt helped her stand.

"No ice cream for either of us, remember?"

Melina twisted her lips for a moment and then wrapped an arm around me. "We've both been so faithful. Mostly. I think one little cheat won't hurt, don't you?"

I shrugged. I still had memories of those horrible pains, and whenever I didn't pay attention to what I ate, I could feel them all day.

"Oh, come on, Sadie," she enticed. "I won't tell Dr. Summers if you won't …"

I stuck out my hand, and she shook it. "Deal."

Becca and Truitt sat at the bar when we entered the ice cream shop on Main Street. At first, I thought they were on a date and Becca had a few things to explain, but when she jumped out of her seat and wrapped me in a hug, I knew something was up. Sure enough, as Becca released me, I caught the smug expression on Melina's face and understood why she'd spent so long in her bedroom "getting ready." She'd invited them to my celebration.

"Congrats, Sadie!" Becca sang. Truitt came up behind her and high-fived me. I returned his smile.

I hoisted Cooper onto my hip to look at the ice cream flavors at the bar. His eyes immediately widened when he saw the Superman flavor. "That one!" he said, pointing frantically at the rainbow treat.

"Figures he'd want the one with the greatest stain potential," Melina muttered from behind us. Trissy and I had been doing laundry the past couple weeks, but lately it seemed Melina went around looking for a reason to make a point, since she wasn't allowed to do much else.

The girl behind the counter handed Cooper a cake cone piled high with Superman ice cream and then took my order.

"I'll have the double-chocolate fudge lava swirl one," I chirped. "Waffle cone, double scoop." Kurt raised an eyebrow. "Go big, or go home, man," I told him.

Jackson, who'd decided I was "pretty good for a girl cousin," also ordered the double-chocolate fudge lava swirl, and Trissy matched Truitt with her Georgia peach. I still found her innocent little-girl crush hilarious, although I was scared of what she'd do to me if she knew.

While we licked our cones, Truitt, Becca, and Kurt discussed the Chicago trip.

"I've never been to Chicago." I caught a drip of ice cream with my finger and popped it into my mouth. Melina handed me a napkin.

"This'll be our third time," Truitt said. "We work with a church downtown. Sometimes they send us out on construction projects. Sometimes we run a kids' camp. You never know."

"Yeah, and then we tour the city a little bit on the last day of the trip," Becca said between bites of her cappuccino cone.

That all sounded more stressful than enjoyable to me, but I still thought it'd be fun to go. I couldn't, though, because Melina had already asked if I'd help with the kids. That was even before her complications, so I knew there was no way I could go now. I shook my head in disbelief when I realized I was wishing I could go on a church trip.

During our conversation, I watched Truitt out of the corner of my eye. His cat scratches had faded into light pink lines, but they seemed to illuminate whenever he laughed. I couldn't understand why he put up with carrying so much of his mom's financial burden. I'd wanted to ask my aunt and uncle or Becca about it but hadn't. I knew what it was like to have a family life you didn't want the rest of the world to discuss.

Thinking about discussing things with Melina and Kurt reminded me I still hadn't asked if I could go to Willow's party. I'd been so busy studying my eyes out for finals that I hadn't remembered it until now. I glanced at my phone in my lap. The party would be starting in a little less than an hour.

I followed Melina to the restroom while the rest of the group mopped ice cream drippings off the table.

"Sadie, I'm just so proud of you!" She gushed as I held open the door for her.

My cheeks warmed. I was proud of myself too. For once, I'd done something right.

"Looks like I'll be a senior in a few weeks, huh?"

Melina's smile stiffened a little. "Let's not think about your departure tonight, okay?"

"Agreed. But I, *uh,* wanted to ask your permission for something."

Melina leaned against the countertop. "Yes?"

"There's this party. And I know you don't approve of certain kinds of parties, but this one won't be like the last one because it's at an actual house and it's for high school students. And I think—"

"Whose house?"

I inhaled, realizing I had failed to do so while I quickly spilled the details. "Willow Crane's lake house."

"Willow Crane? I thought she hated the very air you breathed."

"Wow, thanks."

"Your words, not mine." Melina put a hand on her stomach. "I know Willow's parents, and I can't see them agreeing to a party without supervision." She peered at me from under her dark bangs.

"It's really at their house, honest." I fished my phone out of my pocket and showed her Willow's text with directions. "Totally legit, see?"

Melina sighed. "I don't know ..."

"Please, Mel." I knew begging was unbecoming, but I couldn't help it. "I worked so hard this summer, and there probably won't be alcohol, but even if there was, I wouldn't even smell it because it's bad for my condition."

Melina sighed. "I'm sure the Cranes would never give alcohol to minors, and I'm still not crazy about the idea, but ..."

"Yes?" I leaned in close.

"I'll run this by Kurt, but you can go on one condition."

"What's that?" *I mean I already do the laundry, the dishes, and a good ⁺ of the cooking.* "Just call me Cinderella."

"No, no. Nothing like that. You can only go if you take Truitt \u."

t was a low blow. "Why not Becca?" I asked.

already said her family is having a movie night. I know you \k very highly of Truitt, but Kurt and I trust him. We trust ⁄ou, and we trust him to pull you out of any situation you might find yourself in. Now I need to go to the bathroom. Go tell your friends bye."

I sighed and marched back to the group waiting by the door. It looked like I'd be spending the evening playing hide-and-seek with the kids. Unless ...

After Becca hugged me good-bye, I climbed into Truitt's truck. He was heading to the Elliots' house to return the yard equipment he'd borrowed for the church lawn. I wasn't concerned with seeing the mower safely returned, but I did need to strike a deal with Truitt.

"No," he said, his eyes on the road ahead.

"But all you have to do is drop me off and pick me back up!"

He gave me a sideways glance. "I'm pretty sure Kurt and Mel wouldn't agree to that. I can't believe you're trying to use me to go behind their back." He swerved to miss a stick in the road. "In case you haven't realized, they basically adore me."

"Oh, please. Besides, I never said you had to leave. You can stay if you want, but I can't promise you won't hear something with more than a PG rating."

"What was the reason Hansen gave for why he was kicked out of school?" *That* was a subtle topic change. Truitt pulled into the driveway and cut Beulah's engine. She wheezed and sputtered before finally going silent.

"He said he was defending Willow's honor or something."

Truitt nodded, his eyes still looking out the window. "That's what I thought. No, Sadie, I won't take you to the party."

I felt my blood pressure rise at being told no. It wasn't that I was spoiled and couldn't handle not getting my way, but I'd been told no one too many times recently. My jaw stiffened. "What does Hansen's act of heroism have to do with anything?"

Truitt sagged against the seat and draped his hands over the steering wheel. "It's a long story. And my answer still stands."

"You know Willow?"

He tilted his head to look at me. "I said it was a long story, meaning I don't want to talk about it."

I unfastened my seat belt. Actually, I just tugged a bit and it carr loose because Beulah's belts had a problem with clicking. Glad know I was safe. Truitt motioned for Kurt to go inside, suggesting that I would help him unload the equipment, so I followed him to the back of the truck and watched him fidget with the tailgate.

"Piece of junk," he muttered under his breath. He must've been really annoyed to talk badly about his pride and joy. The tailgate fell open after a few swift kicks, and Truitt hopped into the back of the truck.

"You know, Truitt," I said as I took the weed eater out of his hands and set it on the driveway, "you never want to talk about anything."

He hoisted the leaf blower over the edge of the truck. "What do you mean? Have you already forgotten about our little conversation in the church parking lot?"

I set the leaf blower on the ground and reached for the red, plastic gas can. "That's exactly what I mean. You never mentioned any of that to me before. Don't you think it would've helped for me to know that when you were going off about how you could 'relate'"—I inserted air quotes here—"to my life?"

Truitt slid the mower to the edge of the truck and hopped down. He stood on one side of the mower, and I stood on the other. We slowly set it on the ground, and my finger got caught under it.

Old habits really do die hard, so I cursed and shook my throbbing index finger.

Truitt shot me a stern look. "Watch your mouth. And forgive me for not flapping my lips about my home life. It's not like you've been an open book either. I've tried to be your friend all summer, and you keep shutting me down."

I put my hands on my hips, keeping my injured finger extended. "Then don't be my friend. Why would you keep trying when I made obvious I had things other than friendship to worry about?"

When Truitt looked down at his shoes, I knew. Call it intuition, e are just some things a girl can read on a guy's face. Truitt hing on me. I coughed so I wouldn't laugh.

but looking at me, he tucked the leaf blower under one arm pulling the lawn mower into the garage with the other. behind with the weed eater and gas can.

"You didn't answer my question, Truitt." I lifted my hair and fanned the back of my neck. The sun was almost behind the trees, but its warmth still seeped through the blanket of humidity to warm the earth.

"My reasons are not a part of this discussion. I won't take you to Willow's house, Sadie. I'm sorry."

"Some friend you are, Truitt. The one time I actually ask you to help me with something, and you tell me no. Even though you could ensure my innocence or whatever you're so concerned with, you still say no." I knew it was a low blow, but I said it anyway before I took time to process it.

He had the audacity to shrug. "I'm sorry."

"You already said that. And until you decide to stop being such a self righteous—I don't know—*something*, you can keep out of my business, okay? I know you're ashamed of your home life, but that's no reason to cover it up by pretending you're some super-spiritual guy. I'm not from an ideal situation either, but you don't see me pretending I have all the answers." *Because I don't have any of the answers.*

"I'm leaving now." He backed away slowly, hands extended, like I was a wild animal.

"Yeah, you do that."

As soon as Truitt pulled Beulah out of the driveway, I texted Hansen. I would go to that party, Truitt or no Truitt.

Chapter 24

Hansen held the door open, and I stepped into a haze. I instructed myself to breathe through my mouth and everything would be okay. Somehow I hadn't pegged health guru Mr. Crane as a heavy smoker. But then again, somehow I knew Mr. Crane had no idea about this party. At least I technically hadn't lied to Melina.

I allowed Hansen to take my hand as he led me through the crowded, wood-paneled living room and into the kitchen. He handed me a can from the cooler, and I accepted it. I didn't have to drink it. In fact, I was pretty sure I wouldn't drink it considering how terrible I felt last time, but at a party like this, it was a status symbol. *Here I am. I'm not afraid to have a good time.*

Willow made her way over to us, her long hair stick straight but as sleek as a seal. A green sundress draped down her petite form. When she glanced down at my outfit of gym shorts and a T-shirt—I couldn't get out of the house in anything more partyish—I noticed she'd gone for the smoky-eye effect.

"Hey, Sadie," she said over the den of teen laughter and bass-heavy music. "Good to see you here."

I peered at her and tightened my grip on Hansen's hand. He responded by weaving his fingers in between mine. "Thank you." My voice was cool.

Turning to Hansen, I said, "My lungs are about to explode. Let's go outside, okay?"

Willow sashayed away, and I caught Hansen's eyes lingering on her even as he said, "Sure."

I led him out to the backyard and down to the dock. "Willow is so dense. Does she really think her parents won't notice the smoke when they get home?"

Hansen shrugged. "They're gone for the whole weekend and this is just a vacation home. She'll open the windows and clean the whole house before they get back. They always think she and her sister clean the house to help them out."

"So this isn't her first party?" I eased onto the dock and let my feet dangle over the edge, just out of reach of the water.

"Ha. No." Hansen sat down beside me, our arms touching. "And it won't be her last."

I tipped my can over the edge of the dock, listening to the sound of its contents splashing into the lake. I set the empty can on the dock, silently celebrating my victory.

Hansen looked at me but didn't say anything. The moon was huge and nearly full, so white against the navy-blue sky. I tilted my head back and sighed.

"Happy?" Hansen nudged me.

"Sure." I turned so my chin rested on my shoulder and noticed how the water reflected the moonlight into his eyes. It was dreamy in a cheesy chick flick sort of way. He dipped his head down, and I knew what was coming. I closed my eyes to accept his kiss, but images of Kurt and Melina flashed into my head. I opened my eyes and pulled away before Hansen reached me.

"What's wrong?" His shadowed face registered confusion.

"It's not you. I just—" *I just saw my aunt and uncle and all I can think about is their commitment to each other.* Why would I think like that at a time like this? All Hansen wanted to do was kiss me, and we'd done plenty of that last time. Why was I suddenly so concerned? I closed my eyes and leaned into Hansen, but instead of fireworks, I heard my conversation in the kitchen with Becca. "I'm already his," she'd said about her future husband, "even if I don't know him yet." I hadn't thought of that conversation since it happened. I shoved those thoughts out of my head, knowing I'd always had control in situations like these. I wouldn't do anything irreversible.

This time, I let Hansen bring his face to mine, although I couldn't shake those images from my head. My heart throbbed against my rib cage. He wove his fingers through my hair. From behind us, the din of the party seemed to be a pulse, like the heartbeat of our moment. I felt myself begin to relax into his kiss as his gentleness pulled me farther from my troubles and deeper into the late summer's night.

Footsteps on the creaky dock broke the trance. "That was fun while it lasted," Hansen whispered. I smiled, even though he probably couldn't see it.

"What is this?" *Willow.*

"Oh, hey, Willow," Hansen said casually, as if we'd merely been star gazing the past ten minutes. "What's up?"

"I can't believe you." She stomped—actually stomped—her bare feet on the dock. "You promised me it wasn't like that anymore." She stuck her finger in his face. "You told me that happened when you let your guard down that one time, and you felt nothing for this—"

Willow called me things I hadn't heard since I came to Pecan Creek. They were enough to make me bristle. I tuned her out. *Breathe, Sadie,* I ordered myself. *Come on. Just breathe. Don't murder her.* Wasn't that in the Bible or something?

"It's not what it looks like." Hansen put a solid foot of space between us. "What you saw meant nothing to me, Willow. Nothing." He repeated it as if he were trying to convince himself.

I stood and brought a hand to my hip. "Really? That moment we just had meant nothing to you? How do you think that makes me feel? 'Oh, Sadie's just a toy I can play with until my ex gets jealous.'"

"No ... I ..." Hansen was speechless. I wanted to see him defend himself.

"Save it, Hansen. We're through," Willow announced as casually as if she'd told him she'd decided to stop eating pizza. "But we," she said as she motioned between herself and me, "are not. How could you come to my house—to my party—and go behind my back after what I told you at the bonfire? I thought I'd been wrong about you and that I could trust you."

"I didn't think that. I just …"

"Of course you didn't think, *Princess*." Willow's voice was venomous, and I noticed the majority of the partiers had moved outside, lightheaded with their drinks and end-of-summer reverie. They probably wanted a show, but I was not their entertainment. Willow, however, didn't seem to care. "Does Hansen even know what's wrong with you?" she asked.

"What are you talking about?" He knew about my life back in Seattle, sure. Unless he'd told her, there was no way she would know. Either way, an information leak like that couldn't hurt at this point.

"You know exactly what I'm talking about. First of all, I could call you out on your hypocrisy. How you pretend to be such a good little girl with your family, then how you turn into this at parties." She motioned between me and Hansen.

"At least I don't call myself a Christian like you do," I retorted.

Willow smiled and it scared me. "I do believe in God, Sadie. But I also believe He wants us to enjoy life. Don't you agree?"

I actually didn't agree. I didn't think God was concerned with our lives at all, much less with our happiness.

But Willow didn't wait for a response. "I'm talking about your 'condition.' What's it called? PCOS?" I laughed. Did she really think that would damage my reputation? That a medical condition was cause for a scarlet letter to be slapped across my chest? Yes, I was angry Mr. Crane had told my problem to his daughter, but really, how much would that hurt me? "Sadie just wants to use you, Hansen. She doesn't have to worry about getting pregnant, so she doesn't have any reservations about—"

"Enough, Willow!" I shoved her, catching her off guard. She fell into the arms of another teen and shoved herself away from him. I refused to have her trample my virtue, little that there was. And it wasn't even for the sake of my own reputation. All I could think about was my aunt and how I couldn't risk bringing any more drama into the house. If she heard rumors like that … I was terrified of what could happen to her and the baby with that much stress hovering around.

"Don't shove me at my own party," Willow hissed, pushing me back. Meanwhile, Hansen still sat on the dock, watching the two of us like we were a Ping-Pong match.

Willow slapped me across the face, coming close enough I could practically see her eyeballs swimming in alcohol. That chick needed to chill.

My mouth tasted metallic, and I realized I'd bitten my lip when she slapped me. I didn't want to make a scene, honestly, but what choice did I have? I shoved her again, and this time she fell to the dock, her hands slapping the splintery wooden boards as she hit the ground.

Hansen chose that moment to stand.

"Don't even try to defend her nonexistent honor, Hansen," Willow said as she slowly stood. Her words reminded me of what Hansen had said at the bonfire, of how he'd been kicked out of school while trying to defend her honor. Then I thought of Truitt and his refusal to come tonight. Could the two be connected?

I didn't have a chance to decide before Willow lunged at me. I felt my shoes slip on the dock, my stomach flutter during the free fall, and my nose and mouth fill with slimy water as I landed in the murky lake. I sank down, my flip-flops coming off my feet as I kicked to reach the surface.

I came up sputtering and choking, reaching for the dock but unable to find it in the darkness.

I couldn't stop choking on the lake water I'd swallowed. It tasted like slime. I bobbed down and struggled to come up. Each time I coughed, more water entered my throat. I went under again, groping for the edge of the dock, even though it was several feet above me. A strong hand grabbed one of my flailing arms. I grabbed onto it as the other hand grabbed my other wrist. I couldn't hear anything above the sound of my attempts to stay above water, until I heard his voice.

"I've got you, Sadie. Stop fighting and hang on!" Strong arms pulled me up until I stared into the face of Truitt Peyton.

Chapter 25

"It's okay. I've got you. Let's go." Truitt spoke in quiet, choppy sentences, but I knew I couldn't have processed anything more. Despite the late summer warmth, I shivered on the dock, water dripping from my clothes and pooling on the ground. Truitt took me by the elbow and gently pushed me through the crowd. "Come on, Sadie."

I followed him through the group of teens who continued on with their laughing and chattering like I hadn't nearly drowned. When we reached Beulah, Truitt left me to go search for a towel. My stomach was full of lake water, and it made me sick. I slid to the ground, head in my hands and heart pounding, ignoring the dirt that clung to my bare feet and clothing. I had yet to catch my breath, so I focused on that. *In and out. In and out.*

"Here." Truitt reappeared and handed me a towel. "Wrap up and let's get out of here." He draped the towel over my shoulders, and I scooted into the cab of the truck. I never thought I'd actually take comfort in sitting on Beulah's nasty seat.

"I can't go home like this." My whisper was drowned out by the sound of Beulah coming to life. "I-I can't go home like this," I said louder.

"I've got this" was his only response.

We drove in silence until Truitt pulled back onto the main highway. Meanwhile, I tried to towel-dry my hair, squeeze out my shirt, and silence my chattering teeth.

"Believe it or not," Truitt said, "Beulah actually has a heater. I use it maybe once a year, so don't hold your breath." He turned a knob and air—cold at first, and then gradually warmer—started pouring out of the vents. It smelled like burnt hair.

"I just want you to know," I said, my voice still shaky, "I didn't drink tonight."

"Oh, I believe you. You never could've taken Willow down had you been inebriated. Your aim isn't the best to begin with." I heard the smile in his voice, but the simple fact that he believed me warmed me.

"Is she okay?"

Truitt flipped off his high beams as a car drove past us. "She's fine, I'm sure. She probably won't remember much in the morning anyway."

I slumped down in my seat and leaned against the window. Truitt pulled into a gas station, and for the first time, I glanced at the clock. It was just after nine thirty. My aunt and uncle weren't expecting me to be home until eleven, so that was one good thing.

"Why were you there, Truitt?" I asked.

"I knew you were dumb enough to go even though I told you not to."

"I don't take orders from you."

Truitt unfastened his seat belt and turned to face me. The light from the gas station filled the cab with an eerie yellow color, illuminating his face.

"Truitt," I said as I drew in a breath, "what's up with your eye?" I fiddled with the overhead light in the truck, but of course it didn't work. My phone had been in my pocket and took a dip in the lake with me, so I grabbed his phone off the seat and shined the light on his face, making him simultaneously squint and wince. The bone beneath his eye was a reddish-purple color. Fresh.

"Baseball," he said, his voice low.

"You were playing baseball between when you left my house and came to the lake?"

He shrugged nonchalantly. "I like the game." Then in the same breath, he said, "Hansen, Willow, and I don't exactly get along. That's why I wasn't comfortable going tonight. Or one of the reasons, at least. I also knew there'd be drinking."

"Why didn't you tell me that?" I crossed my arms over my damp shirt.

"You would've accused me of having a holier-than-thou attitude." What could I say to that? He was probably right. "But, see, it's like this: Hansen and Willow have had this weird on-and-off relationship since like sixth grade. It's ridiculous. The three of us always went to the same summer camps. I had a crush on her my sophomore year of high school, and Hansen caught us talking. That's all we ever did: talk. Never even held that girl's hand. But Hansen didn't care. He doesn't like to share. We've known each other forever, and we've always played ball together. He knows about my mom's problems, but to his credit, he never said anything. I don't know why I'm unloading this on you." He ran a hand over his nonbruised eye.

"No, I want to know," I insisted, leaning toward him slightly.

"Okay. Well, he went off the deep end and started spouting things about my mom—some true, but most nasty lies. I pushed him, but a teacher happened to walk by right as he shoved me down and jumped on top of me, ready to rearrange my face. He'd already had some other run-ins and that was the final straw. It was my first offense, so I just got suspension for a day. Willow still hates my guts because she thinks I'm the reason Hansen got kicked out, which means I'm also the reason her dad doesn't want her around Hansen. And that's why I didn't want to go tonight."

"Oh." It was all I could say. I focused my gaze on the trickle of cars driving down the road and wondered how many of them contained happy and healthy people, driving home to the place where they felt safe, the place where they were loved. I shivered.

"Now you tell me why you wanted to go," Truitt prodded, his voice gentle, but eyes stern.

"I thought Hansen liked me. Turns out he just likes himself. He sat there and let Willow blab about my—" I closed my mouth, not willing to divulge anything more.

"Your what?"

His deep eyes were so kind, so patient despite how I'd treated him earlier that night. Didn't I owe him something?

I took a deep breath. "She said I was just using Hansen because I didn't have to worry about ... consequences."

"Consequences?" His brow wrinkled as he tried to understand.

I decided to just go for it. "I probably can't have kids, Truitt. Which obviously doesn't bother me right now, but unfortunately, that's the least of my concerns." I then launched into an honest description of everything I'd learned about my life recently— including my diagnosis and my family secrets. My voice rose in pitch as I told Truitt about how my life in Seattle had started falling apart when the party got out of hand and Gavin and Reese fought it out on my living room floor. About how the neighbors called the police, who showed up at two in the morning. And how the police called my dad, who came home from work and told me to pack immediately because I would be leaving Seattle earlier than planned. I told Truitt everything, including my dad's last words when he dropped me off at the airport: "Get it together, Sadie. I'll see you in August." Finally, I ended with how this God everyone preached so confidently just sat around and watched me suffer. By the time I finished, tears were dripping down my face, mingling with the lake water still clinging to my hair.

"Oh, Sadie," Truitt whispered. I slid across the seat and sat close to him, leaning my head on his shoulder. Sobs wracked my body, and I buried my head in his shoulder. I felt him stroke my soggy hair over and over, saying, "Sadie, Sadie," in a soothing whisper.

He let me cry until I no longer shook. Until I was too weary to care I'd just soaked his clothes with a cocktail of lake water and salty tears. Leaning close to my face until I was forced to look at him, he said, "It's not over."

"But it is," I cried, breaking eye contact.

He squeezed my shoulder, and we both sat there in the gas station parking lot, in his truck.

After I'd brought my breathing back under control, I whispered, "Don't you dare lie to me, Truitt."

"About what?"

"You didn't get hit in the eye by a baseball tonight. You didn't get hit by a ball the other week either, nor did you accidentally get hit by a bat a few weeks ago. I've seen you play. You're really coordinated. I doubt you even have a cat. Who are you fighting? Hansen?"

"I really do have a cat, and no, I'm not fighting anyone." His voice was low, but strained.

The pieces began fitting together in my head, like a jigsaw puzzle. The bruises. The fact that Truitt was never home. How he always seemed to have a smile and could find an excuse to make everything look better than it was.

"Who is hurting you?" I willed my voice not to break.

He opened his mouth, then closed it, then opened it again, running a hand over his jaw. His breathing quickened, and he glanced at me, then out the window, then back at me. If I'd had any doubts at all, they were put to rest. With the calmest, most sincere voice I could muster, I asked, "Your mom hits you, doesn't she, Truitt?"

If I hadn't been looking for it, I would've missed it. But I saw it. I saw the tear drip down his face.

I didn't ask him why he put up with it. I didn't ask him why he didn't tell someone or why his pride was too big to make a change. For all his shortcomings, my dad never hurt me. He'd never hit me, but I'd never told anyone he'd left me alone at night since I was little. Never told anyone he forgot to buy groceries and fix dinner or that he forgot to drive me to school. Somewhere inside, really deep inside, I knew I could never betray my dad, simply because he was my dad, and I was a part of him. He was all I had left in the world, just like Truitt's mom was all he had left in the world.

Truitt loved his mom, even though their situation was very serious. I couldn't tell him to tell someone—even Kurt—because I knew he was smart enough to know what he needed to do. He needed to change, but more than that, he needed the courage to change. Truitt was every bit as broken as I was. I got that. Where was God, really, when we were forced to watch the sky fall, forced to feel the shards scrape us and beat us and leave us broken? We were just two kids with too much pain.

Something inside me shifted as we sat there, side by side, each in our own murky, complicated grief. I saw Truitt sitting there, so tender and kind, and my emotions swelled. I wanted to stay close to him. Despite everything else I'd thought about him that summer, I wanted Truitt Peyton to kiss me.

I tilted my head up again. "Truitt?" I whispered, my voice husky from tears.

His dark, damp eyes locked with mine. "Yeah?"

I leaned up in reply, slowly bringing my face to his. Inching closer, closer ...

At the last second, he turned his head. "Sadie, don't. Please."

I sat up, my face heating. "What's wrong?"

"First of all, we're two teenagers alone in a truck in an empty parking lot at night both trying to process our emotions. That would've been the most unwise decision ever."

I slid back to my side of the truck. I turned to face him and leaned against the door. "And the second?"

"Well," he said as he shifted his eyes to his hands and then to something outside of the truck. He swallowed. I had my answer.

"Oh, I see," I said quietly. The truth hurt and made me angry. "I see you don't like me like I thought. It's because I don't believe the same as you, right? You're so judgmental."

"Listen, Sadie." He sighed and rubbed the back of his neck. "No matter what I feel—and I'm not judging you at all—it's not about that. It's about you thinking you have to pay people for their kindness. Or to feel comfort and belonging."

I crossed my arms over my chest. "What are you talking about?" My voice wobbled, though my teeth were clenched.

"I mean I've seen you do this before. You—"

I started to interrupt, but he put his hand up, all tears now evaporated. "Let me finish. That whole thing with Hansen? I'm willing to bet it was an attempt to make him like you. You were afraid if you didn't 'pay' him, he'd leave you."

"That's not true," I whispered.

Truitt continued like I hadn't said anything. "You think physical affection is like some sort of currency or something. And it's not.

There's nothing you can do to make people love you. Believe me. Nothing." He sighed. "Listen, Sadie. I know this sounds kind of harsh, but I'm trying to be your friend. A true friend. You were about to kiss me just then, but not because you really care about me on a heart level. It's because you want to make sure you've got everything you need. You desperately want someone you can count on, because people have never done anything other than let you down."

I looked down at my lap, my legs covered in chill bumps I couldn't see. A tear dripped onto my leg. I quickly brushed my eyes with my hands. "Why are you saying this stuff, Truitt? What have I done to you?"

He shook his head. "Nothing. But that's the point. I'll let you down. You'll let me down. We're humans; that's how it works. That's also why we need Jesus, who won't let us down."

I sat upright and stuck out my hand. "No, don't go there. He has let me down. Don't you see how messed up my life is? Don't you see how everything I've ever had has fallen apart? Why would I want to trust someone who doesn't care enough about me to let one little thing turn out right?" I was screaming, but I didn't care.

"How can you be so blind, Sadie?" All traces of tenderness were gone, replaced by a tone so sharp I pressed my back against the door. "God's taken you out of the mess you had in Seattle, and He's put you in a family of people who genuinely care about you—who love you. He's worked things out so you could find out why you've been in pain for so long, and He's given you the opportunity to catch up in school so you can graduate on time. He let you live all those years ago; He created you when doctors said it wasn't possible, for Pete's sake! How much more 'right' do you need?"

I tugged at my wet hair, my eyes burning from lake water, from tears, from frustration. "And what about you? You act like you've got it all together in the faith department, when really you don't want anyone to know your alcoholic mother hurts you. Or is it when you try to keep 'evil' away from her? You can't do that on your own, Truitt. You're human just like I am."

Truitt worked his jaw back and forth. "I'm almost eighteen. I'm strong and coordinated. I can't tell people I get beat up by a woman half my size. By my own mother. I'll work it out, somehow. I've done it ever since Dad ran off with Mom's replacement and ever since I became the man of my house. God hasn't let me down so far."

"But God's given you a brain, and He expects you to use it. I know the Bible says that whole 'honor your parents' thing, but she's intentionally hurting you, Truitt."

"You know what? I never should've told you any of that. It's really none of your business." I could tell I'd just picked a scab that wasn't quite healed, and it was about to start bleeding out in Truitt's words.

I turned and looked out the window into the darkness. No stars sprinkled across the sky. No moon shone like earlier that night. They'd been masked by clouds. Just darkness remained. Cruel, inky blackness. That's what I felt like on the inside. Any star of hope I might have had had been covered up or put out all together.

"Take me home, Truitt."

He nodded and cranked the truck. As we drove into the city limits of Pecan Creek, I leaned my head against the window, watching the streetlights pass by. Tears brimmed and then spilled unchecked from my eyes, down my cheeks, off my chin. I couldn't stop them. I didn't even try. I cried for my mess of a life. I cried for Truitt's mess of a life. I cried for two kids who just wanted their mamas back and didn't know the affection of their daddies.

I felt like I was melting, like I was dissolving into a puddle and nothing could put me back together.

I squeezed my eyes shut. *Mom, I need you.* What would my mom do at a time like this? The answer to my question came to me softly, and it gave me chills. *Pray.* No. No way. My mom had prayed all the time, and she still died. Lot of good that did her.

The tears kept coming. On the other side of the truck, Truitt stared straight ahead, seemingly without blinking.

Fine. I'd try it just this once. *God,* I began, feeling awkward to be approaching the One I'd been at odds with for most of my life, *it's Sadie. Why are You letting this happen? Why don't You really care like I once thought You did? I mean every time something starts to look up, I get knocked down yet again. I'm sick of my life.*

I didn't know if you'd call those prayers or accusations, but I decided that was enough. I'd heard no answer, just Beulah's stuttering engine.

We pulled into the driveway minutes before my curfew. Truitt watched me climb out in silence. His eyes looked sad, empty. I looked at them for a moment, unable to turn away from such palpable emotional pain.

But then I did turn away. I turned away, and I didn't let myself process what I'd seen. I'd felt far too much tonight, and the damage could quite possibly prove to be my undoing.

Chapter 26

....

I had trouble sleeping. Every time I closed my eyes, I dreamed I was underwater, watching my life play out through blurred vision as I looked up through the ripples. I could feel Truitt's grip on my wrist, feel the warmth of his strong arms wrapped around me. The only things I saw clearly were his deep, dark eyes. Eyes brimming with tears waiting to fall on his cheeks.

Those dreams were too much. They made me analyze too thoroughly and feel too deeply. I crawled onto the couch that night, leaving the lamp on, imagining it emitted warmth to chill my bones that had yet to thaw from the lake.

At six thirty the next morning, I woke from sleep I didn't know I'd found when Kurt flipped on the light.

"Oh! Sorry, Sadie!" he whispered, clicking it back off so only the lamp's light remained.

"It's okay. I'm up anyway." I stretched my sore shoulders. Unless Truitt had told them, they still didn't know about last night's events. I'd managed to climb into the shower before they could ask questions, so they didn't even know about the dip in the lake. By the time I'd come out, Melina was in bed and Kurt was trying to pack last minute things for the trip.

Melina waddled into the living room, finally looking less stressed after her time on bed rest. Although, at nearly eight months pregnant, she also looked huge, but I would not be the one telling her that.

"Got everything?" Melina asked Kurt, handing him a travel coffee mug and a cinnamon roll. I hadn't heard her moving in the kitchen.

"I think that's it. You sure you're okay with me going?" Kurt sipped his coffee and studied his wife's face.

"I'm sure. I talked to the doctor's office yesterday, and they said from the sound of things, we're all healthy and on track for delivery at the beginning of September, as long as I keep away from unhealthy foods." She hungrily eyed his cinnamon roll as Kurt took a bite, probably before she started drooling on his white Pecan Creek Baptist T-shirt. Temptation gone, she snapped back to attention. "Besides, I've got Sadie, and Lydia Shepherd's on standby since you're taking my babysitter."

She smiled at me, and I waved from my seat on the couch. I realized with a pang that I'd be back in Seattle before Bean came. Those months spent getting to know the baby's movements and reactions to different situations, of feeling him or her connect a tiny heel to my palm, would end soon, but I wouldn't be able to meet my cousin face to face. Sure there'd be video chatting, but it wouldn't be the same.

This was Pecan Creek's public school system's last full week of summer break. When Becca and Truitt came home from the mission trip, they'd only have a couple of days before heading into school again. I flew back to Seattle the following week. I couldn't think like that right now. I shook my head and stood.

"Be careful out there, Kurt, and remember not everyone practices southern hospitality," I said.

"Oh, believe me, I know." He winked at me and set his cup and empty napkin on the coffee table. "Come here, kid." I let him wrap me in his arms, let him strengthen my fatigued frame with his stability. I remembered when he first hugged me at the airport and how I'd stood stiff. This time I wrapped my arms around his middle and realized I'd actually miss the big clown.

"Bye, Kurt." My words came out as a squeak as he squeezed me tight.

"Bye, Sadie. I love you, kid."

He released me and turned to Melina, but I felt a little clamp in my heart as yet another painful realization hit me: Kurt was the first man—not loser high school boy, but man—to tell me he loved me. I'd never heard those words from my father. I didn't even know how often Mom had heard those words from my father.

I sniffed and sat back on the couch.

"Come here," Kurt said to his wife. He placed his hands on her middle. "All right, Bean. You behave now, you hear? Cousin Sadie's gonna be a good influence for you, okay?" He looked at me, and I made a face. He stood and took Melina in his arms. "Bye, Mel. I'll see you Saturday."

He gently took her face in his big hands and bent down to kiss her. I have to admit it might have been the sweetest, most love-filled kiss I'd ever seen. Something about it was different than the movies, different than my own kisses. It was purer, truer in a way I couldn't peg. And it proved to me that their love couldn't be shaken by disagreements or stress-inducing nieces.

Melina leaned back and looked him in the eyes. "Bye, beloved."

That did it. The sun wasn't even up, and I'd already maxed out my sappy quota for the entire week. I tried not to gag. Kurt and Mel exchanged I-love-yous, and then he grabbed his luggage and left us in the living room.

We faced each other, Melina raising her hands and then letting them flop to her sides. "Well, on to business as usual. Want some coffee?"

***

Saturday and Sunday came and went. Kurt, Officer Pete, and my friends were all on the mission trip, which left me and a couple of random people in youth group led by some of the college students I met at the lake.

The weekend exhausted Melina, since she'd been used to lying around the house all day, so Monday morning she invited Becca's mom over for a leisurely cup of coffee. Hope tagged along and entertained Trissy, while Jackson, Cooper, and I attempted to assemble the old baby cradle we'd pulled out of the garage. I tried to remain in control of the situation, but the directions were missing and our conversations ended up being one-sided with a bunch of

> "Cooper, get that screw out of your mouth!"
> "Jackson, seriously, you're too heavy for that."
> "Has anyone seen the screwdriver?"
> "No, that's not a sword!"

We finally figured it all out by lunch. While Cooper and Jackson had their down time that afternoon, and Melina and Lydia Shepherd enjoyed their fourth cup of decaf, Trissy and Hope helped me wash some baby clothes and some packages of spit-up rags and bibs people had given the family. Because Bean was the fourth Elliot baby, Melina said they'd only had a small baby shower at church the month before I flew out to Pecan Creek, but the amount of baby supplies was massive.

All of the preparations made me excited to meet my little cousin, so I had to keep reminding myself it would be a while. Money was tight on both ends, but I hoped I could try to find a job this year to earn money and fly out to Pecan Creek over Christmas break. I also needed to pay them back for some of my expenses they'd covered. My dad barely sent anything, and I'd seen the look on Kurt's face as he wrote the check for Mel's emergency hospital visit. They literally had next to nothing.

It made me hate myself even more to think of how I'd been partying and drinking and sneaking out when they were willing to scrape change and make sure I had everything I needed. When I told them I'd dropped my phone in the lake, they even bought me a temporary replacement until my contract was up. I couldn't understand why they were being so generous. I still had my "We want to convert Sadie" theory, but I rarely even heard them mention Bible verses. They were just … genuine.

The person who wasn't genuine, or one of them at least, was Hansen Avery. And I so knew this, but I foolishly answered his phone call Tuesday after dinner.

"Can we talk?" He sounded like he was in a hurry. Was Willow coming around the corner?

"Fair warning: I'm hanging up on you," I responded, way too into the Veggie Tales movie I was watching to put up with him. How had I missed out on a hilarious talking tomato and cucumber duo for sixteen years?

"No, don't! Hear me out, Princess."

I slid Cooper off my lap and handed the remote to Trissy, who eyed me like a hawk. "Fine," I said, hopping over Jackson's chunky little form on the floor. "You've got five seconds."

"I actually think we should meet up in person."

"Hansen, I—"

"Look, I start school back next week, and you leave after that. It wouldn't be fair if I didn't get the chance to tell you bye."

I walked into the bedroom and studied my face in the mirror while I talked. He made a good point, but … "Willow doesn't have a problem not telling me good-bye."

Hansen groaned. "Forget that, okay? Just … please. Walk down to the end of the street, and I'll pick you up. We won't be gone more than an hour."

I frowned in the mirror, examining the worry lines I'd never noticed before this summer. "Fine. Pick me up at the corner of Magnolia and Camellia in five minutes." I ended the call before I agreed to anything else.

After changing into jogging clothes and telling Melina I was going for a walk but would be back before dark—and that, yes, I had my phone—I slipped out of the house and jogged down the street, loving every pavement-pounding step. I'd missed jogging so much. The Internet said it wouldn't damage anything to jog, but the pain was usually enough to keep me inside. This pain-free interval felt so good.

When Hansen wasn't at the meeting place yet, I jogged back to the house and then back to our spot, just because I didn't hurt.

I was smiling to myself when Hansen pulled up and rolled down his window. "Good to see you too, Princess. Hop in."

We drove through town and out past the church and then kept going past Cobblestone Estates. I thought of Truitt and his issue with Hansen but knew that scab didn't need to be picked. Especially if this was good-bye for Hansen and me.

A couple of miles beyond Truitt's neighborhood, Hansen turned onto a dirt road. We drove through the narrow pathway until he stopped a few feet from a creek. He climbed out, and I followed suit.

"Where are we?" I asked, squinting up at the early-evening sunlight peeking through the treetops and thinking this probably wasn't the wisest decision.

"Pecan Creek."

I gasped. "So it does exist!" I sounded like a little kid, but I'd been curious about this place all summer. "But it's so tiny. You'd think it'd be bigger if a whole town was named after it."

Hansen sat on the grassy bank, and I joined him. "It gets bigger. There's even a little waterfall. It starts at a freshwater spring a few miles farther out of town."

I ran my hands through the grass and breathed in the earthy smell of the woods. "Why didn't they name the town Pecan Springs if that's why this is here?"

Hansen tossed a pebble into the water. I listened to the faint splash and took in the gentle gurgle of the creek as it tickled my ears. "Because that, Princess, would be ridiculous. And as you're well aware, everything about this town makes perfect sense." He winked at me and draped an arm over my shoulders. I shrugged it off.

"What?"

"It's too hot. I just need air," I lied.

Really, though, I knew he'd try to kiss me, and I knew now that's not what I wanted. There was no way it'd live up to the image of a perfect kiss I had in my mind after seeing my aunt and uncle's moments this summer. They weren't even fiery, fireworks moments, but there was something more. Something deeper. And a relationship with Hansen could go no deeper than this measly little creek.

"Come on, Sadie. I'd been drinking. I didn't mean what I said to Willow."

I laughed at that. "You'd had, like, two sips max. You were completely sober."

He lay back on the grass and used his arm to shield his eyes from the sun streaming down through the treetops. He tilted his head just enough to look up at me. "But I'm here now. With you and only you. I want to remember good times with you. And it's my last chance."

I, me, me, I. It was all about Hansen. I shrugged him off again as he tried to pull me down next to him.

"I won't bite, Sadie," he teased, although I couldn't be sure. "Watch the sun set with me." That did sound romantic, but the sunset reminded me of my promise to be back before dark, and the woods were already shrouded in long shadows.

"I actually need to go. I told my aunt I'd be back before dark."

He sat up and rested his arms on his knees. "The one time you care about being a good girl, and it's our last chance."

"I lied to her, Hansen. I told her I was jogging. I've gotta get back before dark."

He plucked a handful of grass and tossed it into the water. "Okay."

I thought that was the end of it until we reached the truck. "Are you sure we can't hang out longer? Let's go to my house. No one else will be there. Tell your aunt you're hanging with a friend. That won't be a lie." He seemed almost desperate to hold onto me longer. He pulled me to him. I pushed back.

"No. I don't like you like that, Hansen. And I may have led you on in the past, but we can't go any farther. It's not worth it."

He scuffed his foot in the dirt. "Willow will disagree." He was trying to make me jealous.

I tried not to gag. The sun was almost completely gone by now. Everything looked gray. "I wish you'd reconsider, Hansen. I'm no expert, but there's gotta be something more to live for than flirty flings and one-night stands, you know?"

He leaned against his truck. "Maybe so, but until I find it, I'll find my own happiness." His words reminded me about how Willow said she believed God just wanted us to enjoy life. That's what Willow and Hansen were doing, but they seemed anything but happy. They still seemed empty somehow.

We climbed into the truck and rode in silence. When we arrived back at our meeting place, he watched me climb out of the truck.

I closed the door and took a step back. "I guess it's good-bye," I said through the open window. "Thanks for being my friend at co-op. I mean that."

He shrugged. "I'd do it again in a heartbeat. And I will, if you ever come back to Pecan Creek."

I nodded. It was all I knew to do. "Okay." I fought everything in me to go back to him, back to the way I was only a few weeks ago when I'd do anything to feel wanted. Instead, I forced my feet to take another step back, to let the fresh air infiltrate our hazy relationship and dissolve it.

"Bye, Princess."

"Bye, Handsome." I smiled. He smiled. I turned and ran back to the house before my resolve crumpled and I returned to the first person who accepted me for who I was and made me feel wanted. I had to believe that somewhere, somehow, there was more to reach for. So much more.

Chapter 27

....

Hansen and I weren't dating by anyone's standards, but I felt like I'd experienced a breakup. Maybe I had. I'd left a part of me, a part of my life, back there at the corner of Magnolia and Camellia all because I couldn't get Becca's words, Kurt and Mel's actions, and Truitt's observation out of my head. I'd followed the wisdom of people I'd disagreed with the most.

I took deep breaths as I stepped out of the twilight and into the kitchen. A cinnamon candle burned near the stove, and Melina had finished cleaning up the dishes I'd promised to do when I got back.

"Why?" My aunt's voice cut through the sleepy evening silence.

I jumped and saw her sitting at the table. "Why what? The sun literally went down, like, two seconds ago."

Melina stood slowly, her hand on her swollen abdomen. "Where were you?"

"I was running." I wiped a trail of sweat off my forehead to lend some authenticity to my statement.

"Is that all?"

I swallowed. I could've really used a glass of water. "I happened to run into someone on my way down the street, but I mean it was no big deal."

She peered at me, her vivid green eyes seeming to pierce through me. "You're lying. This is me calling your bluff. I stepped outside to water the potted plants on the porch and happened to look down the street." She narrowed her eyes even more. "Right as you climbed into Hansen Avery's truck."

I looked at the candle's tiny little flame. I looked out the window into the darkness. I looked everywhere but at my aunt, trying to find my way out of this one. "I—"

Melina held up a hand to silence me. She put a hand on her stomach and breathed deeply. Braxton Hicks. Stress. Melina hadn't had one of those contractions in a couple of days, but still, any stress was bad stress at this point. According to my anatomy textbook, she was still several days from her pregnancy being full-term.

The false contraction passed right as Jackson entered the kitchen, saving me from the grilling I was about to get.

Melina followed him into the living room. "We'll talk about this later," she said over her shoulder.

Fortunately, later didn't come. Unfortunately, I couldn't shake the feeling in my gut that felt strangely like a conscience. I'd been going behind Melina's back all summer and behind others' backs longer than that, so why did I feel bad now?

Melina came into the bathroom while I brushed my teeth that night and said she was going to bed early. Then she did her usual "We'll start over in the morning" spiel and waddled into her room.

I crawled into bed that night and tried to focus on something good. It was hard, really, especially since Pecan Creek had turned out nothing like I'd expected. Next week, I'd start packing to go back to Seattle, but I honestly couldn't think of anything worth it there. I wanted a chance to hang out with Becca more, to fix things with Truitt, to meet Bean.

I rolled onto my side to face Trissy. I wanted a chance to get to know my cousins better. I'd come so obstinately sure I wouldn't let myself form attachments, but I was even going to miss that whacky little redhead sleeping next to me and our random "cousin bonding" conversations at night.

I definitely needed sleep if my thoughts were headed toward sentimentality.

***

I was under water again. This time, when I looked up, I saw a blurry female figure looking down at me, like I was a minnow in a puddle. "Sadie Grey," she said, and I instantly knew it was my mom. "Come with me."

"I'm coming!" I tried to speak, but the water garbled my voice and filled my lungs. I tried to wave my hands and let her know I was on my way, but my limbs were so heavy. I kept sinking farther and farther down. Farther and farther away from my mom.

"Sadie Grey. Come with me, baby."

I began to cry, but my tears just mixed with the murky water until I wasn't even sure I was crying. My chest felt heavy as my lungs continued to fill with water. I tried to clear my throat, but more water rushed in. I started to choke.

***

"Sadie! Come with me!"

I bolted upright in bed, finding myself tangled in sheets and covered in sweat instead of lake water. My eyelids felt heavy; I'd been crying.

Trissy still slept next to me, which meant I hadn't cried out in my sleep. Although knowing that kid, I could've sung opera in my sleep and she wouldn't have stirred.

I started to lie back down until I noticed Melina standing beside the bed.

Light from the hallway made her form glow, although it was still too dark to decipher her features.

"Sadie Grey. Come with me." I recognized the words from my dream. How long had she tried to wake me up?

I unwrapped myself from the bed sheet and followed her into the hall.

Scrubbing my eyes, I croaked, "What's wrong?"

"It's the baby. Or me. I don't really know. I have those pains in my sides again and a headache, but I've been vomiting too, and can't keep anything down."

My eyes were semiworking by that point, so I looked at her and was surprised by the fear I saw in her face. "What about contractions?"

She leaned against the wall. "Every now and then, but I've been having those off and on all along, so I didn't think much of it until tonight. I think I need to go to the hospital."

"What do I do?" I had no idea what time it was, but it had to be the middle of the night. I had a good reason for not being very coherent.

"Go get dressed, and I'll call Lydia Shepherd to come keep the kids."

I rolled my neck, trying to loosen my stiff muscles. "I can keep the kids."

She put a hand on arm. "No. I want you with me."

***

I drove to Augusta while Melina clutched a mini–garbage can in the passenger seat. We didn't talk to each other or turn the radio on, but every now and then I heard my aunt whisper prayers, her eyes closed, one hand on the can and the other on her stomach.

We reached the hospital at a quarter after one in the morning, where my aunt had called in advance. We entered the big lobby of St. Paul's Hospital, which was nearly empty. I was thankful we didn't have to sit in the ER. Thinking about the stuff you might see in the ER at one fifteen on a Tuesday night—or Wednesday morning, rather—freaked me out.

On the elevator ride up to the maternity floor, Melina sat on a bench, shaking. She looked so small and scared, like a little girl.

"Want to know the scary part?" She turned big, anxious eyes on me.

Of course I didn't want to know, but she'd wanted me to tag along, so I knew I should at least make myself useful. "What's the scary part?"

She wrapped both hands protectively around her middle. "I'm not having contractions. This isn't labor."

If she wasn't in labor, then something had to be very, very wrong. I knew that much. I wanted to reassure her and tell her everything would be okay, but I couldn't. Because there were no guarantees that everything would be okay. There were no guarantees that God would stick His hand down here and intervene.

Instead of speaking, I reached over and gently took her hand. The elevator dinged, and we stood, slowly making our way to the nurses' station so Melina's dizziness wouldn't take over. She curled her clammy fingers around mine and squeezed.

We didn't have words, but we didn't need them. Although I was the worst possible candidate for a comforter, I was all Melina had. Her husband was more than eight hundred miles away. *Her husband. Kurt!*

I nudged Melina. "Should I go call Kurt?"

We followed nurse down a stark white hallway. "I don't know. Maybe. No, not yet. Let's see what the doctor says first. That's all I need is to worry about him driving home in the middle of the night." I'd never seen her so indecisive.

"How long does it take to get home from Chicago?"

She brought a hand to her forehead, and I noticed sweat beading on her brow. "Something like thirteen hours, maybe."

That was it. I needed to go behind Melina's back one more time. If Melina was thinking clearly, she'd know how big a deal this was. If something happened, it would kill Kurt to be so far away. So while Melina changed into a hospital gown and began describing her symptoms in her vivid, tell-it-like-it-is (read: gross) way, I slipped into the hall and found a nearby restroom.

What time was it in Chicago, anyway? Were they on Eastern Time, or an hour behind? Remarkably, I'd passed geography on my first attempt the year before. I glanced at the time on my phone as I pulled it out of my purse. Like time even mattered. It was the middle of the night, no matter where you were in the country.

While the phone rang, I paced in the tiny stall. *Half step, turn. Half step, turn. Don't trip on your own feet and fall into the toilet. A self-inflicted swirly is the last thing you need right now.*

"Hello?" Kurt's gravelly night voice answered the phone right before my call went to voice mail.

"Kurt! It's Sadie."

"Sadie? Wha—what time is it?"

I threaded my fingers through my tangled hair.

"It's, like, one thirty in the morning in Augusta. I don't know what time it is in Chicago."

"Did you say *Augusta?*" Kurt's voice rose, and I knew he must've left the room he was sharing with the other guys.

"Yeah. Listen, Kurt. Melina woke me up. Her sides hurt, and she's dizzy. She's been puking. Becca's mom is watching the kids, and we're at the hospital."

"Can I talk to my wife?" Kurt sounded panicked.

"No, the nurse is getting her into bed for monitoring or something. I don't even know what they're doing. I need to go check."

"Tell Melina I'm on my way." I heard a crinkle that sounded like he was ripping open a granola bar wrapper.

"She doesn't know I'm calling you. She told me not to because she didn't want to worry about you driving home in the middle of the night."

"Ah, forget her," he said. "No, that came out wrong. I meant I'm coming anyway. You don't have to tell her. I'll call Lydia and let her know. Maybe I should fly …"

"Save that money for Bean's college fund." I knew they didn't have money to just buy a plane ticket. "She's not in labor."

I heard Kurt take a deep breath. "Lord, give me wisdom … Okay. I'm leaving Chicago in about five minutes. I'll find a car somehow."

"Be careful, Kurt."

"I will. Look after Mel for me, okay? Remind her she's my world."

I swallowed an unexpected lump in my throat. "I will. See you."

I was about to end the call when Kurt spoke up again. "I love you, Sadie."

The lump came back for round two. "I know," I whispered.

Chapter 28

....

Preeclampsia. I turned the word over in my mind, trying to remember if I'd learned about it in anatomy. I hadn't, so I asked the doctor for an explanation.

"It's a very serious condition," Dr. Summers said, her eyes on a blood pressure monitor. "Melina's hypertension escalated in severity, causing her—"

"I'm sorry." I stuck up my hand. "But I'm a kid and it's the middle of the night. Can you give it to me straight?"

Dr. Summers smiled. "Sure. Basically, Melina's high blood pressure condition came back with a vengeance—and it kicked her symptoms into high gear. We have to keep a close eye on her because in severe cases, seizures or stroke can come out of this." She lowered her voice. "Not to mention the baby's blood supply could be compromised."

I felt the color drain from my face. "All of this comes from being a little stressed out?"

"Well, yes and no." Dr. Summers scribbled something on a chart. "There's no definite cause of preeclampsia, but stress can contribute to it."

My knees wobbled, and I sat in the hard-cushioned chair. It squeaked awkwardly beneath me. "How can you cure that?" I looked over at Melina, whose eyes were closed as a nurse worked to insert an IV into her forearm. I quickly looked back at Dr. Summers.

"The only way to 'cure' preeclampsia is to deliver the baby."

What? Bean is going to be born tonight? Will Kurt miss it? Dr. Summers must've noticed the look of panic that crossed my face, because she added, "Melina is just shy of thirty-six weeks pregnant, which is what we consider to be full term. We need to see how developed the baby's lungs are before delivery and possibly give the baby some steroids to speed up the lungs' development. We'd like for the baby to stay for as long as possible, but if we can give the steroids a good forty-eight hours to do their job we won't have to worry so much. At this point, we'll let Melina rest and monitor her and the baby's heart rate."

I nodded and studied Melina's face. She looked so small and pale in the hospital bed. I left the room and paced the hallway as Dr. Summers and the nurses finished situating Melina.

"Get some rest, Melina," I heard Dr. Summer's say through the cracked door. "We could have a baby before long, so consider this a vacation."

Dr. Summers stepped into the hallway, where I'd started doing calf stretches to keep myself calm. "Will you be staying with her?" she asked, peering at me with an are-you-sure-you're-mentally-stable look on her face. I jumped up and nodded.

"Good." She patted my shoulder. "We're monitoring heartbeats, but the volume's turned down so the two of you can rest. We're giving Melina fluids and something to help her rest. Don't let her get worked up about anything, okay?"

I almost—*almost*—made a face but caught myself right as I realized it wouldn't be the mature thing to do. Dr. Summers didn't actually know me well. I mean she knew my insides better than I did, which was weird, but she didn't know me as a person. She was just joking.

I went back into the room. The lights were dimmed and Melina's eyes were closed. I stretched out on the chair next to her bed and unfolded the blanket a nurse had brought me. I took a shaky breath and closed my eyes. My last thoughts before falling into a fitful sleep were *Please, God, don't let her die.*

When I woke up, it was dark except for a faint light coming from the hallway. I glanced at my phone and saw it was just before five in the morning. At first, I couldn't remember where I was until I felt the chair beneath me. I sat up, wincing at the pain in my right hip and shoulder from sleeping on one side. I rubbed my eyes, wondering why I was awake. Then I heard Melina moan.

I jumped up and leaned over her bed. "Melina! What's wrong?"

She shuddered. "Look at the monitor. My baby—"

I looked at the monitor and noticed the baby's heart rate seemed faster than it had earlier. Whereas it had resembled a steady trot earlier, now it was more like a canter.

"Sadie, call the nurse. My baby …"

I pushed the call button on her hospital bed and began pacing the room. A moment or two later, a nurse came in, dressed in yellow scrubs that were way too cheery for so early in the morning.

The nurse gradually slid the dimmer light until the room was well lit. She pushed buttons on the monitor, and the room came alive with the rapid pulsing sound. *Ba-BUMP, ba-BUMP, ba-BUMP.*

Despite her worry, Melina smiled, and her face muscles relaxed a little bit. "Hear that, Sadie?" She laid her head on her pillow. "That's my baby."

While the nurse explained that, yes, the baby's heart rate was up a bit, but it wasn't cause for much concern. I sat still, mesmerized. I'd seen pictures of Bean, I'd felt Bean move, but this? This was Bean's heart. A living, beating heart belonging to a tiny person. Bean's life seemed more real to me as I listened to the rhythmic pulses. The baby was every bit as human and alive as I was. And the baby was in distress.

Melina asked if the monitor could stay on so she could listen to her baby, and the nurse dimmed the lights and left. I sank into the chair, my eyes watery. I could easily blame it on lack of sleep, but that wasn't it. I couldn't help but feel responsible for putting the baby—and my aunt—in danger. While I'd been lying, partying, drinking, cursing, and blurring lines with Hansen, Bean had been growing, developing. And I'd jeopardized that.

I didn't realize I was crying until Melina said, "It's going to be all right, Sadie Grey." Great. I was supposed to be the one offering encouragement. That was short-lived.

I ran a hand under my eyes. "You don't know that," I whispered. "If something bad happens, I won't be able to live with myself. This is my fault."

"Why is it your fault, Sadie?"

I inhaled through a stuffy nose. "I'm the reason you're stressed. If I'd never come, you wouldn't be worrying about finances. You wouldn't be wondering where I was when I snuck out, or what bad things I'm teaching your kids, or what I've been drinking, or what I've been doing with guys. I've gone against everything you and Kurt believe is right." *I'm also the reason you've been arguing with each other.* I grabbed a tissue off the bedside table and blew my nose. "I'm the reason you and Bean are in danger right now, way before your baby should be born. Everything I do is a mistake ..." I paused. "But what can you expect from someone who *is* a mistake?"

"Hush, Sadie," Melina said, her voice stern. "You are not a mistake."

I pulled my knees to my chest. "I'm the reason Mom and Dad got married but were never happy. I'm the reason we were in the car driving to soccer practice the day Mom was killed. I'm a living, breathing disaster." I dropped my head to my knees. "I hate myself so much, and if Bean dies, I won't even try anymore."

"Who says Bean is going to die?" Melina scooted to a sitting position in bed and straightened the hospital gown that had fallen off her shoulder.

In a voice barely loud enough to be heard over the fetal monitor, I said, "I heard about Bailey." Where did that come from? Why did I always ruin everyone's attempts at sweet moments by bringing up something terrible from the past? I fiddled with my hands in my lap. Now was the worst possible time to bring up the death of a baby while this baby was in danger.

Melina opened her mouth and then pressed her lips into a straight line. She took a deep breath through her nose. "Bailey's death was a very dark time in our lives, Sadie. I'll be honest. And though I only got to hold her little shell of a body after she was born, I have hope I'll hold her again someday. Until then, she's in the arms of Jesus, who loves her more than I ever could." Melina rubbed her stomach. "But it pulled Kurt and me closer together right as we were farther apart from each other than we'd ever been. God used Bailey's life to heal a marriage. God had a plan for Bailey."

I pulled my head up and rested my chin on my knees. "I thought you and Kurt had the perfect marriage."

Melina did a combination of a sigh and a laugh. "Oh, dear child. Where have you been all summer? Marriage requires conscious effort, no matter who you are. Kurt was so busy with church things, and I was so busy with home things, that we grew apart. We let stress come between us and stopped confiding in each other. We were still married technically, but at the heart level, we were very far apart. And what good is technical marriage if your hearts aren't entwined? We married young, and Bailey's death grew us up a lot, even though we already had two children. I—I had to confess some ... some things from my past so we could truly move forward. I shouldn't be rambling. I'm just trying to stay distracted ..."

I pulled my blanket into my lap and folded it. I wouldn't be sleeping anymore tonight. "No, it's okay." I needed distraction too. Desperately. "What do you mean about your past?"

A shadow came over Melina's face. "I wasn't always so involved in church and so eager to live for Jesus. After my sister left, I went through some years I'm not proud of. Maybe because I blamed myself for her leaving. I can be a little bit obstinate, if you haven't noticed."

I smiled at that, and she smiled back before turning her gaze to the wall across the room. "I partied. I drank. I did things with guys that I'd always told myself I'd save for my husband. I called myself a Christian because I believed God existed, but I definitely didn't let Him change me."

I was shocked. I'd never pegged Melina as someone with a past. I'd always thought she was the good kid, the polar opposite of my mom. And she'd only been thirteen when Mom left home.

"Wow," I mumbled. "What turned you around?"

Her eyes seemed to look beyond the hospital wall, into the past. "It's not what but who. And the answer is God. And Kurt. See, when I met Kurt, I saw something different in him. Yeah, different because he's kind of a goof, but different as in how confident he was. How kind he was. How he didn't let life get to him but stayed true to what he believed. He was always so full of joy. And he refused to date me."

I felt my mouth fall open. "Seriously?"

Melina nodded. "He was Captain Purity. Literally. That's what people called him. He wanted to save his first kiss for his wife on their wedding day. That's how serious he was. He wouldn't date me because our lifestyles were so different, but he was my friend. My best friend who prayed for me even when I told him not to waste his breath. He loved me like the brother I never had, and he made me crave what he had. He had something so much deeper, so much truer than religion. He had that living, breathing relationship with his Creator. And when I finally realized I'd been so stinkin' arrogant, God changed my life."

"And then you dated?"

"Not for a while. Kurt jokes now that he wanted to make sure my 'conversion stuck,' but we were friends first, lovers second. And although I'd kissed many guys before, our wedding marked the first kiss I gave Kurt. And the first he gave any girl. It was full of so much promise, so much hope, so much purity."

"That's actually really sweet," I admitted, remembering how hollow my kisses were in retrospect.

"You think you're like your mama, Sadie, and you are. But I also see so much of myself in you."

I twisted my hands in my lap, refusing to look at my aunt. "But it's too late for me. I don't have a reason to be here."

Out of the corner of my eye, I saw Melina turn slightly so she faced my chair. "Sadie, listen. What do you hear?"

The only sound in the room came from the fetal monitor. "Fast thumping," I said.

Melina nodded. "And what is that fast thumping?"

My voice quivered as I said, "Heartbeats."

I brought my eyes to hers, and she smiled softly, slowly.

"That's right. They're heartbeats. And heartbeats mean life. Purpose. It's not over for Bean."

I sniffed and studied the shaking hands in my lap, trying to figure out where she was going with this.

"Sadie Grey." I looked up again. Melina's voice was even softer. "Put your hand on your chest." I slowly obeyed. "Now what do you feel?"

"Thumping."

"And what is that thumping?" Her prodding was gentle but earnest.

"My heart beating."

Melina patted the space on the bed beside her. I slowly rose from the chair, hand still on my heart, and sat next to her, careful not to disturb any of the wires or tubes.

"It's the same for you, Sadie Grey. As long as your heart's still beating, you're not done. You still have a purpose. God still has big plans for you."

I fingered the crisp, white bed sheet. "If only I could believe that."

My entire world had crumbled out from under me so many times. I'd done the wrong thing even more times than that. Even if my aunt and uncle loved me, I couldn't possibly be loved by a God who knew all of my secrets, even if there was a purpose in my past.

As Melina wrapped her free arm around me, I dropped my head to her shoulder and sobbed.

Chapter 29

Kurt wasn't coming. Or at least not for a while. He'd texted me at eight o'clock Wednesday morning, telling me he had to wait for a car rental place to open before he could start the drive. His estimated time of arrival was now just before midnight.

I replied to his text, telling him Mel and the baby seemed stable enough, although she'd been having Braxton Hicks contractions on and off.

Pastor Shepherd stopped by to visit and pray with Melina and then offered to take me home to shower and change and gather some things for her. I didn't want to leave, but I couldn't stop thinking about how worried the kids would be, and how seriously Melina needed to rest, so I reluctantly rode back to Pecan Creek, filling him in on Kurt's efforts to make it home.

Back at the house, I hugged Trissy, Jackson, and Cooper, passing on the message that their mom loved them and would see them soon. She didn't want them to see her hooked up to the IV drip and everything, so they couldn't go to Augusta. Instead, I let Mrs. Shepherd, Hope, and my cousins listen to the recording of the heartbeats I'd captured on my phone. While I took a shower and packed a bag for Melina and myself, Mrs. Shepherd called Melina and let the kids take turns talking to her.

Cooper didn't say much, other than a heart-melting "Hi, Mommy." Jackson told my aunt he'd started construction on a second dirt bike ramp. Trissy, who'd been thrilled by the fact that Hope was spending the day with her, lost it when she heard her mom's voice, and I found myself with my arms wrapped around my cousin, telling her everything was okay and desperately wishing I could believe it myself.

After lunch, I volunteered to read the boys their downtime story. I stretched out on Cooper's bed and brought my A game for making authentic train sounds to bring the story to life. Cooper fell asleep as soon as I said, "The end," and even Jackson dozed off with his head on my shoulder. I didn't mean to fall asleep, but something about two little boys snuggled up next to me, combined with the fact I'd yet to have a cup of coffee, made me drowsy.

When I woke up, the boys were gone and my legs were stiff from being curled up in a toddler bed.

"Mornin', sleepyhead!" Trissy sang as I entered the living room. Hope giggled and pointed at my head. I ran a hand through my hair that I'd let air dry after my shower. It felt like it stuck up in a thousand directions. Wednesday was now ponytail day. Cooper ran up to me and wrapped his little arms around my legs and Jackson laughed.

"Was your nap good?" Jackson asked.

I swatted at his arm. "Does anyone know what time it is?"

Lydia looked up from the magazine she was reading on the couch. "It's a little after four thirty."

"Oh no!" I gasped and wrung my hands. "I need to get back to the hospital! What if something happened ..." I trailed off when I realized I was scaring the kids. "I need to go."

Mrs. Shepherd yawned and set her magazine on the arm of the couch. "Peter will take you back when you're ready. He said you can pick up some food on the way so you won't torture Mel with it."

***

After the preacher dropped me off at St. Paul's Hospital, I found myself once again sitting in the uncomfortable chair. From the moment I entered the room, all of the anxiety, emotions, and thoughts I'd had last night hit me again. At least Melina seemed comfortable enough, and the fetal monitor's volume had been turned down again. "How's it going?" I asked her, forcing my tone to sound light.

"I slept for a while, which was good, but now I just feel kind of blech, you know?"

"Yeah."

"Now I have to ask you how it's going."

"I slept for a while, which was good, but now I just feel kind of blech, you know?" I parroted her words back to her, and she stuck her tongue out at me. I never thought I'd be so glad to see her animated personality.

"Oh, and I've been having contractions. Don't you dare say you know what that's like."

"Contractions?" I stood up. "Like, real ones? You've gotta hold on at least until tomorrow."

She shrugged. "No. I think they're false ones. Come sit with me."

I crawled into the narrow bed next to her, feeling like a little girl, which reminded me of a question I'd had since our last conversation. "If Kurt was the reason you turned to God, then what was my mom's reason? It definitely wasn't Dad." A month ago, I never would've opened up a God topic intentionally, but I needed answers.

I let her take my hand—another new thing for me—and she studied my face. "You."

I'd expected guilt, maybe fear, but *me?* "What did I do?"

"I was there when you were born. Did you know that?" I shook my head, surprised. "Melody and I weren't on the best terms, but she didn't have many close friends in Seattle yet, so she asked me to come stay with her."

"But you were a kid."

"I was. And it was also before I hit my rough patch in life. Even though your mom changed and our relationship healed, I still had this guilt that nagged at me and made me want to hide from everything good. But anyway, the doctors wouldn't let anyone other than Mike in the room, so I waited out in the hall. I heard your first cry too." She squeezed my hand. "And do you know what she said to me when I met you for the first time?"

"What?"

"She said, 'Melina, God is real. I can't deny that. Even though I ran from Him, He gave me this gift. Even though I made so many

217

mistakes, He still showed me He loved me. Look at her.' And then I saw you open your wide eyes and stare into the face of your mama. Melody said, 'And see her eyes? They're gray. Isn't that perfect?'"

"My eyes are barely even a color," I interrupted, "so how did she think they were perfect?"

"Because," Melina said as she flipped my hand over, studying it, "she said she'd been living her whole life wandering between right and wrong—between light and dark—but in the middle of her wandering, God gave her you. Something beautiful came out of the gray."

I swallowed and looked at my hand in Melina's. "I always thought she just named me after my eye color."

"She kind of did. But it was more than just a color. She saw it as a sign from God—a sign that He can take whatever mess we're in and turn it into something beautiful. A sign He can take all of our pain and mistakes and doubts and use it for a purpose. Nothing we go through is wasted. He can take all of the bad stuff and turn it into something that works for our good."

I leaned back on the pillow and thought of what Truitt told me after Willow's party. About how God had taken all of the bad things I'd been through and used them to bring me here to Pecan Creek because God had a purpose for me. Could I really let myself believe that? Could I take a chance and fall into the arms of someone bigger than myself, trusting Him to hold me and all of my messy pieces together?

I lifted my head and looked at my aunt. "Even if that's true, why would God want me?"

"Because He loves you." Her church answer didn't answer my question.

"But why would He love me? I've never loved Him."

Melina watched the fetal monitor for a moment. The only sound was the faint *ba-bumps* of the baby's heartbeat. Finally, she said, "It's like this. We were made to have a relationship with God, but we turn away from Him. That breaks His heart. Without Jesus, we're all headed for hell. We're all going to die. Because we're so covered in

ALL OF THIS

our sins, there's no hope for us … unless someone dies in our place. That's the only way for that relationship to be fixed."

I used my free hand to push my bangs out of my face. "That was Jesus, right?"

Melina smiled. "It is. Do you know John 3:16?"

I shrugged. "Sort of. Isn't that on the signs people always hold up at ballgames?"

"Yes. It says, 'For God so loved the world that he gave his one and only Son, that whoever believes in him shall not perish but have eternal life.' That's what God did. As hard as it was for you to see your mom die, as hard as it was for me to hold my lifeless daughter, you know it had to be even harder for God to watch His Son die in the place of people who hated Him."

I drew in a breath. I'd never thought of that. I'd always assumed there was a God—I never thought so much detail in life could result from a random explosion, for example—but I'd never thought much about Jesus being God's Son. If God was real, then Jesus had to be real. If God really had used Kurt and me as a baby to bring people to Him, then what He said in the Bible had to be true too, right? I knew I was a sinner—that much was obvious—but the reality that I was headed for hell terrified me. How could a loving God do that?

"So God does bad things to us? That's not love."

Melina released my hand and tucked a stray piece of hair behind my ear. "He gives us free will. Let's say God created everything and didn't give us choices. We'd be like Jackson's dirt bike drivers. We wouldn't have a living, breathing relationship with our Creator because He would just move us around like little toys. Instead, we choose to follow Him or not. Unfortunately, there are consequences for choices, which means someone's choice can affect the life of someone who does love God. But if you have a relationship with Christ, you'll never have to go through the hard times alone. See?"

I nodded, slowly. "I think so."

"There's another verse—in Romans chapter eight, verse twenty-eight—that says, 'We know that in all things God works for the good of those who love him, who have been called according to his purpose.' Thank God, He gives us the choice to love Him.

And thank God as long as you're alive, you still have the chance to choose Him."

The word *purpose* rang in my ears. *Purpose. Purpose. Purpose.* "What's my purpose then?" The words popped out of my mouth before I even knew they were coming.

Melina rubbed her stomach, being careful not to move the bands of the fetal monitor. "That, dear Sadie, is a question so many people spend their whole lives trying to answer. But it's really simple. It's this: Your purpose is to live your life loving God wherever He puts you. You do that by spending time with Him, listening and talking to Him, telling others about Him and loving them like He does. That's your purpose. Want to know what else I think?"

I nodded.

"I think God's been pursuing you this summer. He loves you like crazy, and He wants you to know what that love feels like. That took taking you away from Seattle, introducing you to some people who desperately love Jesus, and getting you away from mistakes you've made. He used those situations to get your attention. Life doesn't have to be full of so much heartache and frustration. He wants you to experience the joy He gives. He wants *you*, Sadie Grey."

My nose had begun running, and I grabbed a tissue. Shame for how I'd spent my life doing the opposite of what God wanted rolled over me like a wave in the ocean. I'd spent so long growing numb to things I knew were painful or wrong. I'd blocked it all out. Now, though, no amount of focused breathing could take away the shard of shame scraping deep into my heart. I so very desperately wanted a purpose. I wanted to feel loved, and I wanted to love back. Freely. I was tired of not feeling good enough or not feeling wanted.

Melina rested her hand on my back, which tripped the tear switch. I looked up at her through swimming eyes and saw she was crying too.

"I don't think I'd be very useful," I admitted.

"All He wants is your heart," she whispered. "He will only work with broken pieces—a broken spirit—rather than something stubbornly glued together in your own way. Give it to Him. Give it to Him by telling Him what's on that purpose-filled heart of yours. Tell Him what you believe."

I grabbed my aunt's hand and closed my eyes. With wavering voice and quivering chin, I said, "God, I'm sorry. I'm so sorry for being angry with You and blaming You. I'm so sorry for ignoring the purpose You have for me, and I'm so sorry for trying to find happiness in alcohol, in guys, in everything but You. I know I sin, and I know I'm going to hell without You. I really believe now that Jesus is Your Son and that He died for me. Please forgive me. Please be my Father that won't abandon me. Please save me from myself."

I couldn't tell if my sobs were shaking the bed or if my aunt's were. Or maybe both. All I knew was that suddenly, for the first time, I felt free. I felt hopeful. I felt loved. I *felt.*

I put my arms around Melina and hugged her. "Thanks for not giving up on me. I love you."

She kissed my cheek. "Back at you."

Chapter 30

"Your plan worked."

A moment later, my phone signaled Truitt's reply. "What plan?"

With shaking fingers, I typed, "All I'm saying is you'd better get used to me hanging around, because we're gonna spend eternity together."

It took less than a minute for my phone to ding again. "What? That's awesome! Becca's here too. She's screaming. Welcome to the family!"

Family. A word I'd never really known until this summer. Now not only did I have blood relatives who loved me in Pecan Creek, Georgia, I also had a family made up of believers *all over the world*. That would take a while to sink in.

I sent another text to Kurt, even though I knew he was driving, and then grinned goofily down at my phone. I realized that, other than Pastor Shepherd during his sermons, no one had preached to me since I'd come to Pecan Creek. Yet I'd gotten the message. Is that what Pastor Shepherd had meant when he said God's Word was "alive and active" at church one Sunday? That it doesn't have to be read to speak to you? That other people can live it out and God can bring it to life through people's actions?

I looked up to share this realization with Melina, but she had a scowl on her face.

I jumped up from my chair and hurried over to the bed. "What's wrong?"

"I'm …" She stopped to breathe. "I think … I'm in … labor."

What? *Now?* After things had calmed down with Bean? It was nine at night and Melina had been resting for several hours. "Why do you think you're in labor?" I asked, even as I watched a line on the machine spike, signaling a contraction.

We waited for the contraction to pass, me with my eyes glued to the screen and Melina with her hand gripping the edge of the bed. "I feel like I'm being ripped in half. And I'm pretty sure my water broke."

I didn't even pause to ask how she arrived at that conclusion. I pushed the button to call a nurse but didn't wait for one to arrive. I ran out of the room to the nurses' station, hurriedly spilling the news to the two ladies behind the desk. They assured me a nurse would be there in a minute to check on things, and then they'd call Dr. Summers if necessary.

True to their word, a nurse arrived and confirmed that, yes, Melina was really in labor, and yes, her water had broken.

"Told you," Melina said snarkily when the nurse made her announcement. I realized if she had been cranky during her bed rest days, labor had the potential to turn her into a monster.

The nurse left to bring some supplies into the room and Melina started crying. "I'm sorry!" she said. "It's been an emotional day, and these hormones just ... Oh my word! Kurt! He's going to miss everything!" That brought on a fresh round of tears.

I awkwardly patted her hand, still not accustomed to showing affection like that. I decided I should tell her about Kurt before she threw the fetal monitor out the window or something. "Um, Melina?"

"Yes?" She sniffed, trying to get a hold of herself.

"I called Kurt last night." Was that really just last night? "He left Chicago this morning and should be here in, like, an hour and a half. So just—I don't know—cross your legs or something?"

Melina shot me a look. "Not funny." Then her expression softened, and her eyes glistened with tears. Again. "Thank you for doing that, Sadie. God nudged you, and you listened."

I hadn't thought of it like that, but it sounded pretty good. Even though I'd been so filled with doubts and questions last night, He still used me—imperfect me—for His purpose. I just hoped the rest of His purpose held off for a few more hours. The nurse came in to check on Mel's progress, and I slipped out to go to the bathroom. Afterward, I stopped by a vending machine and bought a bottle of water. I was likely to dehydrate after all of my tears, and the last thing Melina needed was for her niece to pass out.

Sipping my water bottle, I walked back into the room, stepping aside as the nurse left.

"Sadie," Melina squeaked, "take my phone and text Lydia Shepherd." I grabbed her phone off the table as she began telling me what to text. "Tell her I'm in labor. Water's broken. I'm dilated five centimeters and—"

I stopped typing and stared at her, my mouth open. "Five centimeters? Don't you only have to go to ten?"

She nodded. "Then call Kurt and tell him to speed home like the Varsity's selling out of chili dogs."

I nodded absently, feeling lightheaded at what was happening.

Thirty minutes later, Dr. Summers arrived and announced we'd be having a baby tonight. Kurt had just called and said he was still an hour outside of Augusta.

The nurses wheeled in delivery supplies and asked Melina if she wanted an epidural, to which she replied, "Don't even waste time asking. Juice me up."

When the anesthesiologist arrived, I sat in my chair in the corner, hands over my eyes. So far, the whole birthing thing hadn't really bothered me, but they were putting a long needle in my aunt's spine. Things just got intense.

Melina leaned back in the bed, her face pinched, repeating a mantra of "Hang on for twenty minutes, Melina Brooke. Just twenty minutes."

I decided to leave her to her chants and focus my eyes on the contraction screen. "I think you've got another one," I pointed out.

That earned me another look. "Not helping."

I put my hands up in surrender. "Sorry."

Dr. Summers came back fifteen minutes later and told the nurses to get everything in place. Fresh blankets were placed on the baby-cleaning station, next to a cart with a heat lamp hanging over it.

Blue paper was spread around the bed, and I willed my stomach not to lurch at thoughts of why all that was necessary. The door opened just as a nurse helped Melina sit up in bed. Kurt stepped out from behind the curtain, panting.

"Kurt!" I yelled. I jumped into his arms and squeezed him around the neck. I took him by surprise, but he circled his arms around me and returned the hug.

"I saw your text. I'm so proud of you, kid."

My cheeks warmed, and I quickly turned the attention back to the situation at hand. "We thought you wouldn't make it."

He set me on the floor and took in the preparations rapidly coming together in the delivery room. "I didn't think so either." He walked over to Melina. "Baby. How are you?" He quickly kissed her damp forehead.

"Hey, love." She smiled. Or was it a grimace? "Go wash up. I don't want you cutting the cord with dirty hands."

He jogged into the bathroom and turned on the sink.

"Okay," the nurse said when Kurt returned. "Are you Daddy?" He nodded, and I was convinced I saw him puff out his chest a little. "We're almost there, so I have to ask that anyone not participating in the delivery go to the waiting area."

Obviously, that meant me, as I was neither Mommy nor Daddy. I walked over to Melina and squeezed her hand. "I'll pray for you."

Melina squeezed my hand back but didn't let go. "No." *No?* "I mean yes. Please pray for me. But stay with me too."

What? Stay with her? "You mean *here,* while the baby comes?" I glanced at Kurt, certain he wouldn't want me intruding on their special moment. But to my surprise, he nodded. "We want you in here."

I didn't know what to say. So I started crying.

The tears trailed down my face as I bent my head close to Kurt's and Melina's while my uncle whispered a prayer for his wife and baby. They kept coming as he added thanks for me and my salvation. They came harder as I stood by the head of the hospital bed and listened to Melina declare the epidural obviously wasn't working.

It all seemed to happen in a blur. Melina whispered Bible verses as she focused on a picture of the ocean hung on the wall. "I can do all things through Him who gives me strength ... The Lord is my Shepherd, I lack nothing ..." And then one that seemed to come straight from God to my heart by way of Melina's strained words: "'For I know the plans I have for you,' declares the Lord. 'Plans to prosper you and not to harm you, plans to give you a hope and a future.'" After she recited that one, she rolled her head over to me and said, "Added that one just for you, Sadie Grey." I smiled. The tears came again.

I couldn't see anything that was happening from my post by her head, but I didn't think I wanted to. Melina began pushing and before long, Dr. Summers said, "The head's out!" Melina moaned and squeezed my hand so hard I felt sure I'd permanently lost blood supply to my fingers. After another contraction, I heard something about the shoulders.

Suddenly, a sharp cry pierced the tense air of the delivery room. *My cousin.* Dr. Summers held up a slimy, bright-red baby. "It's a girl!" she announced.

Beside me, Melina collapsed onto her pillow, uttering, "Thank You, God. Thank You," over and over. On the other side of her, Kurt brought a hand to his mouth, not even caring about the tears falling freely down his cheeks.

And me? I sank down against the wall, overwhelmed by finally seeing my cousin with a healthy set of lungs. Overwhelmed by witnessing such a miracle. Overwhelmed by the love I saw on Melina's and Kurt's faces as Dr. Summers placed the tiny baby in my aunt's arms.

My cousin was so tiny. The nurse took the baby and began suctioning out her nose and vigorously scrubbing her with a blanket. She placed her on a scale and announced she weighed just under six pounds. Small, but perfect. She wrapped her in a blanket and handed her to Kurt.

"Sadie," he said, his voice thick. "Come meet your cousin." I tiptoed around the edge of the bed where Dr. Summers worked to clean up the supplies. I hesitated when Kurt tried to hand her to me, but he insisted.

I'd never held a baby before. She was so much lighter than I expected six pounds to feel, even wrapped in her blankets. She cried out and peered at me with tiny blue eyes. I pulled her closer to my chest so I wouldn't drop her as a sob—a happy sob—shook my body. I gently kissed her on the head and looked over at my aunt and uncle.

"What's her name?"

Melina glanced at Kurt. They seemed to have a conversation using just their eyes. Melina smiled and said, "Evelyn Grey Elliot."

I knew Evelyn was my grandmother's name. And Grey was …

"Did you say Grey?" I asked, and then I lowered my voice so I wouldn't scare the baby. "As in G-R-E-Y. Like Sadie *Grey* Franklin?"

My aunt and uncle nodded, both smiling.

"You named her after me?"

More nods. "God has great plans for your life, Sadie. We've known that all along," Melina said.

Kurt put a hand on his wife's shoulder and looked at me. "You cool with having a namesake?"

I opened my mouth to speak, but words wouldn't come. Tears wouldn't come either. I just gazed down at baby Evelyn Grey and nodded. Once I had a loose grasp on my voice again, I said, "She's got a lot to live up to. She'll be a handful."

Kurt winked at me before taking his daughter and handing her to Melina. "We've had practice. Now go out to the waiting room. There are some people waiting to congratulate you, Cousin Sadie."

I nodded numbly and turned toward the door, and then I turned back around. "I have a question. What would her name have been if Bean—I mean Evelyn—had been a boy?"

Without hesitating, Melina and Kurt said, "Greyson."

Chapter 31

"Truitt!" I yelled as I stepped into the waiting room. Before I could say hi to Becca too, Truitt jumped up from his seat and ran—actually *ran*—to me. Picking me up in his arms, he spun me around, laughing. Then, before I knew what was happening, he brought his lips to mine and kissed me squarely on the mouth.

The kiss was over almost as soon as it began, but it took my breath. I glanced behind Truitt at Becca, who stood with her mouth hanging open. "What did I just see?" she asked.

Truitt let go of me and offered a sheepish grin. "Sorry. It just sort of happened."

I caught my breath. "I-I didn't provoke that," I said.

Both Truitt and Becca laughed. Becca came up to me and hugged me. "Hey, sister in Christ," she said next to my ear. She pulled back and took my hand.

"What are you guys doing here?" I asked. "What about the mission trip?"

"The mission trip's still going on," Becca said, "but we wanted to be here with your family."

"And," Truitt said, "someone had to keep Kurt from freaking out on the drive home."

Speaking of Kurt ... "Y'all need to come meet my cousin!"

Neither Truitt nor Becca moved.

"What?"

"You said y'all," Truitt pointed out.

I shrugged. "I've been contaminated."

Truitt took my hand that wasn't clinging to Becca's. Together, the three of us headed down the hall, our heads bent close, whispering about how our worlds had changed in just twenty-four hours.

"We don't have to talk about this now," Truitt whispered, my hand still in his. "But I told Kurt and Becca everything about the situation with my mom. We're gonna make sure she gets all the help and the love she needs."

I squeezed his hand. "I'm proud of you."

Later, after Melina had been moved to a regular room, Becca sat on the couch holding Evelyn in her lap. I sat next to her, and Truitt sat on the arm of the couch next to me, leaning over to watch my sleeping cousin.

"This couch sure would've been nice the past two nights," I noted.

"I can't stop staring at her. She's so perfect," Becca said. She and I had a total teen girl moment and sighed at the same time—and then started giggling.

Truitt shook his head. "Chicks."

We laughed, but the truth was I couldn't stop looking at her either. I held her tiny hand with my finger. It barely covered the tip. I stroked her wrinkly knuckles and breathed in her fresh, brand-new baby smell.

"You're going to be so spoiled," Becca cooed. "Cousin Sadie's gonna make sure of it, isn't she?" She turned to me and her eyes dimmed just a little. "At least, for the next few days."

I felt a pang in my chest. Somewhere along this journey, Pecan Creek had become home. More than that, these people had become home. Although I didn't say anything, and I didn't know what the future held, in my heart, I knew I was where I belonged.

Lydia brought Trissy, Jackson, and Cooper into the room. All three kids were wide-eyed and sleepy and quieter than I'd ever heard them.

Becca scooted over on the couch so Trissy could sit between us.

"Look, Tris," I whispered as Becca set the baby in her lap. "You finally have a sister."

Trissy looked up at me, her nose wrinkled. "You mean I finally have two sisters. Because I kinda decided you were my sister when you moved here."

I was speechless. My heart really did feel light. No, not just light. Full.

As I looked around the room, I took in all of the faces around me. Cousins who accepted me despite my flaws, a new cousin who I vowed to be a good example to, real friends who told me the hard truth and let me process it on my own, and an aunt and uncle who loved me through it all and believed God had great plans for my life. And you know what? Considering all of the events—each moment that seemed painful at the time, that led up to this moment in a hospital room in Georgia—I believed them. It wasn't over for Sadie Grey Franklin. God really did have a purpose in all of this.

Acknowledgments

I'm overwhelmed by how many amazing people have joined me on this wild and wonderful journey of writing stories. I offer my heartfelt thanks ...

To readers, for hanging out with Sadie and living in her world for a little while. The fact that you invested some of your valuable time in this story is such an incredible honor. You rock.

To the English and creative writing professors at Georgia Regents University, who fueled my love of stories and pushed me to keep growing as a writer.

To Professor Harris, Dr. Maynard, and Dr. Leightner, for meeting with me while I worked on the early versions of this book, offering encouragement and invaluable editing advice and knowing my characters as well as I do. Thank you for helping me chase this dream and for seeing more than just a story.

To Dr. Sadenwasser and the GRU honors program for saying, "Yes, you can write a novel as an honors thesis." My life as a writer would look a lot different if I hadn't had that opportunity.

And to Mom, who reads even my messiest drafts but still calls me her favorite writer.

To Dad, for lots of "yard man" and old truck inspiration.

To Erin, for ideas that crack me *up*, the stick-shift driving lesson, and the infamous video from that first eventful lesson. I get a lot of ideas from our adventures.

To Abby, for answering countless "What if ...?" questions and for making the crazy suggestion that became such a huge part of this story. Sadie wouldn't be Sadie without you, sister.

To Ellen, for being the vibrant breath behind every wacky kid moment I write.

To my grandparents, for modeling lives lived in Christ and believing in the power of the Spirit who lives in me.

To Allison, Brittany, and Emily, my "inner circle." Thank you for the honesty, suggestions, and patience when I go off on random story tangents.

To my team at WestBow Press. Thank you for an amazing first-time publishing experience. It's hard work but so much fun.

To all of my family, friends, and blog readers who continue to pray and believe in the calling given to this quirky twentysomething, and to those of you who asked for a signed copy of this story before it was even written. What incredible gifts you are to me.

And to the Author and Finisher of my faith. You constantly leave this word lover speechless. Thank You, God, for all of this.

Made in the USA
Columbia, SC
11 March 2019